Ian's Empire

Escape to an Era Where True Love Prevails

Other Books by Julia David

Love's Pure Gold Series
Truitt's Truth.
Morgan's Medicine.
Ian's Empire

Leaving Lennhurst Asylum Series
Available on Amazon and Kindle Ebook
Love Covers *Book 1 Elias*
Love Flies *Book 2 Patience*
Love Protects *Book 3 Anna*

Other Historical Romance Books by Julia David
Mighty One Series
Available on Amazon and Kindle Ebook
Burgundy Gloves
Broken Chain
Black Coat

Come visit: https://www.juliadwrites.com for behind the scenes, photos, videos, newsletters, release dates and fun giveaways.

Oregon Territory

Utah Territory

Grass Valley

Auburn

Sacramento Coloma

Hangtown

San Francisco *Northern Gold Diggings*

Pacific Ocean

Ian's Empire

A Novel By

Julia David

Field Runner Press

 Field Runner Press

Published by Field Runner Press
Redding, Ca.
Printed in the United States of America

"These tests have come to prove your faith and to show that it is good. Gold, which can be destroyed, is tested by fire. Your faith is worth much more than gold and it must be tested also. Then your faith will bring thanks and shining-greatness and honor to Jesus Christ when He comes again."

1 Peter 1:7 NLV

One

Chicago, Ill.
Winter 1830

Dr. Walter Bradstreet rubbed the back of his neck as the evening shadows dropped from the window onto his crowded desk. He hadn't meant to stay at the office for so long. His secretary had done her best to handle his appointments, but it was unheard of for him to miss two days at his medical office, and today he'd barely had a chance to breathe.

Restacking a thick medical book on a shelf, he wondered why he hadn't had a replacement come in and see to his patients. His friend and colleague Dr. Maxwell Hastings would have been inclined to help. Unfortunately, the anguish of Dr. Bradstreet's beloved Mona's heart and body had come without warning. His wife had delivered their second stillborn child in the last five years, this one a baby girl.

To pursue his career as a physician, they'd waited to marry and have children. Oh, a healthy baby girl would have made Mona's tender heart sing. She had cried long into the night, and though he tried, he was of little comfort. They had been blessed with a healthy son seven years earlier, making these female reproductive conditions even more inexplicable. Of course, he'd stayed home to attend to her needs. But his frustration flexed in and out, the delivery had been difficult, and now she lay in another despondent state.

Dr. Bradstreet stood; he needed to get home. As he swept his coat off the back of his chair, he noticed a piece of paper where the book had been. He held it up to the oil lamp. His secretary had left a note about a woman who needed his services on Second Street at the Wayside Inn. It was from two days ago. Taking in a deep breath, he tapped the edge of the paper on his desk. It was late, and he knew of the Wayside Inn. Only a block from the docks, it was one of the worst areas of town. Not anywhere close to his usual route. The daylight was fading, he needed to get home. His wife needed him. He could not meet every need placed in front of him. He tapped the paper one more time on his desk before throwing it past the door of the small potbelly stove.

Dr. Bradstreet hitched his small buggy, stepped up, and dropped his top hat onto the black leather bench seat. Grabbing the reins, he unlocked the break and stilled. Unexpectedly, tears filled his eyes. Was it the cold wind coming up from the western shores of the Great Lake, or this unrelenting conscience that often pinched deep in his gut? The desire was real and heartfelt to be a good husband and father, but what of this profession he'd chosen? It came with a heavy cross. He shook his head and swallowed. The strange and sudden emotion rattled him, and he dabbed at his face with his coat sleeve. Tapping his horse forward, he knew he still had some time till full darkness. He would stop by the Wayside Inn and be quick about it.

A few minutes later, he climbed the loose stairs that lined the outside second story of the Wayside Inn. A door hung ajar, and only a sliver of light lit the hallway that hosted ten to fifteen doors. Stepping in, the pungent odor of filth and waste was overwhelming. He reached in his coat for his handkerchief and saw a little boy open a door on the left. The rag-a-muffin pulled up his loose dirty shirt and peed on the wall. *Hence the smell.* Dr. Bradstreet shook his head. *What was the room number on the paper?* he thought, questioning why he'd been so imprudent. "Young man, can you get your mother, please?" The little boy nodded with wide eyes and ran back into his door. A second later, a lantern and a woman's face appeared. She wore a thick band around her moppy hair and peered at him with a cross face. "What you be needin', sir?"

"My name is Dr. Bradstreet. My nurse left a note at my office, was there a medical problem that you know of?"

"Aye." The slender woman stepped from her apartment, holding the door behind her. "The woman two doors down." Her face flinched. "But she didn't make it. The priest was here yesterday and they took her body."

An unseen wave of relief hit his conscience. He needed fresh air and to be on his way. "I had another emergency and didn't see the note till this late hour." Somehow those words were his absolution, and he could leave in peace. "I'm sorry." He turned.

"Wait." The woman called, stepping toward him. "The priest said he would be back today." Her voice rose with desperation. "But he never came." Two other children's moppy heads peeked out the bottom half of the door.

"I thought you said they'd come to take the deceased yesterday."

"They did," she ground out irritably and walked past him to the flimsy exit. The woman searched the alley left to right until her face flared. "You'll have to take her. I can't do this anymore."

"Ma'am, please. You're a bit confusing." Dr. Bradstreet stopped talking when the woman snapped her fingers at the children. "Get her." She walked back to her door.

"See here." She wiped her forehead with the back of her hand. A small bruise made a dark ring under her left eye. "My man is due back anytime. He'll throw a paddy." She reached for a bundle that her child handed her. "He won't take to another mouth to feed, and I can't wait for the priest. You'll have to take her." The woman thrust the bundle into his arms, and Dr. Bradstreet stepped back. It was a newborn. "The woman died in childbirth?" He murmured, everything making more sense.

"I got five of my own in there." She huffed, turning away. "I can't keep her, and my man won't understand. You take her on to the church. The one over on Fourth."

"Yes, I know of it." The infant felt weightless in the crook of his arm. "What about her husband?"

The impatient woman dropped her head to the side, rolling her eyes, her frown conveying the message.

"I see." Dr. Bradstreet replied. "And no other family?"

"I can't say. But if anyone shows up, they can find the babe there."

"Yes. Of course." He sighed, wishing he'd never taken the time to come. A moment ago, his own mercy propelled him to heal the sick, but now he'd become a delivery man. The woman shooed her children back in and quickly closed the door. Carefully Dr. Bradstreet descended the old stairs to his rig, waiting in the alley. It would only be a few more minutes to Fourth Street and then he could hand off the child to a nun or whoever worked there. He stepped up and awkwardly tried to find a place to lay the infant while he drove. Pulling his medical bag from the floorboard, he decided to wedge it next to the bundle, keeping the baby from jostling. A small squeak rang clear, followed by two more.

"Yes, I'm sure you prefer being held."

The baby's face scrunched and let out another tiny wail. Dr. Bradstreet spied the poor thing smashed between his buggy seat and his medical bag. He pulled the bag back to the floor and picked up the child. "Let's see if I can drive one-handed." He took the reins and slowly pulled the horse out to the street. The little scallywag cried out again, and he tried to give it a small bounce. Distracted with his inability to do two things at once, the horse stopped without the proper tension. A gas lantern flickered above him, and finally he looked into the newborn's face. "Those nuns will find you a wet nurse, and you'll have quite the meal."

Open-mouthed, the infant turned its head, straining for sustenance. A cold wind stirred through Dr. Bradstreet's senses, and he took a long look at the pinkish round face cradled in his arm. Brushing his finger across the little velvet cheek, he knew of a woman with milk. A woman in his own home. What would she think? Would it bring her more pain or create a priceless opening for joy?

Two

Sacramento, Ca.

1853

Olivia Bradstreet sat at her large mahogany desk with a pearl-handled letter opener in her hand. Her satin and peach muslin dress with heavy white lace flounces at the sleeve rested on her work. Slicing open the correspondence, another letter from the San Francisco Ladies' Protection and Relief Society awaited her. As the secretary of the Sacramento Chapter, details of the latest news and children's welfare issues was a welcome post. The bottom paragraph was what she was hoping for. They would indeed approve a special night of food and entertainment to raise funds for the two children's homes—the small home run by Sisters of Charity and the one the Beckners had donated on Oak Street. Though they took care of different needs, they would be happy to split all proceeds.

"Delightful." Her chest swelled. She'd only been on the job one month, and the small areas of improvement she brought were looking well. Olivia stood and circled the small front parlor turned office and receiving room. Her thick ruffled gown brushed the floor under the sound of Sister Patricia having the children repeat their lessons. Their young voices flowed from across the hall.

The large front room had been turned into a classroom. Though the home had shrunk under the needs of the orphaned and friendless, they'd retained an excellent, competent teacher in Sister Patricia. Olivia stepped away and stared out the beveled glass front door. Could she ever have imagined after the long wagon ride to California with Dr. Hastings that she would be so fortunate? Unfathomable favor settled inside her to hold such a purposeful position.

Despite wanting to hold the blessing close to her heart, suddenly, her thoughts turned dark. Dr. Maxwell Hastings, her father's closest friend, was the only one to know the real truth for her travels.

The late fall wind twirled the leaves down the dirt street. Like the crackle of the dry leaves, her heart had certainly crackled into pieces after the death of her beloved Ronald in a horrific battle in Mexico. Then not six months later, her father, the esteemed Dr. Bradstreet, passed. Losing her mother five years earlier was the most devastating thing she'd endured until losing Ronald. Surely God had not heard her pleas. And finally, she knew why.

In a time of grief and what should've been solidarity, her older brother had had a fit of rage. Olivia felt her body sway. The drawing-room in the Bradstreet mansion reappeared clear in her mind, beautiful and ornate. Her favorite place to read as a child had been turned into a living nightmare. His horrid shocking words still made her heart quicken in an attempt to squeeze the life from her being.

She was not a Bradstreet, after all. She was a street urchin herself—a child of a harlot long dead.

In one moment, all of her life, her foundation, her past, her future, had turned into an unfathomable lie. Olivia clenched her throat, trying to swallow the pain. She'd dearly loved her mother, who'd fawned over her, giving her every privilege. Olivia had never minded all the music lessons, the fittings, and the etiquette lessons, because she believed she'd gotten her grace and poise from her mother. Now her beginnings were so shameful no one was allowed to speak it, and "no adoption could be done legally," her brother had spewed. He said he would've allowed her misplaced marriage to Ronald, but now Olivia was just a poor single wench, and he alone would be the Bradstreet heir. If she ever spoke of *his* family in a negative light, he would expose her.

She was hardly able to imagine that in her grief and shock, she could have found the strength to tell Dr. Hastings the disturbing revelation of her identity. The wonderful man she almost had as a father-in-law, was sympathetic and nonjudgmental. He, himself, had decided to leave Chicago and his medical job at Rush College to move across the country to the golden shores of California. He was to reunite with his remaining son, Morgan, who was also a surgeon, but due to the effects of the war had gone west to become a gold miner.

With the notice for a mining investment, Dr. Hastings put his money in Grass Valley where he wanted a new life, a new adventure. Dr. Hastings's kindness and patience were remarkable to allow her to come along.

That first week after her brother's rampage, when she could not even rise from bed, Dr. Hastings had the forethought to send a servant to gather her gowns and personal items from her home. *Was it ever really her home?*

"Miss Bradstreet?"

Olivia startled and turned. "Yes." She smiled at young Esther.

"You forgot to ring the bell for lunch, ma'am."

Olivia pulled her hand down her face, alarmed at how lost in her thoughts she could get. "I did. Thank you so much for the reminder." Olivia stepped quickly over to her desk and took the bell. Standing in the hallway, she gave it a firm long ring as the children flowed out towards the back door. Their chatter and smiles lifted the dark mood that had tried to settle on her. Lunch and dinner brought out extra excitement in the children.

"A good morning?" Olivia nodded to Sister Patricia.

"Yes, yes, the expansion of young minds was accomplished...*I hope.*" Lifting the thick cross at her neck, she laughed, the deep lines around her eyes creasing. Olivia set a warm hand on her black habit as they walked out with the last of the children. "I heard from Sisters of Charity. We are going to work together to raise funds for the two orphanages."

"Wonderful." Sister Patricia nodded. They stood in the back of the line while the children helped themselves to soup and bread. Another swirl of leaves and autumn wind rushed around the makeshift dining area. "Maybe we could get new tables and benches built with the money." Sister Patricia filled her bowl.

The children sat around the dried grass, eating and talking. "That and many other things." The women took the only bench seat, a remnant left after the Beckner family had moved to Grass Valley. "The Beckners were kind to leave so many things." Olivia tried to pull the thick layers of her dress aside and balance her bowl. Sister Patricia sat next to her.

"The home is a true miracle." Sister Patricia sipped her soup. "To not charge us rent and allow housing and a school."

"So true." Olivia took a bite of bread. "They are generous and good people. Did I mention that my guardian, Dr. Hastings, has started as a superintendent of some sort? He is helping with the Empire gold mine as he can."

"I'm sure he will be a help." Sister Patricia shook her head. "Poor Mrs. Beckner, losing her husband while her son was away." She gave Olivia a corner smile. "It seems both of you coming West became the providence of God."

"I don't know about that." Olivia turned to watch the children playing tag in the corner of the back yard. Only two people knew the real reason she came to California. All the expensive dresses and the Bradstreet name could not cover the shame she carried. Two young boys approached where they sat.

"Miss Bradstreet." The one with brown hair squinted at her, and Olivia couldn't help but lightly pinch his chin.

"Yes, Mr. Boxner."

"You know my momma, Francine, is comin' today."

"Yes, it's Thursday. Sometime after choir this afternoon, she should be here." Olivia smiled. His mother had traveled from Hangtown, and so far this month hadn't missed one of their weekly visits. Suddenly little Thomas with the thick blonde hair had dabs of water on his cheek.

"Oh no, young Thomas Long." Olivia set her bowl aside and reached out to take his hand. "What is causing this vexation on such a delightful fall day?"

"I think I know." Sister Patricia patted Thomas's shoulder. "His mother, Janny, Janny Long, would sometimes come with Miss Francine." The nun's copper eyes dulled. "We got word she passed months ago." Sister Patricia looked back and forth at the boys. "I'm guessing these are hard days to see your friend havin' a visit and no one coming for you?"

Thomas nodded as the tears rolled down his cheeks.

"Oh, sweet mercy, child." Olivia held him under his arms and drew him into her lap. He smelled like chicken broth and the barn. "I didn't know. What can I do for this pain in your heart?" She rested her cheek over his blonde hair.

Thomas shook his wet face against her ruffled bodice and pushed off her lap.

"I told him he could come with me ma and me."

"So generous of you, Joshua Boxner." Olivia still held Thomas's hand. "Would that be helpful, Thomas? To have a little outing with Miss Francine and Joshua?"

Thomas pulled his hand away and scratched the corner of his eye. "I just, I just…soon stay here."

"All right." Olivia felt the familiar stab of being a child without a parent. "Would you promise to seek me out in my office before supper? I have some new coloring pencils. No one has gotten to use them yet." She waited for his eyes to rise from the ground, before she tipped his chin up. "Please?"

Thomas shrugged, and Olivia regarded Sister Patricia.

"I also need your help this afternoon." Sister Patricia continued. "Do you want to help me gather some acorns and leaves for study time?"

"I can do that, and I know where those squirrels got them hid." Thomas nodded before he and Joshua walked away. Sister Patricia stood and took their bowls. "I'll straighten up while you go ring the bell."

Unmoving, Olivia watched the caring Christian woman. Times like this were baffling. The children seemed to warm up to her daily. How could she explain to them that the façade of lovey gowns and jewelry was like putting a gold crown and satin scarf on a donkey? Moved by each of them, she wanted to be a genuine relief to their plights. Little did they know what lay beneath the frivolity was a heart lonely and wanting just like theirs.

Three

Ian Beckner's thick sea legs stepped onto the narrow plank and found sure footing on the long pier at the San Francisco Bay. Even with the heavy load upon his shoulders and legs that hadn't felt land in weeks, he wanted to run. Relief, shock, and pure disbelief raced in his blood. He'd made the trip to Cornwall, England, and returned with the Cornish workers for the Empire Mine.

It was a fateful journey he would wish on no one. Two families had fallen to the fever, each one losing a child. Five members of the mining group were still weak with sickness. Out of the twenty men who had agreed to uproot their lives and families, two had abandoned the company somewhere in Panama, leaving eighteen who would join him to work the mine in Grass Valley.

The wooden walkway narrowed until he set foot on the rocky shore. He huffed with bliss. A seagull squawked above him, and he dropped his heavy bags on the ground and scanned the bustle of people moving every direction. Streets, wagons, storefronts, hotels, houses. San Francisco had tripled since he'd left this very port.

His eyes wandered through the faces again. He knew she would never come down to the docks to greet him, but a man with a new day and land beneath him could dream. And a reunion with the beautiful Miss Lesandra Grant remained one dream he'd held onto for months at sea. As soon as the Cornish were settled, he'd take a hot bath, have his good suit pressed, then have the beauty in his arms. He jerked his bag back onto his thick shoulders. A hastened step was in order.

An hour later, Ian pulled his fingers through his dark thick hair. He had eaten and shaved, but couldn't wait to find a barber. Lesandra would have to understand. He stuck his finger under the tight collar and pulled at his suit jacket. He'd lost weight since the last time he'd worn the garment. Rounding the fence into the Grant land, he saw a woman pausing from hanging laundry.

"Ma'am." Ian nodded. "I've come to see Lesandra. You may not remember me. I'm her fiancé, Ian Beckner."

Her brows crossed, and she looked like she wanted to say something. Ian waited, wondering if she spoke English. "I haven't had a chance to call. You see, I just got off a ship an hour ago."

"I saw her walking to the stables." Her eyes narrowed.

The housemaid appeared so wary, Ian wondered if he wasn't as presentable as he thought he was. Should he reintroduce himself to her mother first? Come back when he could be announced? The stables beckoned him from the right. After such a long separation, nothing mattered but seeing Lesandra again. His pulse quickened. Finally, joy awaited a weary immigrant now home at last.

Without any way to write his myriad of romantic intentions, he'd held them to himself too long. His steps pounded toward the stable until he stopped at the wide plank doors. Her name burned on his mouth to be called out. He'd pictured her turning in the sunlight to see him standing in front of her. The expression on her face would be worth a bag of gold. Breathing in a deep breath of hay, he thought he heard soft coos from around the stable doors. Probably speaking to one of the horses. He stepped closer with heart pounding. From this moment on, they would never need to be separated.

A man's low chuckle stopped him cold, and he blinked, waiting. Heat prickled his neck and through his stiff collar as he leaned over the side of the stable wall. A scream rent the air before his eyes could register his long-lost love was half-naked, white legs and ruffles wrapped around a man. A scoundrel was accosting his woman; Ian's fist clenched for battle, but the crushing in his chest could not be ignored. The exposed lovers both jumped up and began to straighten their clothes.

"Ian!" Lesandra puffed, pulling her messed brown hair back. "What in the world are you doing here?"

Ian wasn't sure he heard her words. He needed to punch someone fast, and the only thing his eyes could focus on was the young man pulling his shirt over his thin, hairless chest. Ian planted his feet on the ground, rocking his jaw to the side. Round doe-like eyes popped from the shirt as the depraved teen backed away into a corner.

"This is your lover, Lesandra?" Ian seethed. "Is he free from his mother's aprons?"

"I am now twenty!" The terrified young man stepped forward and then just as fast stepped back.

"Ian," Lesandra said, winded. "I wasn't expecting you." She flicked the straw that hung in her face. "I can see how angry you are, but just listen a moment." She had the audacity to give Ian a small smile with her soft tone as she brushed the hay off her skirt.

Ian stood in front of the stall door; neither of them could get out. "I'm listening."

"You *were* gone for a long time." She batted sad eyes. "I missed you terribly, and I got lonely." She tied the little bow together at her bodice. "You can't tell me you never had eyes for another woman in all these months?"

"Before God, never, Lesandra." He scowled. "I made you a promise when I left, and I had every intention of keeping it."

"And you still can." Her tone rolled upward. "We can forget this little mistake ever happened."

"What?" Her beau's face turned red. "Mistake? Is that what I am?"

Ian watched the crushing of his young face. *What kind of bizarre return was this?* Had he stepped into a barn at the Grant home or a gypsy theater?

"No, dear Rafael, you are not a mistake. But this...this...moment we had was a mistake." She popped her shoulders back, brushing more hair from her face. "I come from a good family and should never have let my downheartedness and loneliness invade my good senses. I have fallen waywardly and deeply regret the despair I find myself in."

Ian read Rafael's confused expression before he asked, "How long has she been in this kind of deep despair with you?"

The sad doe-eyed man found solace in Ian's calm question. "For months." Rafael frowned, rubbing his temples. "We've been together for months and...and...I know she needed time to tell her family. I am a worker here, and I know her family may not approve, but you..." His eyes switched over, narrowing on Lesandra. "You never said you were spoken for. You lied to me." His eyes blinked rapidly while his chin began to quiver.

Lesandra released a quick huff, sneering at his emotional display before turning back. "Really, Ian, this was all for you."

Ian rolled his tongue inside his cheek. "I might believe you have gone mad since I was away, but how would you account for this liaison being for me?"

"You were such a gentleman." Her soft green eyes beseeched his. "We'd one, maybe two, chaste kisses. How would I know how to be a good wife? How does a woman learn what a man wants unless she has a *little* experience?"

"Ha!" The barrel laugh left his chest before he realized it. "You *have* gone mad!" Wide-eyed, he shook his head. Poor Rafael slouched, physically crumbling under the false façade of *his* Miss Lesandra Grant.

"The only experience *I* want is with my wife!" He rubbed his eyebrows. "I can't decide if you are that stupid or that manipulative!" Ian stepped back, the desire to choke Rafael fading. "Likely, Lesandra, you are both." He nailed her with his stare. "Whatever promise I made to you is over. I *am* a gentleman, and I thought you were a lady—"

"I still am." She whined. "Now you are just being mean." Her bottom lip wiggled downward. "You were the one who left *me*," she snarled. "What will I say to my family? My father gave your mother money when your father died. We made sure the house at Empire Mine was finished properly. We were at the funeral service. You weren't." Her nostrils flared, and her lips pursed in a tight line. "The Empire Mine, that large rock home is supposed to be part of *my* future!"

Rafael released a whimper.

Ian felt the sharp hate in his belly rise higher at her every word. He should've been here for his father passing, to comfort his mother. The Grants had come to her aid instead of him— Lesandra's indictments stung like sand in his eyes.

After a moment of swallowing months of ridiculous hope and today's fury, Ian cleared his throat and stepped back and nodded to Rafael. "Thank you for your impeccable timing, stable boy. One day you will forgive yourself for falling for her beauty and vices." He stepped toward the wide, stable door. "I will count this day one of my most fortunate—a rescue from matrimonial death. For you, Rafael, you may have all the petticoats and lies to yourself." Ian turned to Lesandra, pinning her with his eyes. "As for you, you will never want to lay eyes on me again. If you do, I may not be of a sound mind. Our land has many dark descending mine shafts, and I will find a long narrow one. Once I drop you down, I will not look back."

Four

A stunning silver candelabra sat in the center of the Beckner grand table. The light flickered with all the opulence and poise of the Bradstreet home, only this was the Beckners' fine Empire Mine home in Grass Valley. Bewitched, Olivia could only stand and stare. The glowing dining room walls were covered in deep wood paneling, and the room centered a large, well-appointed table for ten. The china and silver glistened under the radiance of the presentation. Olivia straightened her back in her lovely three-tiered lavender walking dress. With the half-jacket of purple velvet, she would've thought she was back in Chicago waiting to step out with Ronald. Quickly chiding herself for her melancholy, she gently fingered the linen napkins.

"You are a splendid sight, Miss Olivia," Katy said as she set the dishes on the serving sideboard. "I know Mrs. Beckner should be down at any moment." The sturdy-boned housemaid smiled at Olivia. "You do your hair yourself?"

"I try." Olivia patted the three buns she'd tried to raise into a pretense of sophistication. "My secret is the combs and my hats." She smiled at Katy. "This one with all the beading and feathers can cover up my poor hairdressing."

Both the women turned as Dr. Hastings stepped past the parlor and into the dining room, sporting his own fine attire. He stopped and blinked. "Olivia, I've not seen that dress. You are surely the finest young woman in this territory." He winked and gave her a fatherly kiss on the cheek.

Katy wiped her hands on her thick white apron. "Now, Dr. Hastings, you never told me if the little cottage was to keep ya warm? We've had a few cool nights."

"The stove is just right." He nodded. "And I thank my good fortune to take my meals here in the Empire Home. You are a fine cook, Katy, and Mrs. Beckner has been an accommodating hostess. A man couldn't ask for..."

"And you all are talking about me." Mrs. Beckner smiled as she came down the wide, carpeted stairs. Maxwell Hastings face lit up as he lifted his left elbow to meet the matron of Empire Home at the bottom. "You are a sight to behold," he murmured, his eyes glowing tenderly. The stately woman linked her hand under his arm and offered him a warm smile. Their gaze held each other's a bit longer than Olivia had seen before.

"It is difficult to move from my black mourning dresses." Judith Beckner said to Olivia as she stepped away from Maxwell. Olivia offered a compassionate expression, and Judith took her hands, giving them a quick squeeze. "This ruffled gown, my love, is breathtaking," Judith fussed, fingering the velvet flounces around the small collar. "Something you brought with you, I imagine."

Olivia nodded once. "Yes, from my past in Chicago."

"Yes, of course," Judith said wistfully while rubbing her hand down Olivia's dress sleeve. "A bit more than the headmistress of the Oak Street Home for Children could afford." Judith squeezed Olivia's wrist before letting go.

Olivia felt a small shiver run up and down her arm. So much of Judith's kindness and attention reminded her of her own mother. "And I applaud you, Mrs. Beckner, for bringing your lovely sapphire gown out for tonight. If I may speak for Dr. Hastings and myself, though you are still in your year of mourning, you have gone beyond what is necessary to help two weary migrants adjust and feel welcome in your two homes and mining industry."

"And I would be remiss not to mention that you both are an answer from the heavens." Judith's face creased with humble thanks. "To have your care and insight to the needs of the Oak Street home after Mrs. Todd took her leave. You, Olivia, stepped in with such grace and intuition, I could not have found a better replacement."

Katy nodded to Maxwell, and he pulled the high-backed chairs out for the ladies. "Thank you, Maxwell." Judith blinked up at him.

"It has been a blessing, a true calling to my life." Olivia took her napkin and drew it across her lap. "The children, the home fills my heart."

"Speaking of children, I asked Katy to set an extra spot. And my dress is a bit of happy color only a happy mother could wear." Judith glanced toward the parlor. "I wonder how long we should wait." She smiled back at her dinner guests. "I'm not sure if Max…Dr. Hastings mentioned it. After a long season, my son, Ian, has returned with the Cornish workers for the mine. He's spent the day getting them settled, and he did promise to make it to dinner to meet both of you."

Olivia squeezed her hands under her napkin. Maxwell had shared that Judith had asked him to help with the managing of the mine while her son was away. How would the Empire mine's heir feel about Dr. Hastings's help? Katy came from her left and poured her goblet full of cider.

"Thank you." Olivia's breathing stopped as a tall, imposing man approached to her left. Every muscle in her being stiffened.

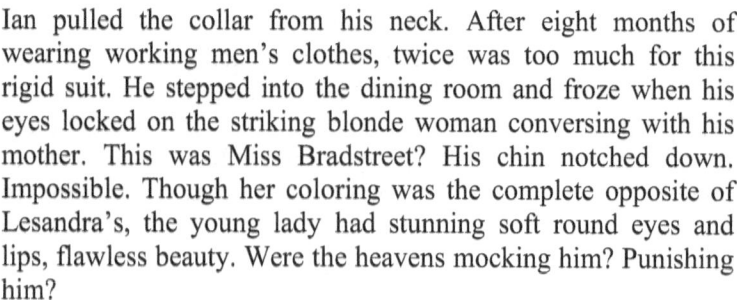

Ian pulled the collar from his neck. After eight months of wearing working men's clothes, twice was too much for this rigid suit. He stepped into the dining room and froze when his eyes locked on the striking blonde woman conversing with his mother. This was Miss Bradstreet? His chin notched down. Impossible. Though her coloring was the complete opposite of Lesandra's, the young lady had stunning soft round eyes and lips, flawless beauty. Were the heavens mocking him? Punishing him?

"Mother." At least his voice worked as he bent to kiss her cheek. "You look lovely." His tone was a bit tart as he pulled down on his cuffs.

"Dr. Hastings, I presume." Ian reached out, and Maxwell stood to shake his hand.

"Pleasure to meet you, Mr. Beckner." Maxwell nodded. "May I introduce a close friend of the Hastings family, Miss Olivia Bradstreet from Chicago."

Ian barely gave her a tip of the head. How dare she sit at his family table with all her chilled splendor, a loveliness so striking that her return greeting barely reached his ear. *Women.*

"Suddenly, I'm in need of a real drink." Ian wondered how he could judge the beauty so quickly. Beautiful women had never left a bitter taste in his mouth before. Blowing out a quick breath, Ian walked over to a small cabinet. "Dr. Hastings, may I pour you a shot of whiskey or bourbon?" The bottles and glasses rattled as he set them on top of the glass tray.

"I'll take whiskey." Maxwell nodded his thanks as Ian handed him the small glass. His mother's eyes narrowed as he took his own amber liquid down in one swallow.

"Now, may we eat?" Judith asked.

"Yes, please. Thank you, Katy." Ian eyed the empty chairs at the far end of the table. It was highly unfair for him to be accosted by the lovely Miss Olivia Bradstreet from Chicago on his first night home. Though he finally pulled the chair out from across her, he had enough to discuss with his mother to fill the entire evening.

"Dr. Hastings, you know I've been away nigh eight months." Ian tried to focus as Katy set a bowl of fresh vegetable soup in front of him. The sight was like a brilliant watercolor portrait after the corn mush served on the ship day after day. "And I…I understand with the loss of my father…" Ian couldn't wait. He took a spoon full. "…That my mother had selected Mr. Wright to move up from the mine shafts and oversee the daily functioning of the mine." *The soup was mouthwatering. Oh, how he'd missed Katy's cooking.*

"Yes, of course." Maxwell glanced at Judith. "Your mother and I talked at length about this. As you know…" He dabbed the corners of his mouth with the napkin. "I was only to invest in the mine. Your father and I corresponded regarding this. But with the loss of my eldest son and my other son making his living in Auburn, I felt the inclination to come west. It was in no way to come in…" Maxwell took in a deep breath, "…and take over." He nodded. "Please hear that clearly. We were just saying, Olivia and I…" Dr. Hastings talked on, but suddenly an incredible peace came over Ian's being. This young, innocent beauty was *not* so innocent. He called her by her first name. The postured close family friend was *with* Dr. Hastings. His lover, no doubt.

Wonderful, somehow, he'd a renewed opinion of the man across the table sitting elbow to elbow with his blonde beloved. She didn't look like a trollop, but things were freer here in California. *No need to hide in the stables.*

The vision of Lesandra, in such a situation as he'd never imagined, seeped into his mind. Taking a quick glance at his mother, he wondered what she thought of it all. She mentioned that they both were staying in the little guest cottage. Had his own mother really approved of the uncivilized situation?

"… and again, I have no knowledge of the actual working of mines." Dr. Hastings continued. "Besides medicine, I only have a head for facts and figures, and so I hope I've been a help in watching over the best use of your family's money and mine."

Judith nodded at Dr. Hastings. "After the shanties were done for the Cornish families, we had a small manager's office built." His mother added. "Two to three desks fit nicely." She waited, trying to read his stiff expression. "It was what we'd talked about when your father drew out the plans."

Ian speared the meat Katy set in the middle. Pulling his chicken apart with his knife and fork, he realized his mind had wandered. The whiskey was likely dulling his senses. Should he be upset about this intrusion or count it as a blessing? He chewed and risked a glance at Miss Bradstreet. Dr. Hastings was old enough to be her father. He was judging her again, and he didn't even know her. There was an unmistakable burr in his saddle the longer they both looked comfortable at his family table.

"I should thank you for your assistance, then." The benevolent words fell out before he had found a true place of goodwill for any of it. While he'd spent his weeks with the Cornish men drawing up plans for the use of their hard-rock mining techniques, his fiancée had found a lover, and his mother had found a new manager for the mine. He stabbed a carrot. It didn't matter, he was back now, and things would change rapidly with the Cornish men at work. Dr. Hastings had put his own money in. Indeed, he could find a place to be of help somewhere else.

While everyone finished the meal, his mother told a sweet story about having a doctor around. Colbert Levy, one of their older mine workers, had lost only a day of work thanks to the medical attention he received from Dr. Hastings. Ian rose a faint half-smile.

"If you would all please forgive me." Ian stood, too annoyed to listen to any more silly stories. Dropping his napkin on his empty plate, he'd other things to tend to. "It is the first night for the Cornish families. I noticed none of the shanties had stoves."

His mother started to open her mouth, and Dr. Hastings spoke up. "That would be my doing." Maxwell scratched his head. "I didn't want to speak of only business with this being the first night at your family table."

"No, please do." Ian had held himself at check this long, but he felt the heat rising up into his stiff white collar. These three, sipping from fine goblets, did not want to hear his stories of watching sobbing parents hug their children and grandchildren goodbye on the docks of England's shores, likely never to see each other again. The Cornish people had sacrificed home, land, and heritage to come to California at his bidding. Though he loved his mother, they'd become closer than his own people, and he would not disappoint them or let them go cold.

He gripped the back of his chair. The money had been set aside, and the orders were more than clear when he left. They deserved what he'd promised them. Suitable housing was expected when they arrived.

"It was the supplier from San Francisco." Dr. Hastings replied.

Ian was about to tell him to stick to the healing profession and keep his hands out of his mine *and money.*

"The price you agreed on was somehow tripled." Dr. Hastings said.

"Three times what they'd said?" Ian walked over and poured himself another drink. He'd known how bad the prices had risen all over. A dozen eggs were over two dollars in the mining towns. Swallowing the drink, he felt as if the fire in his throat was trying to burn into his once-satisfied belly.

"We'll figure out a solution." His mother glanced at the glass in his hand and frowned as he poured another. "We'll have Mr. Wright work on an earthen oven for their cooking for now, and then we'll look into another supplier. I can personally speak to the women if you like."

"No, thank you, Mother." Ian turned to Dr. Hastings. "Your intervention in my absence is appreciated, but from now on, your interference is neither necessary nor desired. I alone will handle everything to do with the Empire Mine."

Walking around the table to squeeze his mother's shoulder, he tried to pull his eyes away from the pretentious Miss Bradstreet, but the faint narrowing of her eyes into daggers was hard to miss. Forcing his temper to remain in check, he nodded once, "If you'll please excuse me, I will take my leave."

Five

Olivia waited by the front door as Maxwell took a moment to speak to Judith. Looking away, she felt like an eavesdropper as they shared confidences with each other. After finally saying their goodbyes, Maxwell escorted Olivia back toward the small Empire cottage as the evening's autumn air held its soft warmth. The English manor design had been Mrs. Beckner's idea for the family's grand new home, creating a small quest cottage with the same rock and touches as the large two-story home. The woman was talented in many ways. Olivia reached out for Maxwell's elbow as they stepped down the pebbled path to the smaller cottage.

"I'm wondering what you are thinking," Olivia said gently. Mr. Ian Beckner's crossed brow and pursed lips had tried to mask his naturally handsome features. The man was rude, practically booting Dr. Hastings from the propriety.

"I...I'm feeling for Mr. Beckner." Maxwell held the door open, but Olivia stopped, wondering why he felt that way.

"He's lost a father. All he has is the mine, and I show up unannounced. The weight for the Cornish workers is evident on his shoulders."

"You carry such empathy, so much like Ronald." Olivia sighed. "Or maybe more like Morgan." They both chuckled at how different the Hastings sons once were.

"What will you do?" she asked. They stepped into the small front room, and Olivia pulled the combs and pins from her hair.

"I will back off for a bit. Give him his lead and see if he will warm up to me." Maxwell slipped off his suit jacket. "If he does not, I suppose you could find me a cot with the friendless at the orphanage in Sacramento."

Olivia smiled. Dr. Hastings was a wise, noble man. She glanced at her door and then out the front window. "I've missed the grand flower garden path here on the property. I think I will take a stroll tonight before it's completely dark."

"I will retire. Goodnight, then. Tomorrow is my *day off,"* he smirked. "I will take you to Sacramento whenever you are ready."

"Thank you." Olivia stepped out, walking back down the shadowy path that headed towards the garden. After being ignored the entire evening by that rogue, Ian Beckner, she could almost hear Sister Patricia coaxing her to find her quiet peace with God. These gardens would suffice.

Without the tight pins in her hair, she shook out her soft locks that flowed down her back. A light, musical sound sifted in the air. Confused, she looked behind her. She knew the grand home and mining camp were not far, but the soft strumming seemed to be coming from before her. Stepping down to the rows of lovely flowers, she saw a large, dark shadow moving out of the corner of her eye. Wide-eyed, Olivia jerked back, clutching her chest.

"Mr. Beckner," she gasped.

He'd jumped off the bench so fast, his guitar almost flew to the ground. Stumbling to keep it in his grasp, he stood straight. "What are you doing here?" His dark hair fell across his forehead, making his previously impeccable features now look like a child caught stealing the cookie jar.

"Strolling in the garden?"

Ian stood, gripping his guitar over his untucked white shirt. "It's getting late, I...I...would think Dr. Hastings would worry."

"I've done this many times, always safe from man and beast. He does not worry." Olivia stifled a tingle of amusement. Dare she linger long on how shaken and uncomfortable he appeared? "You play the guitar?"

"Only when I think I am alone." He raked his fingers through his hair.

"Of course." She tilted her head to the side, watching his eyes scrutinize her. "I will finish my stroll and allow you your privacy." Olivia stepped down the next tier of steps and turned to enjoy the changes in the row of roses from the last time she was here.

"I didn't realize it was you who has taken over the administration of the Oak Street Home for Children." He walked behind her. "How is work approved of for a lady from such a fine family?"

"What do you know of my family?" A clipped tone escaped with her question. She stopped and peered over her shoulder. Irritated, she kept walking. "Only poor women can work?"

"Well, the Bradstreet name is well known back east... my mother says." He mumbled the ending. "You have a point. I dare say many of the women of your family did not hold service occupations."

Olivia's cheeks turned pink, and she quickened her steps around one row and stepped down to another tier. *What would he say to her birth mother's occupation?* Wishing he'd never spoken to her, it was her turn to ignore him. The man was uncouth, brash, and far too handsome for his own good.

"She said you only wanted to volunteer." Ian continued to keep pace behind her evening garden stroll. "I suppose with old family money that would be more respectable for a daughter."

Olivia wondered if it was her own annoyance or if his words were as smarmy as they seemed. Turning through the last row of the garden, she'd had enough and stepped up the center path to take her leave.

On the top step, her backbone stiffened, and she stopped. What had she done to deserve this scrutiny? "How dare you ask me such personal questions?"

With the darkness and such a quick halt, his guitar bumped into her backside, smashing it between them. The strings twanged, and they both stepped back awkwardly.

"I didn't mean to offend you." Ian laughed without humor. "Forgive me. My mother speaks very highly of you."

"That's because instead of behaving like I wasn't in the room, she took the time to get to know me, without judgment or malice." Olivia whisked her hair behind her ear and turned on her heel.

"Wait, it is fully dark." He stepped up beside her. "Let me see you to the guest cottage."

Olivia let out a low growl and marched on. It was so unlike her to snap at anyone.

"Wait, please, Miss Bradstreet." He lightly touched her arm, and she stopped. Though he was obviously taller, she shouldn't have looked up, leaving only inches from his face. A strange shudder rose inside her.

"I...I...admit, I could've been more cordial tonight." Ian released her arm but didn't step back. "You might not believe me, but just a week ago, I sported a bit, of...of a...romantic heart."

Olivia dropped her chin, her eyes rounding wide with doubt.

Ian gave a half chuckle. "I can see you find that hard to believe, but it's true."

"And what happened to this romantic heart?"

Ian huffed and Olivia smelled a faint smell of alcohol. That explained the strangeness of the man and his chasing after her tonight.

"My betrothed found another. The wait for me to return was too much for her."

Olivia quickly covered her mouth with her fingers. "I'm sorry. How terrible."

"And for an unfathomable reason, you are the first to know. I haven't even broken the news to my mother." He pulled back, tucked the guitar under his arm, and strummed two low menacing notes.

"I see that I disturbed your brooding tonight. Music is a balm for the soul." Olivia hesitated, thinking of the many late-night talks about God that she and Sister Patricia had. "So I've heard." She carefully glanced up and met his soft gray eyes. "I will pray that God will heal your wounds and…" Blast it all, those empathetic words were touching her. Months of praying for absolution of her own past, of losing Ronald in the war, all were causing her own eyes to mist.

"What is this?" Lowering the guitar to his side, he carefully pulled a loose strand of hair from her cheek, leaving his fingers lightly holding her hair back. A touch of compassion broke through his confident guise. "I see tears gathering. Do you also have a romantic heart?" For the faintest moment, she didn't know what to call her heart. But with only a few moonlit shadows highlighting his tender expression, she could almost believe his pain made him a kindred soul.

Coming back to the moment, Olivia had utterly forgotten her hair hung loose and accidentally met his hand as she tried to pull it away from his touch. His fingers held over hers, and with barely a twitch in his smile, he gently tugged her closer until he could place a soft kiss against her lips. Before she could form a protest, he kissed her again. This time it felt like slipping into a warm bath. Liquid warm chills seized every inch of her skin as their breath and lips continued forming sweet sensations she'd only dreamed could happen. Releasing his fingers from her loose hair, he pressed her firmly against him. Her heart pounded in time with his own pounding beats. His kisses weren't demanding, but with each tender touch, he massaged his hand up and down her back. No doubt, he was taking, and she was freely giving. A heady carelessness started to wax over her good sense. The man was a…a…what? *An ardent… scoundrel.*

"I must go," she squeaked and pushed him away. Holding her heated face, she covered her scandalous mouth. She wished she'd covered her eyes. His surly and dark smile appeared a touch too humorous…*or pleased?*

Shock at what she'd just participated in fueled her limbs. Olivia hurried down the dark path, spying the low candle waiting inside the guest cottage. Entering quietly, she held the door closed and rested her flushed face on the cool wood. *That was ridiculous.* Her heart raced furiously from the brisk walk, and she clutched her chest, willing it to slow down. That man...those...those kisses meant nothing, except to play her like the sad notes of his guitar. Those perfect gray-blue eyes pursuing hers, as if he really saw into her heart.

She groaned under her breath. Nothing more than a moment of digression. Why could she not catch a full breath?

Ian Beckner was a wicked tease, impetuous, and she wasn't prepared. His warm lips, his need looking to awaken hers. She rolled her eyes. She'd given in to him for what... one minute...maybe two? It was nothing. Likely his broken romantic heart should now be called desperate. For heaven's sake, they didn't even know each other, and what she knew she did not care for. The shadowy encounter was nothing more than a nonsensical physical diversion mixed with a few too many drinks. It would never happen again. In the darkness, the cad had just pressed upon her before she saw it coming. Any woman would find herself unprepared. That's all.

That's all it was.

Six

I *an teetered on the edge of the ship's gate in nothing but his*
breeches. Where were his clothes? Suddenly to his right was
Lesandra in nothing but her corset and pantaloons. What the
devil? Had they...? Her face was afire with scorn and she spun a
long steel dagger only a hair away from his exposed ribs. Just as
he dodged away from the blade, Dr. Hastings was on the other
side with a war saber pointed at his belly. With hollow, yellow
eyes, the man pulled back to pierce him through and Ian had
nowhere to escape but over the side. Falling, his limbs fought
against the air. There was no water below, only jagged rocks,
falling faster and faster, the impact...

Gasping for air, Ian flew upright in bed. His chest rose and
fell deeply, and he gripped his bare belly. No marks, just a
dream. He flopped backward, still wondering where he was.
Breathing like he'd won a race, he dropped his arms over his
face. He was in a room, in a real bed at the Empire Home. Not
on a ship, thank God, it was just a dream. Lesandra had been
about to gut him like a pig. That made a small fleck of sense,
since he'd behaved like a pig at their parting. And the Dr.
Hastings apparition was like the ghost of death, ready to haunt
him as retribution for his brash behavior.

Ian bolted up like his bed was full of hot coals. He'd kissed
Dr. Hastings' woman!

He clutched his hands into his hair and squeezed. What kind of murky madness had possessed him last night? Releasing a long, low groan, he stood and carefully peered out the second-story window. Was the good doctor waiting for him now? Breakfast and a duel at dawn? *But they were not married.*

Ian growled and spun from the window. He punched his fist into his hand. Now he was the Rafael, dabbling and toying with a lady who was not his. Snatching his work clothes from the chair, he jerked his pants on. Would Miss Bradstreet tell of his misbehavior?

Of course, unlike the witty Lesandra who led everyone on, Miss Bradstreet seemed truly more vulnerable, more honest. The young lady had tried her best to get away from him last night. Maybe she would keep his indiscretion to herself. Unlike Lesandra, at least she wasn't intentionally playing the strumpet with two men.

Ian took an extra look around the entry before completely descending the stairs. The parlor was empty. He peeked in the dining room. All was quiet, such an eerie sound after months of the ship's tight, noisy quarters. Walking into the kitchen, Katy turned from the sink.

"There you are." She smiled. "Your mother said she'd hoped you'd get a good sleep. Something about 'a bit short nerve last night.'" Katy had filled a bowl with grits and buttered a piece of thick bread. After setting it in front of him, she poured him a mug of coffee. Ian took the stool next to the kitchen counter.

"Thank you, Katy, this is a fine breakfast."

"Too much to drink, your mother wondered?"

Ian sipped the hot coffee, judging the benefits and losses of being back at home. "Something like that."

Katy continued to clean and straighten. Taking another sip of coffee, he peered over the rim. "What of Dr. Hastings and Miss Bradstreet? Do they take breakfast in the big house?"

"They have in the past. But Dr. Hastings had his own cookstove put in just recently. But now I expect them back."

Ian shook his head. He didn't feel like he was hungover unless he was still intoxicated from the softest lips a man could hope for. He tried to reign his thoughts back. "What are you saying?"

"Only an hour or so, Dr. Hastings had a wagon brought to the guest house. A few of the men were told to take the stove out to take to the miner's row and let one of them use it."

Ian dropped his spoon in the empty ironstone bowl, and the clanging smarted his head. "That wasn't necessary. I told him explicitly that I would handle the...the needs." He rubbed his eyebrows, where a headache had started.

"I think he's just trying to be helpful. Do what he can." Katy took his bowl and cup. "Would you like anything else?"

"No." Ian stood and patted her back. "I didn't mean to sound cross. Forgive me."

"Oh, no." She shook her head. "It's not my place to say. But you might want to get to know them. Dr. Hastings is a kind, reasonable man. Miss Bradstreet has been good company for your mother. A bit of the daughter she never had. You should give her a chance too."

Ian hesitated with his mouth open, but no response would come. He'd given her a chance already...a chance to hate him.

The fertile land and trees around Grass Valley provided a colorful Autumn. The cooler air brought on the most vivid reds and yellows. Ian remembered when they'd first bought the property, when it had been nothing but rolling hills and scrub oaks. Now he stepped out to groomed front lawns with rock fences and walkways; the changes to the land were everywhere. He spied his mother wearing a wide-brimmed woven hat with a brown ribbon around her chin. Deep in thought, she looked back and forth in front of the new water feature. Her ideas had taken shape in the design of most of the pools and fountains. Two workers unloaded the rocks while she gave them directions.

"Mother, can I have you for a moment?"

"Ian." She wrapped her arm around his back, giving it a squeeze. "How did you sleep? I wanted to see you rest well after such an arduous journey."

"I...I don't know about rest for me." He feigned a grin. "I have a lot on my mind."

His mother tilted her head, and he noticed that there were more strands of gray peppered through her hair. "We haven't had a chance to talk about what is important." She took his hand. "Walk with me for a moment."

Ian took in a deep breath of the Autumn air. Nervous energy pulsed up his back. He had a feeling he knew where she was leading him. As if orchestrated, the breeze turned gentle and the birds flitted away to give them their privacy. The headstone stood erect in memory of Quinn Wallace Beckner. Breaking away from his mother's grasp, he brushed two leaves from the monument.

"I'm sorry I wasn't here." Ian rubbed the back of his neck.

"I felt you here." She nodded. "He was failing when you left. All that was important was that you had your time with him then. He trusted you with his mine. He was so thankful to have a smart and caring son to carry it on."

Ian felt his gut twist watching the leaves ruffle around on the ground. "I was just thinking I don't even recognize the place from when I left. I guess I thought I would pick up just where I had left it." He squatted in front of the stone and drew his fingers over the engraving.

"The Grants were so generous," His mother said. "They wanted to see the mining continue, and they helped out in—"

"I know." Ian rose and sighed. Stretching his head from side to side, he pushed out the words. "Lesandra and I are no longer engaged."

"Oh, I'm sorry." Judith gripped her collar. "I didn't know."

"Whatever they invested in the mine," Ian offered his arm as they slowly stepped back down the path, "we will need to pay them back."

"A dowry already spent." His mother frowned. "It was six."

"Six hundred?" Ian turned to her.

"No, six thousand."

Ian's feet stopped cold. His chin and stomach dropped at the same time. "How could that be?"

"Her father has done very well in the lumber business. San Francisco has burst open with people. Buildings on every free corner." Her eyes creased. "I suppose they saw it as an investment for her too."

"I'll need to get to the books and settle it right away."

"Maybe they would agree to repay it in seasonal increments." Her tone lifted. "When the mine starts to produce."

"What are you saying?"

"Listen, Ian." She stopped and turned to him. "I know you didn't take to Dr. Hastings. But there wasn't one decision he and I didn't make together."

"Such as?"

"The cost of the buildings and the living quarters for the Cornish families. The equipment for the mine expansion and the finishing touches on the home, gardens, and…" She stopped as he turned away, shaking his head. "Salaries for the men, the new workers, for Katy, for the needs of the Children's Home. The children have filled every inch of our old home on Oak Street. They have to eat out on the grass. Olivia and I just spoke about ordering some simple benches and tables."

Ian rolled his lips, waiting to speak. His mother had had a lot to maintain in his absence. "I can tell you have worried far past what father or I would've wanted. The home and the grounds are like you, detailed and full of loving care and time. But from now on, mother, please come to me, not Dr. Hastings. Katy tells me that he had the stove removed from the guest cottage just this morning. That wasn't necessary. I'm sure Miss Bradstreet would like to make his coffee without soiling her gowns at the fireplace."

Taking a full breath, they walked on. "I will thank him again for filling in. There are many areas near us that have no doctor to speak of." They walked across the grass to the front door of the Empire home and he chided himself for his harsh judgment and reckless behavior. "With her in Sacramento, I'm sure he would like to be closer than Grass Valley."

"I think he wants to be here." Judith brushed her hands across her full skirt. "There must be a way," she said softly.

Ian had another second of confusion. "He doesn't want to be with her?"

"I don't know if you even took a full look at her, Ian. She is a grown woman."

Ian shook his head, blinking. "Aren't they together? A couple?"

"Oh, son!" She laughed. "What made you think that?" He's a family guardian of sorts. Olivia's father and Dr. Hastings were medical colleagues in Chicago. Olivia was engaged to Maxwell's son, Ronald. He was killed in the war." She sighed, looking down. "With the death of her parents and mourning Ronald, I think she needed to make a change." Judith looked up and smiled curiously at him.

"A lady as refined and attractive as Miss Bradstreet could find no suitors in Chicago?" His mind spun with the truth. "So she just followed a family friend all the way to California?"

Judith tiled her head. "So, you think she is beautiful?"

Ian opened his mouth, but shut it quickly. His mother's smile incited a warm flush up his neck. Though he was relieved he hadn't kissed another man's woman, he'd been far too forward. "Where are they now? I need to speak to Dr. Hastings."

"They left over an hour ago. Back to Sacramento."

Seven

Olivia took another deep breath, trying to settle her ragged nerves. After a month of details and preparation, the small and narrow Sacrament Hall had been filled with the wonderful local men and women of Sacramento. Tonight they'd all agreed to attend the fundraiser for the Sisters of Charity. Father Gilbert and Sister Patricia had just spoken poignantly about the need to protect the less fortunate. The small choir she led from the Oak Street home was up shortly. They'd spent the last month practicing their two songs for the crowd, but the children looked as terrified as she was. Why hadn't she spent more time teaching them to stay poised in front of a crowd? Her childhood flashed around her; she'd had so many recitals where she'd thought she would pass out.

"Children, don't forget to open your chest. Without air, your sweet melodies won't carry far." Not one child met her eyes, all kept their eyes on the crowd. Everyone froze with fright. "God is with us," she tried.

Joshua Boxner came near. "Miss Bradstreet, I don't feel so well." He'd gone pasty white, and just as she was going to make another encouraging platitude, his cheeks puffed round.

"Oh, Lord, not this." She practically pushed him to an open side door before he lost his dinner of beef and gravy onto the church lawn.

"Miss Bradstreet? An oval-faced nun and her wide habit filled the door. "The Oak Street Children's choir is up next."

"Yes, we are ready. Could you keep an eye on him?" She squeezed past the nun. "Children, it is our turn. Please follow and watch me." She stepped a few feet into the front of the room and heard a wrenching cry. Bonita Rodriquez began to wail at the top of her lungs. Without a moment to think, she straightened all the children in front of the room and casually turned on her heel to escort the crier out to the nun watching Joshua. "Her, too, please."

Olivia found her own chest pounding as she tried to smile at the children. "Just as I am, without one plea," she prompted, while they all looked past her to the silent faces watching them. Raising her fingers like a conductor, she growled under her breath. "Children, please watch me. Just like we practiced in choir class." Finally, when she had three wide-eyed faces on hers, she started the song and prayed the others would follow along. The point was not to hear her, but each time she'd try to lower her voice so the choir could be heard, like ducks who couldn't see their mother, their singing fell off. With six never-ending stanzas, the applause was as weak as the performance.

Sister Patricia wiggled a finger to come near. "Stand with them, facing the crowd and gather them close."

Why not? Olivia went back to her line of children. "I'm standing in the middle. Everyone comes in close around and on the sides so we can face them together." Hands gripped the layers of her full skirt so hard, she could feel them pulling her side to side. Fighting against her own fear, an unknown Bradstreet gust of courage infused her.

"Ladies and Gentlemen, thank you for your patience. The Oak Street children are a bit intimidated tonight. And I can testify that none of you are *that* scary." Her smile and dimple worked the crowd provoking a low chuckle that swirled across the room. "Our next song…" Olivia tried to clear her throat. At the back table sat Judith Beckner, whom she had invited. But the handsome smile with steeled eyes reached across the room and stared at her. Blood rushed from her toes to her neck. *Mr. Beckner, what is he doing here? Oh Lord, what was I saying…?*

A squeak escaped her throat, sounding just like the one from the night in the garden. A child tugged on her skirt, and she sucked in a thin breath.

"The Cows in the Orchard." Came out weaker than her last words. "Let's sing it together, children." She wrapped her arms around the ones near. While starting out the fun song about the farmer's wife, her voice brought wide eyes and pleasant expressions from the crowd. The children relaxed and finally sang out their parts. The boys mooing in time as the cows and the girls clucking like chickens. Weakly they all joined in the chorus.

The cow's in the orchard again.

The farmer has to fix the fence

The cow's in the orchard again

Could his wife be so dense?

Smiles and applause brought their silly tune to the end. The girls curtsied, and the boys bowed, just as she'd taught them. Her fledgling choir exited to the left where Sister Patricia waited with Joshua and Bonita. Before they could organize the children, a well-dressed older woman appeared, extending her card. "Miss Bradstreet, may I give you my card? I would love to have you to tea. I am familiar with the Bradstreets from Illinois."

"Oh, thank you." Olivia smiled, wishing she had changed her name. Sister Patricia helped the children get in line for a cup of punch while another couple introduced themselves, commending her on her lovely voice. They wondered if they could call upon her to sing for any other occasion. Olivia politely brought the conversation back to the needs of the orphanage, and they eventually nodded and left. Standing behind them, thoroughly regal in his dark suit from the first night, Mr. Ian Beckner smiled. Olivia's breath caught in her throat.

"You do have a *lovely* voice, Miss Bradstreet." Ian bowed towards her, and she answered by forgoing her own curtsy.

Was there a sliver of mocking in his compliment? Her gloved fingers entwined and gripped in front of her dress, crushing her own knuckles. "And if I had been aware that you were attending our humble fundraiser, I would've asked you to bring your guitar."

"That or my pocketbook?" His eyes turned serious, and she didn't like how quickly his tone challenged her.

"Thank you for coming tonight, Mr. Beckner. I'd hoped to greet your mother." Casually, she tried to look over his shoulder, but her pulse betrayed her.

"She wants to come by the house tomorrow."

"Wonderful." Her eyes wouldn't come near his. "You are staying the night?"

"Yes." He tilted his head to the side. "I understand our Oak Street home is full to the brim. Strange, we have to stay in a hotel."

Olivia glanced around to the people taking their leave. He didn't sound as benevolent as his mother when discussing the use of their home. "I really should be mingling with the patrons." With the perfect excuse, she feigned a modest smile.

"Wait." He took her gloved hand and she could feel her fingers tremble beneath his touch. "I need to apologize." His voice dipped low. "For the time we were in the garden."

"Humm." Olivia winced. She looked from left to right. The air had seemed to leave the room. She tugged her hand loose. She'd spent an entire month blocking him and their kiss from her hourly thoughts. How rude of the man to confront her like this. A sweaty chill came up her back. His domineering presence had commanded her attention from the moment their eyes met, and he knew it.

"I accept your apology. Your romantic heart wasn't as broken as you thought."

He nodded a half-grin. "Your time is commendable here with the nuns. God must have heard the earnest prayer you offered that night."

"Maybe so." She smiled, needing to leave.

"I've made peace with Dr. Hastings."

Olivia stilled, finally meeting the striking blue-gray of his eyes. "How is that?"

"The months at sea were rough for many passengers. In our company, we lost two children to smallpox and others were still feeble from the fever when we arrived." Pressing his lips in a line, he seemed genuinely contrite. "Dr. Hastings came in with care and remedies for the sick. Two of the Cornish men had sustained deep cuts after falling from one of the narrow scaffoldings. Thanks to his care, the stitches show no sign of infection. The families like him, and they are thankful for his care and concern." His eyes seemed to struggle with the humble confession, and Olivia felt a quickening in her heart. He'd taken the time to see Maxwell for the man he was. Ian lifted a shoulder. "I guess you would say we're working… together."

For the first time all evening, a calm peace settled inside of her. Ian Beckner had put his pride aside to give Dr. Hastings a chance. His words, his attention tonight brought another wave of masculine allure she'd worked so hard to stifle.

"And I wanted to apologize for when I first saw you sitting at my family table," he said. "I made a hasty assumption. I didn't realize I was so bruised and short-sighted. I'd thought you were with Dr. Hastings."

She angled her head and leveled him with her eyes. "With?" Thinking she understood the word, she swallowed hard and dropped her chin. "You mean as a couple?"

"A man too long at sea." He rolled his eyes with a crooked smile. "Just a clumsy misunderstanding on my part."

Suddenly she stifled an impolite word that many a ruffian used on the wagon trail. "If you… thought…" Her words came out in short spurts. "Then… why…?"

He looked to his feet and slowly grazed up her form like a lover's soft caress. That boyish handsome jaw rocked to the side. "In case you didn't know, you're *very* attractive. You stroll into the dark with your hair down? What do you expect an unstable man to do?"

Olivia felt like a piece of cheese left in the corner for the rat. The air finally entered her lungs. "For one sunlit moment, when you spoke tonight, I had a feeling I might have misjudged you. But no. I was right." The room seemed to fade away as her heartbeat began pounding in her ears. "You are a rogue and a scoundrel. All this nonsense about your broken romantic heart. Do you use that line often?" Taking in a needed quick breath, she took a step closer. "How dare you kiss me." She growled with clenched teeth, praying no one heard her. "You thought I was already a corrupt woman?" Her eyes began to fill with hot mist. Did she reek of her own indecency and fraudulence? Could the man see into her disgraceful birth?

Ian took a step back and offered his handkerchief from his corner pocket. "I've, I've...please. I...never meant my impressions to insult you. It came out wrong." He bit the corner of his mouth. "I meant it as a compliment."

Olivia snatched the cloth from his hand and quickly dabbed the tears from the corners of her eyes. "Never mind. It doesn't matter. Believe me, it really doesn't matter." She took his hand and pressed the handkerchief into his palm. "Tell your mother I look forward to her visit." Shoulders back, she turned on her heel and walked away, thankful her life here in Sacramento was full of purpose, far away from the snare of Ian Beckner.

Eight

The next morning, at the front door of the Oak Street Home, Olivia's rehearsed greeting stuck in her throat. Ian had escorted his mother quickly to the steps and, without even a nod her way, turned and went back to their wagon. Disappointed she didn't get to ignore him as she practiced, she reached out her hand.

"Judith." She smiled, but her eyes followed the wagon as it rolled away.

"Ian asked me to tell you he would be back before supper to gather me." Judith waited. "Have I upset the order of the day? You look distressed."

"Oh, no." Olivia reached in to hug her. Why now, after tossing and turning all night, did she wonder if she should lower her defenses and give consideration to Ian's apologies? Blinking away her befuddled state, she smiled. "I'm so sorry I missed you last night, Judith. Thank you for coming." Olivia patted the hair at the nape of her neck. "Let's move into the office."

Judith turned to watch the children working over their slates as Sister Patricia walked the rows, checking their work. One little girl smiled at them.

"My front room as a school." Judith removed her gloves and hat and set them on the side table. "It warms my heart."

"May I bring you a tray of tea or coffee?" Olivia offered.

"I just finished a cup of tea at the hotel, but thank you, dear." Judith sat on the soft leather chair across from Olivia's desk and rubbed the faded arms. "These two chairs were from my parents' home. The way you've arranged the office is quite handsome."

"I find this room very special and yet..." Olivia sat at her desk, searching for the words. "Often painful."

Judith squinted. "Oh."

"I've had the joy of seeing one of our students placed into a good Christian home," Olivia said. "But then *we* miss them." She huffed skyward, shaking her head. "Many of the children's mothers come on certain days for visits. There is so much excitement and love shared, and then at parting, so many tears." Olivia felt emotion rise in her throat. "Including mine." She tried to lighten the moment with a laugh.

"Umm, yes, I see what you mean." Judith nodded. "It really is God's work, yes? Caring for the least of these. You are so wonderful at it."

"I know you applaud me for taking on this position, but I will confess I couldn't do it without Sister Patricia and the other nuns. They have mercy that has no bounds, but yet unlike me, they don't crumble under the weight of the needs." Olivia shrugged. "I just want every orphan in a good family."

"Of course, but you must not despise your youth." Judith tilted her head to the side. "Those beloved nuns were all once like you. Sojourners from afar, hearts full of hopes and dreams."

Olivia let those words settle in her. She was young and much too idealistic for her own good. One would think after losing Ronald and being kicked from the Bradstreet family, she'd let go of her childish ways. Her mother had said her heart was as golden as her hair. Something in her mind's eye flitted to Ian Beckner. He'd seen the hapless, naive woman in her and possessed the skill to make her feel worse about herself. What a cad.

"What did you think of last night's attempts to solicit funds?" Olivia released a chuckle. "A bit of a mad-hatted caper with its ups and downs."

"Oh, no. It was delightful, heartfelt. *And...*" Judith's eyebrows rose. "I know some of those in attendance. The gold rush has been to their favor. I can only hope they dug deep into their pockets with charitable hearts." Judith patted the arm of the thick leather chair. "I saw you and Ian talking. It didn't look like it went well. I wondered if he admitted we are in a bit of financial plight. He might be feeling embarrassed not to give our usual amounts to the charities."

"Oh, no. He said nothing towards that. And please..." Olivia leaned forward across her desk. "How could we begin to count the value of the use of this lovely home? The Beckners and I suppose the Empire Mine has done more than anyone to support this work."

"Perhaps I should've not talked of the pressure he's under." Judith sighed. "His fiancée's family helped us out considerably after my husband passed. But Ian has told me she is not the person he thought she was." She paused, her tone faint. "In so many words, Ian found her with another man."

Olivia barely nodded. His broken heart was not *all* alcohol speaking. Still, he was a rake, to assume she was a fallen woman. "Would you like me to speak to Dr. Hastings? I don't know what kind of money—"

"Oh, no, dear," Judith said quickly. "Maxwell has done so much. His forbearance with Ian is quite noble after the things said at our first dinner together."

Olivia smiled. "Maybe Dr. Hastings' forbearance has more to do with *you* than Ian?"

Judith released a soft wide-eyed laugh. "How do you have such uncanny sight in the back of your head, young lady?"

Olivia smiled with her. Just the two eyes in front had seen enough to wonder if a romance was starting between them.

Mary Ellen appeared in the doorway. The young teen didn't have to say a word.

"Yes, the bell." Olivia stood and gave it a good ring. "The children have a morning routine of exercises and chores for the older ones. "Shall we tag along?"

That afternoon, Ian drove his wagon away from the Grant yard, irritated and relieved. By his own admission, he'd never wanted to see Lesandra again, and thankfully she was nowhere to be seen. Did she expect he would expose her unfaithfulness to her father?

Mr. Grant, on the other hand, treated Ian as if the plague entered his house with him. He was gruff and short, demanding the gift was really Lesandra's dowry. It was meant for her future only. Ian handed him all he could scrape together, and Mr. Grant threw the five hundred dollars on a table. He wanted to be paid back in full in thirty days, or he would get a lawyer and put a lean on Empire Mine. Knowing it was near to impossible to raise the cash in thirty days, Ian kept his cool and asked for a signed receipt for the first payment. With nothing left to say, Ian bid the man a good day.

On the next stop, he would use his own injustice to sway the owner of the San Francisco ironworks. They also had a price set for the purchase of the five shanty cookstoves. Truth be told, the Cornish women hadn't voiced one complaint. Using their fireplaces and the earthen oven for their baking, they were just like their men, resourceful and hardworking. His pride was more pierced for not having everything he'd promised. Maybe he should just be thankful to be able to provide enough food for now.

Ian stood back as the men loaded three of the stoves, the weight bearing down in his wagon. Two he purchased at only double the price, the third one he took on credit. Reaching for his glass jar, he took off the lid and took a long drink of water. The day had been exhausting, and he still had to drive back to Sacramento and gather his mother. It would be another two hours to Grass Valley listening to his mother recount the day with the lovely Olivia Bradstreet. Would Olivia tell of their harsh words at the fundraiser? Would she weave a tale of his long list of indiscretions?

Lesandra Grant was surely deserving of his wrath, but Miss Bradstreet had received the whiplash of his jilted affections. He jumped up to the wagon bench and tapped the horses forward. *A dark night and loose hair,* could he be so cavalier to use her to prove he was still a man? The truth raked his gut. He was borrowing misfortune, and he knew it. Miss Bradstreet was not just beautiful; she was engaging, unique, and benevolent, holding her own in a room full of stiff wealthy people.

He had a certain admiration for her, and that is why he'd wanted her forgiveness. Truth be told, he could not take his eyes from her. The moment he'd seen her in the Sacrament Hall, it was a reaction he'd never felt before. Her kisses were innocent, but only for him. In a room full of people, the desire to single-handedly possess her heart and attention was overwhelmingly strong. Many of the families the Beckners knew had made polite conversation, but as soon as they turned to his mother he moved away to watch Miss Bradstreet.

Almost as sweet as their stolen kiss was the moment their gazes met from across the room. Her glowing expression faltered and her words sounded labored until she looked away from him. Her response was enchanting—from bow to stern, he felt the same way. Now who was behaving the victim?

Women like her, all fancy with tons of old family money, could not be trusted. Olivia Bradstreet had clearly shown she could chew him up and spit him out. Blast it, he'd deserved it. He tapped the horses east to Sacramento. Why had there been pain and tears in her eyes? Had she begun to care for him? Why had he opened his mouth about her relationship with Dr. Hastings and put his foot straight in? Frustrated, he shook his head and gripped the reins tightly.

As if their stolen shadowy kissing wasn't enough, her desire to shun him just made him all the more attracted to the interesting young woman.

Nine

Groggy from the long drive the day before, Ian sat up in bed, unable to welcome the new day streaming through his window. He'd slept little, hearing Mr. Grant's words about taking the mine. They played over and over, and in his torment he'd offered up a beggar's prayer to God. He thought of sitting in the church as a child, the reverend speaking of a God who loves His creation as they conduct their lives in righteousness. Yet the stain glass above the organ showed a lamb being sacrificed on an altar. Ian rubbed the tired thoughts from his brow.

What foolish thought or action was he paying for now? He'd tried to be a respectable man. Obviously, God, in the form of Olivia Bradstreet, knew differently. Ian rose and hovered over his desk. Picking up the receipt with the Grant's letterhead, he held it, waiting for some other possibility to appear from the sky.

Tossing it back on his desk, he picked up the mine reports. They just needed more time. The new shafts were going deeper every day. The chip and drill method the Cornish workers applied were hauling out more rock than he could imagine. The stamp mill was rudimentary, just donkeys pulling the large crushing rock, but it was all working for the good. Knowing he'd been awake for hours rehearsing what might help the mine produce, Ian rolled his eyes and stepped over to the window. Mr. Grant told him thirty days, and now, with the lien coming against the mine, he had to repay the dowry, and there was only one thing he could do.

⌒

Thirty minutes later, Judith was scowling at the breakfast table. "Absolutely not," his mother clipped. Upset, she set her cup and saucer down and stood pacing with her hands on her hips. "Those children have no home. You can't sell the Oak Street home, the only home that keeps them from being vagrants on the streets."

"I knew you would feel that way, and I've examined every side of it." Ian sighed. "Mr. Grant has a good lawyer, and they will take the mine, the house. The only reason father wanted the Sisters of Charity to use the house was that the mine could sustain it. When this is all gone, it would fall anyway."

"This breaks my heart." Judith's chin quivered. "And what of Miss Bradstreet? That home, those children are her lifeblood. Do you expect her to send the children packing?"

"No, of course not. I was hoping you would go to Sacramento this week and ease her into the transition, help her understand."

"Me?" Judith gasped, her lips pursed tight as she walked around the table. "I…I cannot do it. I don't have the constitution. That home is her domain. As the headmistress, she runs it with care and intuition. The children are loving and disciplined and…I could…never." She sucked in a breath. "You'll have to carry this eviction out yourself."

"Fine." Ian shrugged. "You have more connections, but I'm sure we can secure another position for her. Maybe the church will find another home for the children, and she can carry on as usual in that one."

"Humph." Judith's eyes creased dark. "That doesn't seem likely when they have to do a fundraiser just to obtain benches and tables. Oh, Ian." Her voice sank. "Are you sure there is no other way? Perhaps I could speak to Maxwell?"

"It's Maxwell now? You mean Dr. Hastings?" Ian felt his gut pinch. He'd started to make excuses to miss dinners in his own home. His mother and Dr. Hastings appeared to be in their own new world. He was the one supposed to be starting a home, a family, not losing sleep over repaying an exorbitant dowry. "The Empire Mine is under our control mother and I will spare you my good humor in suggesting assistance of any kind from Dr. Hastings."

Judith held her flushed cheeks and shook her head as Ian walked out. He was the devil incarnate living in the Empire Cottage home, and tomorrow the devil would arrive at the Oak Street Home for Children.

Olivia felt the Autumn winds pull her skirts to the side as she helped Mary Ellen hang the laundry in the back of the yard. Today it was the boys' bedding and clothes that flapped back and forth, mimicking the chatter of the children helping with the various morning chores. "Did you see the pumpkins the neighbor left yesterday, Miss Bradstreet?"

"I did hear of that gift." Olivia smiled as she pinned the sheet to the line. The young teen, Mary Ellen, was almost her height with a splatter of freckles across her nose. "What do you think Sister Norma could make with them?"

"Oh, that's a fun thought. I knew a lady when we were panning by the big river." Mary Ellen smiled, and then it faded. "This was before my ma died. She would cut them in fourths. Add a little sugar and molasses and bake them for two hours. She brought a chunk to us, and I shared one with my little brothers. It was wonderful."

"Miss Bradstreet," Thomas called from the barn. "There is a man here. I just took his horse, I thinks he's comin' around to the door."

"Thank you, Thomas." Olivia handed Mary Ellen an apron. "Will you finish for me?"

"Yes, ma'am." Mary Ellen tilted her head. "I wonder who would use our barn instead of the hitching post out front?"

Olivia stepped away. Someone familiar, she knew. Her insides twisted as she walked in the back door and down the hall. Coming in without knocking, Ian stood in the foyer and dropped his hat on the hall tree. Confusion competed with jangled nerves at seeing him. Olivia quit biting her bottom lip and straightened her windblown hair. "Mr. Beckner. Is everything all right? Has something happened at the mine?"

His eyes did that familiar quick rove over her being, finally reaching her eyes. "Good day, Miss Bradstreet."

"Forgive me, Good day sir." She bent a small curtsy.

"You look well," he said, tucking his hands in his gray wool slacks, then quickly bringing them out to pull on the bottom of his tweed vest. His eyes wandered around the entrance.

"To what do we owe your visit? Please tell me, is everyone all right?"

"Yes," he nodded. "Everyone is fine." He scratched the back of his neck. "So, that is the schoolroom?"

"Yes." She took a step closer to the wide opening. "The children are on their morning exercise or chores. When each one takes the opportunity to milk the cow, feed the chickens, do laundry, muck the barn...." He seemed almost nervous or distracted, making her ramble on. "...then we accomplish trade skills along with reading and writing. Sister Patricia teaches the primary lessons. And I teach the boys... needlework, curtsying, and how to hold a fan," Olivia teased, trying to gauge his attention.

"Could we talk in the office?" He glanced over to her desk.

She knew he wasn't listening.

Broad-shouldered and preoccupied, Ian Beckner walked in before she finished rolling her eyes.

"Would you like to sit?" She extended her hand to the leather chairs and hesitated to sit behind her desk. Clearly distracted and void of any social graces when she was near, he glanced out the window. Swallowing hard, she prayed he wasn't here to call upon her or offer another awkward apology.

"I'll stand." He rubbed his temple. "I wanted to inform you in person that this Oak Street home is for sale."

"For sale?" She steadied her wavering body and gripped her tall chair. "This home?"

"Yes, I found a facilitator to handle the purchase. I know you have your hands full." He glanced back toward the entry where children began to gather again in the front room. "So, if there are any inquires, you may direct them to this address." He pulled the paper out of his pocket and set it on her desk.

Her body froze, and her mouth hung open. "You can't just sell this home out from under these children." She met his gaze boldly. "It takes months to find one good Christian home who wants an older child." She glanced at the piece of paper, waiting for any reasonable explanation. "They have nowhere to go. That is why they are here." Her chest rose and fell.

"There are other orphanages. Maybe not in Sacramento, but I'm sure there are in San Francisco." His jaw clenched. "I don't want to do this. But I've no choice."

"Why? What has happened? Is the mine out of money?" Olivia implored.

His tongue rolled inside his cheek. "It's really none of your or Dr. Hastings' business," he said sternly, eyes narrowing.

Olivia fought the urge to spring across her desk and take him by the throat. "Could you be any more capricious? I have a right to know. Did you have a falling out with Dr. Hastings? Is this your way of getting rid of us?"

"No, don't be dramatic." He scowled. "It's just business. The sale of the Oak Street house will save the mine from being taken from my family."

"At the cost of the children's security and my job?" Her eyes flared. "How dare you treat us like disposable country bumpkins. There must be another way!"

"I will help you find another position." He huffed. "And trust me, Miss Bradstreet, you may be naïve, but you are no country bumpkin."

Her face flushed red. He was doing it again. *How dare the man be so pompous?*

Ian shrugged. "It's possible the church will find another location and all the children can be moved together."

Olivia stilled, Ian Beckner had turned into an indifferent brick wall, removed from all feelings and care for God's children. She'd told herself a hundred times, she should've never dithered over a handsome face. The mask was off now, and her stomach dropped to her feet. "How long?" she said dazedly. "How long until we must vacate."

"As soon as possible." His words were faint over Sister Patricia calling the class to order. Returning to their seats, the children began to recite scripture verses with Sister Patricia.

Yea, thou I walk through the valley of the shadow of death, I will fear no evil...

"I'd like to come back in two weeks. If it's not raining, I'll need to move our families furnishings to the Empire Cottage."

What did he say? Two weeks? Would they all be out on the streets?

...for thou art with me; thy rod and thy staff they comfort me.

Olivia felt a stab of shock and then embarrassment. She'd paraded about the area as the secretary of the Ladies' Protection and Relief Society, believing her life calling as the headmistress of the Oak Street Children's Home could overcome her past. But very soon she would be without a position and back to being an orphan all over again. How many more times in her life could she withstand being thrown out and her security pulled out from her? The heated silence lingered between them, and Olivia finally lifted her stunned gaze to his.

"I am sorry." His tone held a measure of defeat. "I have thought it over a hundred ways. I know you believe I am the ruin of your worthy cause." He stepped closer, fixing his eyes on hers. Leaning his hands on her desk, he was close enough to reach for her and her skin bristled. "I believe that the lives of the miner's families and *their* children are just as important. They are my cause."

Surely goodness and mercy shall follow me all the days of my life: and I will dwell in the house of the LORD forever.

The children's voices, repeated, like a melodic chorus. Did she even believe those words herself? Could that familiar verse ever be true for one moment of her life? Crushed in body and soul, Olivia numbly showed Ian Beckner to the door.

Ten

Two weeks later, Olivia sat at her desk with her face in her hands. The couple who were interested in Mary Ellen had only wanted a nanny for their twins. After Olivia had gently explained the need for a child to have a real family, not just employment, they had scowled. *No cast-off would ever be their real kin*, they'd said.

Olivia rubbed her forehead. At least she hadn't done introductions and given Mary Ellen false hope. Olivia looked down and crossed off the couple's name. She vacillated between frustration and desperation her paper of possible placements for the children held little promise.

Standing and stretching her back, she moved to the front window and stared out needlessly. The sky was clear and there was still nothing new to see. How long until Ian Beckner sent workers to move their belongings? Her own trunk sat packed like a daily reminder of the inevitable. She also had no offers for another position, and being hauled back to the Empire Mine like all the Oak Street furnishings felt like another dreaded wagon trip to the unknown.

"We have the third room cleared." Sister Patricia sat a box down in the hallway and stepped into the office.

Olivia struggled to find a smile for the saintly woman who worked tirelessly. "Thank you, Sister. Any word from Father Gilbert?"

Sister Patricia grabbed her large wooden cross that hung in front of her chest. "We must have hope, we must trust," she said matter-of-factly. "But no, he said no one has come forth to offer a home for all of them."

"And the rectory could hold four if possible?"

"Yes." She hesitated. "I feel as if we should have those with mother visits move there. If they are placed too far out, I fear they will lose the only connection they have with their families."

"We don't want that," Olivia said, unable to hide her discouragement.

"And the older brother of Franklin and George is coming tomorrow. He's found a steady job and wants them with him."

"Well, that's good. I suppose." Those two brothers were pure mischief and energy, needing constant supervision. How would an older brother who worked from dawn to dusk be able to—?

Sister Patricia took her by the arm and held her hand. "I see the fear and grief all over your countenance." She squeezed their hands together.

Olivia tried so hard to stay positive in front of the children. "The family for Mary Ellen was not suitable." Her voice cracked, and weary tears filled her eyes. "You are the dearest friend I've known." Olivia squeezed her warm hands back before she let go. "I am ashamed to say I grieve for myself and my inabilities." The tears rolled loose, and Olivia swiped them away. "And this is no time to think of one's self."

Sister Patricia wrapped her arms around Olivia. "You don't have to be strong every minute, Olivia. God sees your heart. The depth of your hurt reveals the depth of your love." Sister Patricia rubbed her back. "So, just take a moment for yourself." She pulled back and offered a sad smile. "Will you go back to Grass Valley?"

Olivia found her hankie from her pocket and dabbed her wet face. Fighting the words forming on her lips, she sighed. "I don't want to, but just like the children, I have nowhere else to go."

Sister Patricia tipped her chin. "One of the hardest things we must accept with God is that He has a way and timing that is unlike ours. You know, I shared my deep despair when I lost three of my dearest Sisters of Charity while crossing the Panama jungle."

Olivia nodded. "And you were on assignment for God, doing His work." The irony of their deaths seemed incomprehensible.

The wise nun gripped her arms. "But here you see me today, teaching the children. I do not grieve as one forsaken anymore." She patted Olivia's cheek gently. "Let me pray over you. *Our Loving Father and Creator, we surrender our lives anew in this time of need. For Olivia and every child that craves Your security, would You come and show us the depths of love and care You have for us. In the name of the Father, Son, and Holy Spirit, I pray.*" Sister Patricia kissed her cross rosary and touched it to each shoulder and her forehead.

A soft settled calm rested on Olivia. "Thank you. I have one more interview for Clara Brown this afternoon. At this point, I can only rely on God."

By dusk, Olivia knew God had mercy on her fragile heart. She pulled the brown draperies over the front window and turned her attention back to her desk. The family interested in Clara had turned out to be loving parents with four older boys, and the mother had longed for a girl child to dote on. Olivia wrote the word *"placed"* over Clara's name. It was a miracle, along with the fact that Father Gilbert had gone personally to many of his parishioner's homes asking for help.

Franklin and George had left earlier today. Olivia walked into the schoolroom. This room would feel empty without the children's energy. She blew out the oil lantern hanging on the wall. A sound at the front door startled her. She turned as the door opened. Olivia hung back in the classroom while Ian Beckner dropped his hat and jacket on the hall tree. Her lovely calm sparked to anger, and she longed to tell him it was only courteous to knock. But the home belonged to him. He turned to her as if he knew she would be there, waiting to give what was rightfully his but so incredibly wrong for her.

"Good evening. Miss Bradstreet."

Olivia nodded. No good manners could be found in her.

"I'm sorry for the evening hour. I've been in San Francisco all day." His voice was flat and his jaw tense. "I wanted to tell you. I made one last attempt to try to persuade Mr. Grant's lawyer."

Olivia walked past him and back into her office. It was aggressive of her to ignore him so blatantly, but she cared little for his last attempts. Straightening the papers on her desk, she returned the quill to the round glass holder.

Little Thomas came around the office corner. "Miss Bradstreet?" He squinted upward, frowning at Ian Beckner. "Are you the man who sold our house?"

"Thomas Long." Olivia cut in. "That is not how you greet an elder." She huffed. "And the truth is, it is not *our* house. This fine home belongs to Mr. Beckner."

"Why can't we stay just a little longer?" Thomas scowled. "Last year, the church brought pudding and cream, and each of us got new socks."

Ian Beckner opened his mouth. Confused, he turned to Olivia.

"Christmas. He's remembering Christmas." She crossed her arms over her chest.

Mr. Beckner rubbed his chin, appearing at a loss for an answer.

Good, Olivia mused. Let the confident brute feel what it's like to turn a child out with no loving family or orphanage to care for him.

Uncomfortable, Mr. Beckner shuffled his feet and looked to her again.

"Thomas." She touched the boy's shoulder. "What did you need from me?"

"We'd hope you'd sing to us tonight? We all got our hands washed and will get in bed early if you will sing." A sly smile rose across his face. "Or we can play with the costumes in the attic while we act out a story for you."

Olivia opened her mouth, but nothing reasonable would come out. On Saturday evenings, she'd brought the children up into the attic for a makeshift theater. Using the Beckner's old clothes for costumes likely would not set well with Mr. Beckner. She doubted he'd ever even been a child. "Thomas, I'm not sure how long I will be at Mr. Beckner's disposal." Her eyes bobbed upward. That didn't sound proper. "Thank you for getting ready for bed without supervision. It reminds me of what a responsible boy you are." She turned him back towards the stairs, but before she looked away, a fierce frown was leveled at Mr. Beckner. The boy pounded up the stairs.

"How many children remain?" Ian's tone stiff.

Olivia walked over to her desk, feigning ignorance. She already knew without looking. "Ten," she conceded. He'd every right to be angry. "Three were placed this very afternoon."

"And how many tomorrow?"

She drew her fingers across her forehead and patted her hair. "I couldn't say. I suppose that's in God's hands."

"God's hands?"

"Yes, Mr. Beckner." She emphasized. "I have the entire Ladies' Protection and Relief Society helping and the Catholic Church of Sacramento. Despite the position you've placed me in, God is in control."

"I'm not implying you've been slack, Miss Bradstreet."

"Then it must be the sudden weakness of my prayers." Wide-eyed, her rigid expression was meant to challenge him, but a small smile danced around his mouth. Yet there was nothing humorous in her tone or words.

"I seem to remember a garden stroll and the fortune of your rich prayers. I find them very effective."

A sudden heat rose up to her neck, how dare the man tease her. Why couldn't they both forget their lapse in judgment? For heaven's sake, it was months ago. "It's getting late, I must see to the remaining children."

"Is there a place I could sleep? It's too late to begin the move, and I assumed the house would be empty."

Olivia folded her arms across her chest. "You can have my room."

"You would share with me?" Those taunting lips could not hold back a smile.

"Mr. Beckner!" she fumed. "I meant that as in lending, *not* joining." He inched back.

Thomas Long bounded down the stairs, slid across the foyer wood floor in his nightshirt and cap, and exclaimed joyfully. "We're ready!"

"Thomas. Get. To. Bed." Her arm and finger thrust straight out. The wide-eyed boy turned like a mouse about to be pounced on by a cat and ran back up the stairs.

"I will sleep in the girls' room, "she defended herself curtly, heart thudding. Oh, how she longed to wipe that handsome smirk off his face. "Humph, actually, I may leave before dawn." Her voice simmered sarcastically low. "I'll let you handle putting the last of these children out on the street. Sister Norma is gone, so don't forget the stove is temperamental, and you'll need to feed them breakfast before you kick them out." Before she could cross from the room, he grasped her elbow.

"Miss Bradstreet, please. You would never…" Genuine fright showed in his eyes. "Please say you're joking!" A small groan escaped from the back of his throat. "I am completely at a loss why I behave so ridiculously when I'm in your presence. I've agonized over and over, and I can't seem to make my words sound proper."

"Agonized? Certainly, you exaggerate," she puffed, pulling her arm loose from his warm fingers. "Mr. Beckner, these last two weeks have been torture for me." She prayed to keep her voice steady. "Let's just stay out of each other's way and get this over and done with." Gripping the sharp pain at her chest, Olivia stopped at the staircase. "I'll be here in the morning."

Eleven

Ian should've never accepted the use of her room. It was tidy and polished, her silver brush and mirror set atop the thin dresser, all waiting innocently to be disrupted. Careful to make no sound, he pulled each drawer out. They were all empty. His guilt only multiplied. Not only had he made her move, but could he not have one conversation that didn't end with her disgusted with him? He picked up a small unused bar of milk soap and brought it to his nose. It smelled like fresh lavender, just like she did.

The room was small, and the single bed and thin dresser took up most of the area. He dropped his vest on the chair and sat, pulling his boots off. This room had been used for storage when his parents lived here. That seemed like a lifetime ago. When had everything gotten so demanding and complicated? Blowing out the candle, he pulled her blanket loose and laid down.

Agonize? He could still hear her mocking him. Like many nights before, his mind drifted to her. It *was* agonizing. He flipped to his side and adjusted the blanket. Her beauty would keep bears awake in the winter. Her feminine form would keep a swarm of wasps from their nests. His eyelids closed as he envisioned her before him. Her soft full lips would stop a bull from charging. Her voice would make… His eyes flung open, good lord, he was lying in her bed, evoking the worst ideas ever! What if she was to come to him tonight? His breathing quickened.

He imagined her sweetly apologizing for all the unnecessary fretting she'd done, softly saying that she was sorry for pushing him away. Maybe she would sit on the corner of the bed and tell him she desired him as much as he desired her. Would he reach his fingers up into her loose flowing hair? It was that easy last time. And this time, instead of a guitar hanging attached to his side, he had both arms to surround her and pull her close.

A loud thud radiated above, interrupting his dreams. Did they all still go to the attic for story time? He rose on one elbow and listened. No other sounds were heard but the small grating reminder of his own agony. Miss Bradstreet and her endearing body and soul was only a dream. The truth was in all his ridiculous attempts to draw her into his good graces; each one fell flat. Or worse than flat, whatever that is. Laying down again, he closed his eyes. The romantic heart he thought he possessed was a sad joke. The former headmistress of Oak Street would never have anything to do with him.

Like the creaking on the ship across the ocean, a noise roused Ian from his sleep. An angel stood next to his bed with a white gown and long blonde hair. Blinking back the sight, he almost smiled. His dream was so real, he thought he was seeing the candlelit face of Miss Bradstreet.

"Mr. Beckner."

It was her! Ian flew back so fast he hit his head on the wall. "What? What are you doing?" He rubbed the dull pain under his hair. No air would reach his lungs as he scrambled for the blanket. Suddenly he remembered he'd slept in his trousers and shirt.

"Maybe it's nothing. But I smell something burning. Could you look? Maybe it's coming from outside."

"Yes, certainly." He jumped up before he realized she didn't have time to step away in the tight closet turned bedroom. His arm went around her waist to steady them from falling. "I'm sorry," he ground out as her warm curves collided against him. Quickly holding his guilty arms up in surrender, he tried to lean back. "You go out first."

Olivia struck a match to a sconce in the upstairs hallway. "I'll look around up here. Maybe leaves got caught in the flue. That happened one time in our home in Chicago." She brushed her loose hair behind her ears.

Ian must have looked the fool standing in the hall, jaw hanging, staring at her. The soft sconce flickered, highlighting her incredible femininity beneath her white gown as soft, loose tresses trailed down her form. He blinked, this was no dream. This was the real Miss Bradstreet talking to him and kindly asking him for help.

His mind finally awoke to her request. "I'll check downstairs, the kitchen, and the outside barn." *Of course the barn was outside.* He raked his fingers through his hair as his bare feet descended the stairs. Searching around quickly, he headed into the kitchen. There was a faint smell of smoke. He set his hand upon the black cookstove; it was barely warm, with nothing burning inside to his knowledge. He opened the back door, a strange pull like a strong wind almost taking the knob from his hand. It was a bit gusty in the blackened night as he walked back from the two-story home.

Without seeing anything out of place, he jogged into the barn. Animals, hay, peace and quiet—even in the dark, everything seemed as usual. An instant panic made his blood surge and he ran out the back of the barn and searched the property. His wagon was here. His horses were in the corral and, spotting the few neighbors' homes left to right, nothing looked amiss. Deciding to check the front of the house, Ian stepped back through the barn.

A faint scream rent the night air. Running at full speed, Ian flew over the back steps and into the hallway. The sconce in the hall upstairs illuminated billows of gray smoke coming down the staircase as Olivia screamed *fire* at the top of her lungs. Ian took the stairs two by two before he was blocked by Miss Bradstreet, pulling children down the stairs.

"Take them all to the barn," he panted.

"Go, Mary Ellen!" She coughed and turned back toward where she'd come.

"No!" Ian yelled, grabbing her wrist. "Go with them." The smoke now burning his lungs, he jerked her down from the steps as she fought against him.

"Boys!" She screamed up into the smoke, fighting to get loose from Ian's hold." I don't have the boys!" Three boys coughed into their nightshirts as Ian released her, and they stumbling into her arms.

"Now go, Olivia. Now!"

"Wait!" She cried as the boys ran away from her hold to find air. "I don't have Thomas. Thomas!" She started back up the stairs, and Ian grabbed her around the waist, pulling her off her feet. "You're wasting time." He growled in her ear. "Go now and I will find him." He set her roughly below him, pushing her forward. Squeezing his eyes shut to relieve the burning, he yelled. "Thomas! Come this way!" The heat and smoke suffocated his lungs, so he laid on the floor and crawled. "Thomas!" The narrow stairs to the attic loomed forward, but his lungs would not cooperate. If he could just go back and take one breath. He hugged the floor as he tried to return to the wide stairs. *With just one good breath*, he hung his head over the stairs and breathed deep. Just as he was about to turn and try again, the ceiling cracked with red embers and violently collapsed where he'd just been. The heat and another falling beam pushed him like a rag doll, scorching his feet as his body slid down the stairs. Struggling to turn on all fours, Ian fought against the heat only to see the top floor completely engulfed in dark smoke.

The blistering heat and the popping red embers were coming closer. Swearing under his breath, he reached for the front door and crawled out. Struggling to stand, one last hope flicked across his weary mind. Had the boy found a window? "Thomas!" Ian cried while fumbling toward a window, almost tripping. The bottom of his feet were raw and burnt, but he couldn't be stopped. "Thomas!" He stumbled into the street as the heat and flames blazed hungrily through the night air.

Running toward him was a man with two boys. Just as his eyes began to adjust to the dark, he noticed the smaller one in a nightshirt and cap. He'd seen him before.

"Thomas!" Ian grabbed him and held him up in his arms. "Are you all right? Did you get burnt?" Ian panted.

Before the boy could answer, they stepped aside for a large wagon filled with four large water barrels, and carrying three men.

"The fire brigade." The neighbor said before jumping up to start the bucket line.

"I've got to check on the other children, and see to the barn." He set Thomas down and took his hand. Running around the burning house, he almost couldn't believe his eyes. Olivia was at the well, pulling the hoist with all her strength as the other children were taking the water buckets and dousing the yard. One of the older boys stood on top of the ladder leaning against the barn. Reaching for the bucket of water below, he tossed it on the barn roof to keep sparks from taking it, too.

"Thomas!" Olivia cried, spotting them. She handed off a full bucket and raced to them. "Oh, dear God, thank you, Ian." Quickly stooping to hug the boy, Olivia stood and squeezed her arms around his chest, trapping Thomas in the middle. "Thank you." Her fingers dug into his skin as she shook with unrestrainable broken sobs.

"Are they all here?" Ian moved from her grip.

"Yes, with Thomas. Yes." She sniffed, drawing her hand across her wet cheeks. "All ten." She bent down to hold Thomas.

The sound of hot cracking wood and smoldering ash barely beyond them brought Ian back toward the flaming structure, and he felt his body waver. The house would not be saved. The sting of reality was as great as the pain in his feet. This home had been his only recourse for keeping the Empire Mine away from Mr. Grant's control. Now what? Without the sale... Clenching his teeth, he went into the yard and began to stack the new benches. Hefting them to his side, he marched them away and stacked them into the back of his wagon. Next, he took the end of the long wooden tables and dragged them across the dry grass. The older boy from the ladder came to the far end and lifted, helping Ian load them into the wagon. Passing Olivia, the other children huddled around her as they watched the bucket brigade try their best to douse the flames. Ian held onto the railing of his wagon and let his head fall forward.

A noise had come from the attic. He'd heard it himself. A miserable laugh escaped. Why poor orphan children? It had been just a matter of time before one of those little urchins burnt the place down. He banged his forehead on the railing. *It happened while he was under this roof.* Ian's eyes lifted when another wall collapsed into the center. It was a miracle they'd all got out in time. The Victorian was a fine home, one week away from being sold for top dollar. He groaned aloud. His parents' misguided benevolence was now nothing more than an unrecognizable burned pile.

Twelve

An hour later, the neighbor and the fire chief stood in the back yard, watching the smoke rise into the air. Ian gazed upward, mesmerized by how the gray swirls moved and dissipated into the black sky. Like ghosts in the night they flew away with his last hope of keeping Mr. Grant from confiscating his mine. *Where had the previous gusts gone?* he thought oddly.

"My boy there went and brought these blankets from our barn for the children," the neighbor said, waiting for Ian to respond. "I suppose they don't got anywhere else to go."

Ian finally acknowledged the short reddish-haired man. "No, they don't."

"I can have a man stay and watch for embers." The chief faced Ian.

"No, no, I can do it." Ian barely felt the squeeze of a thick hand on his neck. "Just glad you all got out." The chief slapped his back. "Sorry about the loss, Mr. Beckner."

Ian swallowed, "Thank you… for coming." His tongue would barely move, it was late they were all exhausted. "And, thank you for the blankets." He nodded to the neighbor. "I'll have one of the children return them tomorrow." Both men stilled at the sound of a faint soft soprano voice floating from the barn.

"I've heard that before." The neighbor scratched the top of his head. "When the windows are open, sometimes her songs carry to my place. Mighty pretty voice."

Ian sighed, rubbing his brow. He'd not spoken to Miss Bradstreet since she hung on him crying. Rubbing his hands along his dirty shirt, he knew there were a hundred things he should've done to help her with the children. *Blast it all.* He had been so lost in his own regret, he'd had little to offer.

"Well, I'll go now. Maybe I can have the Missus bring some bread and eggs in the morning."

Ian nodded to the neighbor, knowing the light of day would only reveal more despair. Walking twice around the soggy grass, he inspected the low red coals. His feet felt like they walked on broken shards, and blowing out a long breath, he turned to the barn. He would need to sit and watch. Walking was too painful. One of the double doors was pulled closed, and he glanced through the other to see Miss Bradstreet sitting huddled in the center, her arms wrapped tightly around her knees. The children, all tucked under horse blankets, appeared sound asleep. He stepped in as she rested her head on her knees, then looked up to see him. Rising in her white gown and dirty robe, she carefully stepped between the children and came to where he stood.

"Ian…I mean, Mr. Beckner."

"Just call me Ian. I have little care." He noticed soot on her chin and a red scratch across her cheek. Her eyes searched his as if she could share his defeat.

"I have the deepest sorrow for the loss of your home." Her chin wiggled under her frown as she tried to keep it still.

His feet could take no more. He slowly slid down against the barn door facing the smoky remains of the grand house. With his toes pointing skyward, the cold air brought some relief to the bottoms of his feet.

"Oh, no." She whispered. "Your feet are burnt." Her white nightclothes billowed around her as she knelt by his feet. Quickly she stood and went to a bucket of water. Reaching under her robe, she ripped the hem off her gown and sank it in the water. Before he could stop her, she knelt back at his feet and began to carefully clean the burned skin and blood away.

He wanted to scream at her to stop, but the gesture was so kind that he clenched his teeth against the searing pain.

"I suppose you...are a nurse too." His voice sounded like gravel. "Your time with Dr. Hastings." He rolled his lips tight, not to groan from her ministrations.

"No, no such thing." She went back to the water, cleaned the fabric and started to dab the wounds again. "But I saw a woman, a mother, on the wagon trail here to California. Her little one stumbled right into the fire pit, hands first. And before that child could get out a second wail, she'd snatched the child up, torn her petticoat and found clean water, and had it salved and dressed. A month later, I walked with her and the child, and I could barely see the scars."

Ian wondered if he was in another dream as she tore another long scrap of her gown and gently wrapped his feet. After securing the fabric into a knot on the top, she came and sat next to him. *Who was this refined, educated young lady who walked across America with the rustics and bound men's burnt feet?* "You never cease to amaze me, Miss Bradstreet."

"I suppose after I've flung myself into your arms, you may call me Olivia." Her golden hair hung splendidly loose and tousled, and her eyes held little hate as she looked up at him.

"All right." He coughed, the smoke still burning his throat. She rose and carefully handed him a tin of water.

He nodded his thanks. Her small fingers pressing into his made his skin tingle. "You've got a red scratch across your cheek."

Olivia sat again and ran her finger down it. "I...I guess I learned more protective instincts from that mother I just told you about." She hesitated. "The smoke overtook the second story so fast; I've never been so scared in my life. I grabbed those poor girls by their hair or gowns, whatever I could to drag them from the room. The smoke was already choking us and in the mayhem one of them scratched me." She released a long sigh, considering the dark glowing night. "I have to wonder, do you believe it was providence?" Silence lingered with her unanswered thoughts. "What if I was in my room? Would I have awoken too late to locate all of them? What if you were not here?" Her eyes locked on his. "I apologize for fighting you on the stairs. I wasn't thinking. You likely saved my life." She held her hand over her mouth. "And poor Thomas." Her watery eyes filled.

"I found Thomas with the neighbor."

"What?"

"I didn't pull him from the house."

Olivia glanced back at the sleeping children. "Where was he? I looked him over, not a bruise, or burn on him."

"Was he in the attic?" Ian's face was stoic. "Did he start the fire and then run to the neighbor?"

"Why, why would he? You heard him tonight. He wanted to live here."

"And he was angry." Ian swallowed the burning in his throat.

Olivia swung her head in a circle. "I just don't think he…he would ever do that. To endanger the other children." She crossed her arms and squeezed her elbows.

"Where is he from? Why is he here?"

"There's not much in his file. His mother was Janny Long, a saloon girl in Hangtown. No father or other family listed. I understand there is a Chinese woman in Hangtown who runs a laundry and helps some of the…the *troubled* women. Joshua's mother, Francine, works there, and she was the one who brought the devastating news. His mother, Janny, went missing for a few weeks and they found her dead."

Ian released a long sigh. "Unless he unloads his conscience about tonight, we may never know. You work with the priests at the church, maybe we can get him into confession." His eyes narrowed, and he gave her a quick shoulder bump. It worked; she managed a half-smile. "Nothing's going to bring the house back," he said, pulling his knees up, wincing as his feet touched the ground. "Thank you for the careful nursing. Daylight's around the corner, you might as well get some sleep."

Olivia rose, rubbed her hands together, and wrapped them around her front.

"Do you have a blanket?"

"No. I'll be fine." She stepped away. "Maybe I can sneak in with Mary Ellen."

"Olivia." Her name felt natural as if he used it all the time. "You tore up the bottom of your nightgown, you can take my shirt." He began to unbutton it.

"Oh, no. I couldn't."

He stood and caught her arm, bringing her back in front of him. "Take my shirt. It's smelly and full of soot, but it's better than nothing. He removed it and felt the chill on his bare arms before he wrapped it over her shoulders. Holding the collar at her chest a minute longer than needed, he met her eyes. "I should've helped you earlier. I apologize, I was preoccupied with my own burdens."

Olivia took the collar in her hands, and he released it. "I know we've had our differences." She stepped back. "But never in a thousand years would I want this to happen to your home. I think I've been lost in my own burdens as well and I've been a poor example of Christian grace and mercy."

"We are unfortunately too much alike, Miss Olivia Bradstreet. I want to secure the mine and I want the families to thrive and prosper just as you do these children. You asked earlier about the providence of God. Here we are now, both in the same place—without a miracle to speak of.

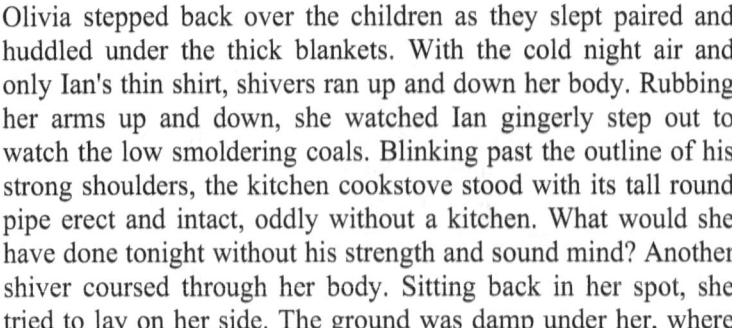

Olivia stepped back over the children as they slept paired and huddled under the thick blankets. With the cold night air and only Ian's thin shirt, shivers ran up and down her body. Rubbing her arms up and down, she watched Ian gingerly step out to watch the low smoldering coals. Blinking past the outline of his strong shoulders, the kitchen cookstove stood with its tall round pipe erect and intact, oddly without a kitchen. What would she have done tonight without his strength and sound mind? Another shiver coursed through her body. Sitting back in her spot, she tried to lay on her side. The ground was damp under her, where the water from the roof had found its way through. Curling in a ball, she tried to pull his shirt taut over her. At least she would not burn in her sleep.

Thirteen

Olivia opened one eye to daylight and closed it again. Praise the heavens, just as she thought her bones would crack from the cold last night, one of the children had snuggled up to her backside, and pure warmth took her into true sleep. Was it Mary Ellen's arm that rested in front of her chest, holding her close?

"Miss Bradstreet." Someone whispered.

Olivia forced her eyes to open. "Yes, Mary Ellen." She drew her hand over her face and pulled the warm bare arm down to her waist.

"The neighbor's wife is here. She brought a pot of porridge."

Bare arm? Olivia gripped it and peered down at a thick manly dark-haired arm? *Mary Ellen is standing over me?* Olivia bolted to a sitting position, and Ian Beckner rolled back, blinking at her. "Good morning." He rubbed the back of his neck.

"Sir!" Her mouth fell open, and just as she was posed to slap his face, her head whipped to the side, spying the neighbor's wife holding a metal pan with two potholders and two wide eyes. "Oh, my goodness." Olivia yelped and puffed, standing in nothing but her nightclothes. His shirt slipped off her shoulders, and she gripped it in her hand before flipping it back toward in his face.

"This is so very kind of you." She realized most of the children were awake huddled under their coverings. "Maybe we could put that pot on the tack bench." She smiled and walked over. "So, so kind of you, ma'am." Olivia's face still burned red, and she could not seem to catch her breath. The neighbor pulled a stack of spoons out of her apron pocket and sat them on the bench.

"I didn't have enough bowls."

"Oh no, this is so generous." Olivia choked. "To aid so graciously in our hour of need."

The woman's eyes widened as she looked back at Ian, then even wider when she scrutinized Olivia. Finally, as she walked away, Olivia felt herself waver. What had happened with Ian Beckner last night? Did he have a concussion? Why would the man take such liberties as to sleep curled around her?

"Hey, is he your husband?" Joshua asked.

"Her name is *Miss* Bradstreet," Mary Ellen piped up.

Olivia's mind raced between anger and embarrassment as Ian sat casually, checking the bottom of his feet.

Joshua frowned. "I thought Sister Patricia said you couldn't sleep with anyone unless they were your husband."

All the children's eyes seemed to look at her, and Olivia opened her mouth. "Ah…I…think Mr. Beckner and I have…ah…because of the fire…ah…that we didn't expect… we…have a special…ah…we are engaged! Yes. True, we are not married yet, but when you are engaged, and there is nowhere else to sleep." Her words came slower as she tried to explain or lie to the impressionable children. "And…and…we had no blanket." That sounded reasonable…until her eyes caught Ian's, gazing at her with a roguish smile.

"When are you going to get married?" Milton asked innocently.

Ian pressed his lips together and raised his chin smugly at her.

"We've not set a date. As you know, we…we…" She glanced out the barn door. The sight of the black rubble slammed her heart against her chest. "Have a few other things that are more important." Her voice faded out.

"Like eating breakfast." Joshua piped in.

Mimicking chicks breaking out of their eggshells, they all jumped up and formed a line. Mary Ellen took charge, telling them each one could take a spoonful and then get back in line.

Olivia felt dizzy. A memory flashed of the Bradstreet carriage passing a church once where sad, needy children stood outside with bowls extended. A substance like watery soup ladled into each one. It'd broken her heart then, and now these poor ragamuffins had nothing. No clothes, no home. Each took one bite and ran to the back of the line. Could their situation possibly get any more bleak?

Ian came up behind her. Gripping her elbows, he steadied her. "I said last night you never ceased to amaze me," he whispered close to her ear. "But never did I imagine I would be engaged without asking the woman first."

"I couldn't wait for you to ask so that I could adamantly say *no*," she said on an angry lark. Turning on him, she poked his chest. "You should've never slept next to me." She growled. "As if the fire wasn't enough last night, are you bent on ruining my reputation? Did you see how the neighbor's wife stared at us!" Her nose flared. "How am I to ever find another position if I am the talk of the town!"

"You don't need another position." Ian quirked a half-smile. "After your sweet care last night, I think we'll keep the engagement, so I'll keep you for my own."

Olivia tried to suck in a much-needed breath, but it got caught between the constriction of anger and the panic overtaking her. He was close enough to slap, but her arm felt like a cloud in the wind. He was pompous and had no manners. Icy tingling rose from her feet as her faint breath competed for words that would not form. "I…I…" Black spots blurred the face of Ian Beckner. *Good riddance.*

⌒‿

Ian observed Olivia's eyes roll into the back of her head and grabbed her before her knees buckled. Sweeping her up into his arms, he noticed the children watched them, but not one pipsqueak broke the food line.

"Children." Without all those thick dresses, of course, she was lighter than he thought. "Miss Bradstreet is distraught and has fainted. So, no more talk of engagements and weddings. She is a fragile flower, and we need to all help her." The extra weight on his feet seared up his legs as he placed her on a nearby blanket.

"It's a good thing she gonna get a husband," one of the children murmured as Ian tried to fan her face.

A gasp pierced from the barn door. A nun in a flowing black habit covered her mouth with wide eyes. "I came as soon as I heard! Oh, heavens be praised! All the children were spared?" She pushed past the food line and knelt next to Olivia. "What has happened? Was she injured?"

Ian scratched his forehead. "She fainted."

They watched as Olivia tried to open her eyes and then closed them again. "Oh, Sister," she whispered. Her hand wandered upward until the worried nun took ahold of it.

"I'm here, I'm with you." Sister Patricia gently patted her cheek.

"The worst nightmare imaginable— Mr…Beckner was…was here. I was sleeping…with the girls one minute, then with him the next. Oh, the horrid smoke…" Pale, Olivia opened her eyes, more shock and pity lining her face, and they drooped closed again. Suddenly awake, her vision shifted to Ian's, and she closed them again. "He's still here," she murmured and tried to sit up. "What did I say about him?" Olivia groaned. Sister Patricia held her steady as she sat.

Milton stood nearby with his breakfast spoon still in his hand. "Do you remember that you and him are getting married?"

"Boy." Ian grabbed him by the arm. "What is your name?"

"Milton."

"Milton." Ian tried to calm his tone by running his tongue along his bottom lip. "Do you remember what I said just moments ago?"

"Ahh…that we shouldn't say anything more to Miss Bradstreet cause she's a flower?"

Ian gave Olivia a pinched smile. "Close enough."

"Oh, Sister." Olivia leaned into her embrace. "It was just terrifying. I'm sorry, I...I..." She tried to pull herself to standing, clinging to the black habit. "I suppose it all just caught up with me. Forgive me."

"Child." Sister Patricia held her steady. "I can only commend you for the saving of these lives."

"And Ian." Olivia murmured.

"And to God be praised." Sister Patricia held one arm tight around Olivia as she lifted her rosary cross and kissed it.

A strange emotion twinged in his gut. They were obviously close, and for some reason, he felt excluded, no longer needed. His eyes floated out the barn door to the empty air that had once held his family's home. After a frustrating meeting with Mr. Grant's lawyer, he'd come to gather the furnishings and make sure the house was empty.

He stepped away and stood at the barn entrance. The smell of smoke still wafted in and out. People from the neighborhood stood to the left of the rubble, shaking their heads. It was one of the finest Victorians built in the budding town of Sacramento. Twisting to see over his shoulder, two girls in dirty nightgowns squealed as they threw hay at each other. The facilitator said he had people ready to look at it, but no one would pay top dollar with the orphans running amok. Ironically, now only the orphans remained. Ian huffed, pinching his temples. No house, no sale, and no way to pay back Mr. Grant.

Fourteen

B y afternoon, the small barn had been turned into a charitable receiving station. A pot of beans still remained after neighbors had come and gone with food and bread. Three more nuns had come with clothes and shoes. As people stood around visiting and the children ran in and out, one might mistake it for a holiday.

Needing private space, Ian stood near his wagon where he'd tossed the benches and tables in last night's frustration. Tired and ruminating over the loss of the house, he lowered the wagon gate and jerked the items back out.

"I hate to interrupt you." Olivia stood close, transformed. A simple blouse and matching cape and woolen skirt, her hair pulled back in a plain knot at her neck. He'd never been able to keep his eyes off her, and even now, his heart pushed against his chest. She radiated even more beauty with her simple vulnerability, increasing his undoing.

"I know you don't want to hear this." Her jaw dropped toward the ground and she took in a deep breath. "Four of the children are going now with Sister Patricia, but that still leaves six."

Ian turned to stack the benches and faced the wagon. Was she asking for his help or his sympathy? Why had he goaded her about coming back to the Empire Mine to be with him? Why did he goad her at every chance? Slowly turning, he leaned his arm along the wagons side rail. "Why don't we take the last six back to Grass Valley? There is a new church being built, my mother mentioned it. Led by a Father Dalton, if I remember. Maybe you could speak to him and start over there." That sounded fair and helpful, without his usual superior tone mixed in.

"The thought had occurred to me." She tapped her chin. "Do you think your mother would mind if they stayed there until I find a suitable home? I think Dr. Hastings and I could find room in the guest cottage for them."

Ian couldn't imagine the tight guest quarters spacious enough for eight, but it held only a second of his attention. The color had returned to her cheeks and she was speaking to him calmly. The idea of having her close at the mine brought the only spark of optimism to any of this. He scratched his head. "Tell the children about the move, gather up the donations, and we'll see how much we can take. I can have someone come back for the cow and chickens."

Her eyes softened, and she reached out to touch him. "Thank you, Ian. I will oversee them at all times. Schooling, chores, everything."

Fighting the worst urge to pull her into his arms, he smiled, not wanting the moment to pass. "Am I forgiven? I was tired and cold last night."

"Umm." She shook her head, stepping back. "I can't say. Perhaps a bit of forbearance is needed for that romantic heart searching for comfort."

"And you *were* the only one that could meet the need."

She smirked, dropping her head to the side.

Ian's brows narrowed. He couldn't hold back from prodding her. "And since we are engaged. You said it with your own words we—"

Olivia stiffened, interrupting him. "That was said to rescue young minds from careless imaginations. They will forget and…and…we will too." She patted at the little bow at the collar of her second-hand cape.

"I could never forget." He shrugged. "Sleeping next to you with my nose in your hair, I've smelled glory. My arms have held your softness, better than a hundred feather pillows. My lips have also tasted…"

"Mr. Beckner! You *will* hold your forked tongue." She pointed her finger at his face. "How do you ever expect me to believe in any of your fine qualities when you behave like this?"

Ian laughed and jerked a bench up onto his shoulder. "As long as you remember, I do have some qualities."

She shook her head and strode away.

"And call me Ian." He called after her. "Or dearest, now that we're engaged." He laughed again, surprised he had any humor in him. But something about the way she clutched her hands over her ears was truly amusing.

An hour later, Olivia patted Bonita's back as she bawled into her skirts. "Sweetheart, I know this is hard. But I will be with you the entire time."

The child's muffled cries were for a mother who would never come for her, a night of fiery terror, and now a long journey away from everything she'd come to trust.

"Here, Bonita." Mary Ellen held out her hand. "I have a nice spot right here. You can sit with me."

Olivia felt the child shake her head no and clutch Olivia's skirts with all her six-year-old might.

Ian finished hitching the horses and came around to the back of the wagon. "Let's go." Without warning, he picked Bonita up at the waist and deposited her in the wagon. Angry and shocked, Bonita let out a blood-curdling scream.

Ears ringing from the ghastly shrieking, he held his hand out to Olivia. "I guess you are riding back here, now."

"Can I ride up with you?" Milton jumped up while Bonita began to stomp and rage.

Ian finished locking the wagon gate and nodded yes to Milton above the racket. Olivia put the stiff, fuming child on a seat and pulled her on her lap. On top of the screaming, the child began to rock and kick, and Olivia winced as the child's heel slammed into her shin. Wondering who gave the small child such stiff shoes, the wagon rocked forward, and she moved Bonita to sit beside her, where her feet could fling and kick uninterrupted. Olivia rubbed out the pain in her shin and held the side of her face as Bonita's screams flicked at her last testy nerve. How did mothers do it? Though she'd hoped one day to embrace the high calling of motherhood, right now, if Sister Patricia had room, they would be heading to drop this one off.

The oldest at thirteen, Mary Ellen sat brave and tall with an arm around her younger brother, Lester. Olivia tried to offer a weary smile to Thomas, sitting across from her. He'd sulked quietly through most of the day. When she tapped his knee to get his attention, he didn't move. The wagon turned onto the next dirt road. Esther took advantage of the turn and nestled into Olivia's quieter side. At ten, she was a plain girl who didn't talk much. Olivia felt Esther's arm curl under hers and patted her hand. What were all these children feeling? Likely Bonita was the only one to express how the rest of them felt.

An hour later, Bonita fell asleep with her head in Olivia's lap. Ian turned and spoke over his shoulder.

"A stop for water?"

Olivia nodded; her head had had bobbed for sleep more than once in the last few minutes. Ian pulled the wagon along a small creek and set the brake. Pulling the back gate down, he helped the children get out. Olivia hated to wake the screamer, but her backside needed to stretch. She woke Bonita and pulled her to standing. Still dazed, Bonita stepped into Ian's arms and rested her head on his shoulder.

"Maybe we can let her sleep a little longer." Ian held his arm under the child's legs and offered his free hand to Olivia.

As her feet touched the ground, she looked twice at him. He held the child like he'd done this before. "Your mother never said, are you an only child?" She asked as they walked to the creek.

"I was an older brother." Pain flickered in his eyes. "My sister died at four. My mother was sure leaving New York for the west would bring health to her future children. But then she never had any more."

"I'm sorry for your family on both accounts."

"And you? Where do you fall in the Bradstreet line?"

"I…I." Flustered, Olivia watched as the children scooped drinks from the creek. "I'm the only daughter. And I have one older brother."

"And this brother granted permission for a younger sister to travel to the wilds of California?"

"Quite enthusiastically."

Ian's eyes narrowed slightly. "That seems a bit of a mystery. Your curt words are hiding something."

"I'd had an *advantageous* loving engagement." Her words escaped pricklier than she'd intended.

Ian stopped walking, adjusting Bonita higher on his shoulder. "My mother said he was killed in Texas in the war. I am sorry."

"Not as sorry as my brother. A sister's mourning and pouting around the house was too much. Considering our father…" Those last shaky words made a knot form in her belly. Her brother would make sure they'd never have that inheritance together. "Considering our father had passed and Wally was never home, Dr. Hastings was the only one to share my grief." She shook her head and gaze toward the ground. "My so-called brother had no use for me. It was best to make my own way." She mumbled.

"What a cad. To dismiss his own blood through her season of grief?"

Olivia straightened her cape, ignoring the concern on his face. "And now you see why I am diligent in my cause for orphans. I feel a bit of what they feel, except…I was given everything." Weary emotions and the truly broken heart of missing her parents rose back up and misted her tired eyes. "The finest home, the most beautiful clothes, a nanny and governess, a teacher who taught me to speak Latin." Her hand rested on her chest, and she sighed. "A wonderful fiancée from a loving family, *everything.*" She swiped under her eyes. *Everything but acceptance. Everything but security and a bright future. Everything but a dirty secret withheld—one that should've never been spoken.* Olivia brushed a loose strand of hair back. Even in her weariness, she'd picked her words carefully. The Beckners were good stock. In so many ways much like the Bradstreets. The fortunate, the few that had done well with the old and new money in America. If they knew her true bloodline was born from a vagrant prostitute, they would also show her the back door. And that was one more loss, one more rejection she could not live through.

Fifteen

Just before dusk, all that was left from the Oak Street Home for Children rolled onto the Empire Mine property. Ian took the road to the left. Desperate for a sight of anything solid and stable, the sight of the rock-walled guest cottage with the small swirl of smoke from the chimney made Olivia's chest swell. On cue, Dr. Hastings peeked out the front door with a book under his arm. "What do we have here?"

"A large number of guests for the guest cottage." Olivia raised a weak grin. Ian carefully ambled down and nodded at Dr. Hastings.

"Are those bandages around your feet?" Maxwell's brows narrowed.

"Burned in the fire," Ian answered briskly as he skirted around the man to help the children from the back.

"What fire?" Maxwell's face turned alarmed. He reached for Olivia.

"The Oak Street Home for Children burned to the ground last night," she said somberly.

"The Beckners' Sacramento home?" Maxwell reached for the bundles of clothing and blankets she handed him.

"That's the one." Ian shut the back gate. "I'll ride to the main house and ask Katy for some food."

Olivia instinctively counted six heads, then went to thank him for everything, but she stopped. He'd already pulled the wagon from the guest cottage.

"Boys and girls, I would like you to meet Dr. Hastings." A low greeting murmured within the group of children.

"I'm so sorry, Maxwell." Olivia's eyes pleaded with him. "We've been in dire straits, and there was nowhere else to go."

"No, no, please, children, come in." Dr. Maxwell patted Thomas on the head as he led the children through the door. "They seem to have fared well enough, any breathing problems or burns?"

"They all came out of this unscathed," Olivia sighed. "Girls, please set your things in this room. This is where I sleep. And boys, perhaps, umm..." She glanced around the small area. "Put your bundles in that corner. We can push the furniture back and find some places in this room to sleep." Like weary soldiers, the children did as she said and then turned to look at her for more directions. *Heavens, the little cottage was lacking everything they were used to. Now, what to do?*

"Dr. Hastings, may I introduce Mary Ellen and this is her brother Lester." Both siblings nodded and looked at their feet. "This is Thomas Long. Suddenly she couldn't remember the other last names. *Did it matter?* "Milton is here." He nodded. "Then there is Esther and Bonita." *Why did this temporary guardianship idea with Sister Patricia make any sense?* At this moment, she could barely hold herself upright. *What was she thinking?*

Awkward silence hung in the air.

"I'm hungry." Milton murmured.

"Yes, ahh, I think Mr. Beckner is coming back." Olivia felt like the woman in the nursery rhyme. The old woman who lived in a shoe, who had so many children she didn't know what to do.

Ian found his mother and Katy in the kitchen. His mother gaped wide-eyed at his feet. "What happened to your shoes, your feet?"

"My shoes burnt to ash along with our Oak Street Home."

"What?" both women said in unison before they covered their mouths in shock.

"Yes, I would never exaggerate anything this calamitous." Ian raked his fingers through his hair.

"All those children." His mother stepped forward, grabbing his arm. "Tell me they were all gone elsewhere?"

"There were ten left with Miss Bradstreet, and they were all able to get out in time."

Judith stumbled back as her hands flew to her face, "Oh, thank you, Lord." Straightening, she held herself steady. "The home was completely destroyed?"

Ian nodded, feeling the grating in his gut.

"Oh, son." Judith shook her head, sighing. "And poor Olivia. Did the church find room for them?"

"Not the church." He moved to pour a glass of water.

"Then who?" She waited as he drank his fill, swiping the back of his sleeve across his face. "The number of guests in the cottage has increased by seven."

"Seven?" Judith and Katy said in unison.

"It seems that despite the sale of the house, Olivia was only able to place half of the children. The other half were still there when I arrived. One of the nuns took four this morning." He spied the women's shocked expressions. "I...I would've given her more time." He shook his head." But without a place to live and..."

"Oh, oh." Katy crooned. "You did the right thing, the charitable thing, sir."

"Is there a basket of food you could prepare? I said I would bring some back."

"Of course." Katy turned to gather the items. Ian gingerly stepped closer to his mother. "We're in a dark pit, I'd say. Now with the sudden loss of our Sacramento house, there is nothing left with which to payback Mr. Grant."

Judith huffed, wrapping her arm around his waist. "I'm just so glad you all made it out. Oh my, my..." Her head shuddered into his shoulder. Releasing a low groan, she pulled back. "This is all my fault. I should've never accepted such a large gift. With your father's passing and your engagement, I thought— "

"No, this mess is my doing." He hugged her. "Well, more like Lesandra's." He rolled his eyes. "Let's just blame everything on Lesandra." Ian gave his mother a half-surly smile. "Right now, my feet are throbbing, so I'll blame that on her too."

"Ian, sit!" His mother jumped, pulling out the chair at the square kitchen table. "I'll go with Katy and bring back Maxwell to tend to you."

"No, thanks." He propped his feet up on the next chair. Seeing Olivia tenderly wrapping his wounds was all he wanted to remember. "I'll be fine." Judith bent and examined them closer. "They don't look fine, and you smell like a smokestack. Katy, can you take the basket yourself? I'll stay and start the hot water for bathing."

"I've got this, ma'am." Katy pulled the basket into the crook of her arm. "Would they be needing anything else? I'll make the poor things a big proper breakfast in the morning."

"The church brought the orphans used clothes, shoes, and some bedding." Ian winced, carefully pulling the bandages away from where they'd stuck to his raw skin.

"All right then. I'll head over." Katy nodded as she went out the back door.

Judith added another pot of water onto the stove. "After the dirt and bandages are off, I want you to let Dr. Hastings look at those feet."

"Maybe tomorrow. I'm sure he's a bit overwhelmed now." Ian's face grew serious. "Mother, it's all hardly believable. Our Oak Street home was one of the finest Victorians in Sacramento. I have a feeling one of the boys might have started the fire in the attic."

"An orphan child? Why, why would he?" Her hand brushed over his shoulder.

"When I got there, Olivia, I mean, Miss Bradstreet and I were having a discussion. I'd expected the house to be empty."

"Discussion?'

"I…I might have sounded upset. A boy, Thomas, wanted her attention, and in the middle of our discussion, she shooed him away. Then, later, when I was in her room, I thought I heard a noise in the attic."

"You were in her room?" Judith's tone rose. "I think there is something else you're not telling me."

"No." He squinted. "She slept with the girls. Thank God she woke me. Olivia smelled the smoke before we could see it."

"Olivia?" His mother had a strange look in her eye.

"We've asked to call each other by first names." Ian gently stood.

"Humm." Judith tried to carry the water around the corner to the bathing room, but Ian took it from her hands. "I'll do this if you can take the stairs for me and bring me clean clothes."

"Yes." She stepped away and turned. "Ian, you know I care for Olivia like a daughter. She's bright, caring, and selfless. Now that she is back, it's like she's home, like she was meant to be here."

Ian nodded and finished filling the water.

"Just think for one moment about a possible union with her."

His head shot up. "What?"

"The Bradstreets are well known back east. Let's just say they don't skim and scrape like the Beckners. Maybe the two families would make business and bedfellows?"

"Mother," he whined. "Oh, no." He jerked his shirt off. "Beautiful women and family money. No, no, and never. This whole mess we are in, don't you think I've learned my lesson?"

"But her parents are gone; certainly, her inheritance would…"

"Stop," he chuckled, holding his palm toward her. "I thought *I* was desperate to see this mine survive. Now I think I've met my match. You would sell me off like a chattel deed for a woman's inheritance?"

"Call me selfish." She shrugged, walking away. "But I would have the most beautiful grandbabies on the west coast." She held her hand over her heart.

"And that would be *my* gold mine."

Sixteen

The next morning, Ian descended the stairs, balancing his weight by holding tight to the thick banister. Sporting a pair of soft leather slippers his mother had bought him years ago, he felt half-dressed. He'd never found the leisure time to wear them before, but today they would have to do. The Empire Cottage was strangely quiet, and entering the kitchen, the evidence as to why was before him.

It appeared as if his mother and Katy had cooked for a mob and fled. At least a bit of coffee was left. He poured himself a cup and grabbed a flapjack left in the pan. Sitting with his feet propped up, he pulled out a piece of paper and looked it over. The fee he'd paid on the bottom of the paper made the flapjack stick in his throat. He hoped it was worth it.

While he'd been in Sacramento, he'd retained his own lawyer. The man assured him the court was not likely to put a lean on the Empire Mine if it showed he was making regular payments to refund Mr. Grant. He had the receipt for the first five hundred dollars. Now he had to make another payment *and* make payroll for the miners.

He'd convinced the miners the voyage to America would be worth it. With wives and children to feed, they deserved a fair wage, a promise he could not skip out on. And now, without a choice, he had seven more mouths to feed. Ian went over the numbers and rubbed the back of his neck. The walk would take twice as long as usual, but he needed to get to the mining office. He folded the paper and took his last drink of coffee as Katy, his mother, and two of the children came in the back door.

"Mr. Beckner." Katy beamed. "I have a question for you."

His mother had a bright grin as well, resting her hands on the children's shoulders. "A solution."

"Yes," Katy started again. "With my Bernice gone and married, I still have the extra bed in my room. I'm asking what if Mary Ellen and her brother stayed with me. With the extra mouths, I could use the help with milking, gathering eggs, cleaning." Katy huffed a smile, glancing around the messy kitchen. "Lester here could haul the water, keep the woodpile chopped."

Ian pushed up from the table. "Children, Katy runs a tight ship. You would have to work."

"It's fine, Mr. Beckner." Mary Ellen nodded. "This is a grand house, and the other one is a bit small."

"And Miss Bradstreet? Is this good in her opinion?"

His mother nodded. "She agreed it would be a temporary solution until she has time to find housing."

Ian blinked, picturing another possibility. "And the other boys?" He glanced at Mary Ellen. "When you go back to get your things, would you have Dr. Hastings bring the boys to the mine office?" He squeezed his mother's arms. "We need every hand to increase production."

"But they're children." His mother scowled.

"I'm not sending them down to chip rock." He met her gaze. "But there is work to do." He clapped his hands once. "God speed to all of us." He kissed her cheek and stepped gingerly out the door.

Ian grit his teeth as he walked along the rock and dirt into the mining area. The donkeys were pulling the stamp rock, and tracks were running back and forth with cars of rock. Everywhere it looked like mining was happening at a steady pace. Catching sight of Mr. Wright, Ian waved him into the mining office and sat behind his desk.

"Good to have you back." Mr. Wright entered and sat.

"Our Oak Street Home burnt to the ground." Ian pulled his paper out of his pocket.

"No." Mr. Wright shook his head. "That's horrible news."

"Isn't it supposed to get darkest before the dawn or something like that?" Ian's tone soured as he shuffled papers. "I just know it's getting dark." Ian eyed Mr. Wright. "Can we increase productivity?"

"What did you have in mind?" Mr. Wright scratched his chin.

"Blasting another shaft."

"Whoo." Surprised, Mr. Wright leaned back in his chair. "We could, I suppose." His brow creased. "Who ya gonna hire to work it?"

"I can't pay another employee. But most of the lightweight, above-ground labor I want to go to two boys who will be helping. Then the teen boys can be trained to help in the shafts."

"Might work."

"I'll personally chip and drill."

"Now that won't work." Mr. Wright lowered his chin. "We need a boss without rock dust filling his lungs. And talking with the Cornish workers, I think we should try their pump. That would replace the mud diggers, giving us more hands."

"Approved." Ian stood to shake his hand.

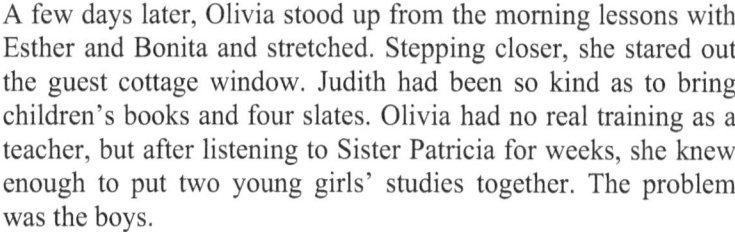

A few days later, Olivia stood up from the morning lessons with Esther and Bonita and stretched. Stepping closer, she stared out the guest cottage window. Judith had been so kind as to bring children's books and four slates. Olivia had no real training as a teacher, but after listening to Sister Patricia for weeks, she knew enough to put two young girls' studies together. The problem was the boys.

Maxwell had left early for the mine with the boys in tow. By the time they got home to wash and eat, they would fall asleep at the table. Their studies were suffering. She never imagined four out of the six children would be put straight to work for the Empire Mine. She could've allowed Mary Ellen the job as a nanny back in Sacramento if this were to be the case. Sighing, Olivia rubbed her eyebrows.

"Try this problem again." She erased Bonita's simple numbers. "Count it out with the beans." Bonita counted the pinto beans sitting in front of her, taking four away.

"That makes one?" Round brown eyes awaited her approval.

"Yes. Very good. Do the others the same way."

Olivia stepped to the simple kitchen and set the tea kettle on the stove. There was one other very large, handsome, brash boy who eluded her. Maxwell told her Ian worked from dawn to far past midnight. *Like a man rowing a ship to shore with his hands,* Maxwell had said of his fervor.

Was he trying to avoid her? Did he know she would disapprove of the children's chores around the mine? Goodness, Thomas was only eight. What would Sister Patricia or Father Gilbert say to the conditions? Olivia poured the water over the tea steeper and added a touch of sugar. She wrote them both updates but had no ride into Grass Valley. Maxwell knew of her desire to send the post and possibly meet with Father Dalton, but he was also weary from long hours and retired early. Everyone seemed to be occupied, and what she had hoped to accomplish had taken a back row to all things surrounding gold mining.

"Good, do two more." Olivia squeezed Esther's shoulder and sat with them at the table. Sipping her hot tea, she felt irritated. Her mind kept drifting to Ian and the frightening ordeal they'd shared. Fingering the book of fairy tales she had read the girls earlier, she huffed. The man was no prince on a white horse. But in the smoke and cold of night, he had been everything she needed and more. Though his self-assurance often worked against her best plans.

Olivia took another sip. She could hold no malice over the children's home; it was gone now, and he bore the finality of the loss. The same self-assurance he carried also came to effortlessly shelter most of her insecurities. She rubbed her temple. What a strange dance they did. Maybe she missed him? A low growl rattled in the back of her throat. *That could not be true.*

It was funny to think that months ago she'd arrived without notice or fanfare here at Empire Mine with Dr. Hastings. It had been Maxwell's dream to come to California, see his son, and invest in a gold mine. Certainly not hers. But after meeting Judith Beckner and finding favor with the kind woman, she'd been offered the headmistress job for the Oak Street Orphan School. A commendable occupation.

Her time on the board of the Ladies' Protection and Relief Society had been a true gift from God. Favor and friendship with the Sisters of Charity was a healing balm after months of travel and hardship. Judith had spoken here and there about the loss of her husband, and now her son would be seeing to things. But with all the new surroundings, Olivia hadn't paid much attention to who Ian Beckner was. Everything had changed when he returned. The rogue had kissed her, thinking she was some trollop in Dr. Hastings's bed. Olivia twisted in her seat and dismissed the girls to play with the yarn Katy had dropped off.

What a scoundrel, head to toe. That night in the barn, full of himself and taking liberties at his own whim. *Warm, humph.* Ronald would've never tested her sensibilities like that. Olivia sighed, resting her elbow on the table, and held her chin on her palm.

When had she stopped thinking about Ronald daily? It had been months since she'd pondered their courtship. Maybe it was the same time she'd stopped pretending to be Miss Olivia Bradstreet. The fire took the last remnants of her fine dresses, shoes, and hats. Judith had given her two day-dresses from the charity box to replace her clothes, but the truth was she was at another impasse.

Wearing another's clothes, sitting idly back in the guest cottage was discouraging. The Oak Street home had always been abuzz with people, work, and children. She looked back out the window. The gray skies outside seemed as dreary as the inside, and self-pity nicked at her. Hadn't she learned never to have expectations?

They only belonged to the naive and hopeful.

Seventeen

It had rained miserably for two days, and the clouds were finally breaking up. The boys returned soaked head to toe each evening and Olivia prayed they would not catch their death of cold. She'd asked Maxwell to speak to Ian, but he admitted to hardly ever seeing him, and being a doctor, he reminded her, he wouldn't allow them to work if they were sick.

A soft knock at the door caught her attention. Was it Judith or Katy? She smiled at the girls sitting playing by the warm fire. "Who could it be?"

She opened the door to two women dressed in working clothes. One was possibly Judith's age, one perhaps hers. "Good day, ladies." A little girl with a tattered bonnet leaned out from the younger one's skirts. "And hello to you, too."

"Good day, ma'am. Mr. Beckner asked us to come by and introduce ourselves." The older one smiled, exposing a missing front tooth.

"Yes, wonderful." Olivia held the door open, inviting them in. By their accents and plain clothing, she determined they were the wives of the Cornish miners.

"I'm Miss Bradstreet." She smiled, taking their shawls. "But please call me Olivia."

They both nodded, and the little girl leaned around her mother's side to spy the girls playing with yarn dolls.

"These little ones are Esther and Bonita. Would you like to see their dolls?"

Her head nodded up and down as the mother tried to untie her bonnet. "This is my lovey Lydia. I'm Mrs. Camille Hocking." The thinner young woman with brown hair said. "This is my mother-in-law, Mrs. Doretha Hocking."

"Wonderful to meet you all." Olivia felt befuddled with the sudden guests. Where was her proper etiquette? "Could I offer you a cup of tea?"

Both women nodded sheepishly. "We don't want to be no bother."

"No, I have the water warming." Olivia turned a few feet to the kitchen. "Please, sit." The corner of her eye caught their muddy shoes and hems. "So much rain." Olivia murmured, nervously reaching for the cups. "What do you all think of California?"

"Well enough, well enough." The elder Mrs. Hocking nodded.

"Mite better than being on a ship for a day and forever." The daughter-in-law smiled.

Olivia was about to ask another question when small arms wrapped around her legs. "Bonita, what?" She pulled her away. Seeing her watery eyes, she wondered if the child had an injury.

"She took my doll." Bonita frowned, red rising in her cheeks.

Olivia knelt down and whispered close. "She won't take it, I promise. Lydia is younger than you. Can you please just share for a few minutes?"

"No." Bonita pouted.

"May I be of some help?" Camille Hocking stood near, and Olivia rose and forgetting what she was doing.

"Tea." Olivia turned to pour the water and tried to pat Bonita's shoulder at the same time. "Cream or sugar?"

Before the woman could answer, Bonita let out a wail and jerked hard on Olivia's skirt, almost making her spill the hot tea over both of them. Carefully, Olivia handed the cup over to Mrs.

Hocking. "Could you excuse me for one minute?" Olivia pulled Bonita off her feet and carried her into her room.

"Listen to me, young lady," Olivia set her on her feet, speaking over the wailing. "You will stay in this room all day if you continue. I mean it. You can share your doll for a moment. I will not let her take it." By the pure grace of God, Bonita looked up through tear-soaked eyes and hiccoughed. "And if you dry your face and come out with me, I'll see you girls have a bit of tea party."

A small nod without a piercing wail was all Olivia needed as she opened the door and smiled at the ladies.

"Thank you for your patience." Olivia gave Bonita a tap forward. "The children have had so many difficult transitions of late."

"Mr. Beckner said as much." The elder Mrs. Hocking nodded. "We wondered if you might want to join in with the ladies on Thursday. With the rain, Mrs. Beckner invited us into her parlor for quilting and bible study. We bring the little ones."

"Oh, how wonderful." Olivia found three more teacups and served the little girls a cup of tea and half a biscuit each. Wide-eyed, they came and sat at the small table.

"He also said you sing like an angel." Camille sipped her tea.

"Did he now?" Olivia wondered how he'd had time to converse with all the Cornish women, but had not found one minute for her. "He's being generous." How dare he talk about her with other people? The man was as erratic as the clouds and rain.

"And there was another thing besides quilting and singing," Camille said softly.

Olivia blinked. Was the younger woman's eyes filling with tears? "Yes, please go on."

The woman rubbed her finger back and forth over the rim of the cup, trying to settle her shaking chin. "We lost our Kara traveling...here." Her mother-in-law handed her a handkerchief, and she dabbed her face. "About halfway over the ocean, the pox broke out."

Olivia covered her mouth before she could find the words. "I see how you loved her. A wise woman said to me the degree we grieve is a sign of how we love."

The younger woman took a deep breath and looked up with watery eyes. "Thank you, ma'am, that is a true sentiment." She glanced at her mother-in-law and then back to Olivia. "My husband, he works at the stamp mill with Milton and Thomas."

Olivia nodded.

"And with only this one,' she nodded to Lydia. "And Mr. Beckner saying they were orphans and all." She sat straighter in her chair. "My husband and I talked about having them. You know, see if they would take to us and see if you would care if they came to live at our place."

Olivia felt like a brick was pushed into her chest. *Ian was not only working the poor children but placing them with families?* How could he possibly know all the discernment it took to make a good match? "I...I... have found myself as their temporary guardian." Her tongue seemed to stick in her mouth. "I will take into consideration what you are suggesting." *They seemed like good people, but the conditions at the mine were...were...* She huffed. She'd never been there, but she could only imagine the hardships. *Hadn't the children been through enough?*

"Well, then, thank you. And please call me Camille. My husband is Edward." She stood and took her cup to the basin and whispered in Lydia's ear. Lydia slid the little yarn doll across the table back to Bonita.

"Can we go on Thursday, Miss Bradstreet?" Esther asked. Waiting, she squinted her face. "Please? You said we could see the big house one day."

"I...I'm sure we...can," Olivia said, without much conviction.

"Well, we just wanted to introduce ourselves." Camille popped Lydia's bonnet back on and reached for their shawls. "Thank you, Miss, for the tea."

"We look forward to seeing you on Thursday." Doretha nodded. "And don't worry if you have no sewing. We'd love to sing the hymns with you."

Olivia found a weak smile as they crossed the doorstep. As she watched them walk across the soggy grass and down the trail to the mine area, a cool breeze seeped through her blouse and chilled her skin. She'd never intended for the last remnants of the Oak Street Home for Children to be consumed by the wants and needs of the mine.

Why could there not be one thing in her life that was hers? Certainly, her family of origin was not truly hers, a truth they'd kept from her that still cut as deep as the day Wally had threatened and dismissed her like rubbish. Ronald was not to be hers. The journey out west was not her wish. But the Oak Street Home was under her guidance, under her say, part of her heart.

Well, it had been.

She clenched her jaw, thinking of Ian Beckner. Why couldn't he leave her and the orphanage well enough alone? And now he likely believed himself helpful, yet if the man had any sense he'd know it was quite the opposite. He was taking the last threads of her fragile identity. How could she allow even one kind thought toward him?

A stupid notion festered like a splinter under her nail. Had she felt in her heart that Ian might actually care for her? The man was as handsome as the day was long. Eyes of blue and gray surrounded by dark lashes, deep enough to take your breath away. Especially when they softened into true sincerity. Had she been swayed into more girlish nonsense? *Hair that smelled like glory and softness like a hundred feather pillows*, he'd said.

She shut the door and sagged against it. The same place she'd leaned for security after their kiss. This was impossible. She stood up straight. At the beginning she'd been thankful for the refuge of their home, but now being back at Ian's Empire Mine exasperated her inside and out.

Eighteen

The following Thursday, Olivia rapped on the front door of the stately Empire Cottage with Esther and Bonita flanked on each side of her. The grand design of rock and mortar was like a European fortress against the simple terrain of rugged California. Another woman carrying a large basket on her hip came up the walkway as Mary Ellen opened the door.

"Good day, Miss Bradstreet, Bonita, Esther." Mary Ellen gave them a stiff nod before breaking into a wide smile. "Just trying out my parlor maid tone," she giggled, showing them in and taking their wraps.

Olivia noted the new dress and crisp white apron and matching cap upon Mary Ellen's sandy hair. "You look well. Is everything all right here?"

"Right as rain," Mary Ellen piped up before greeting the next woman as she arrived.

Olivia wanted to talk more openly with Mary Ellen, but the woman behind her could not be ignored. "How do you do? I'm Miss Bradstreet, and these little ladies are Esther and Bonita." Olivia bowed.

"I've heard of you." The shorter woman smiled, and Olivia bristled. More idle gossip at the Cornish shanties, no doubt.

"I'm Mrs. Kitt. Please call me Sarah." Toting her large basket, she followed Olivia past the entry and into the parlor. Nine or ten women sat in a circle of chairs. Mrs. Kitt took it upon herself to introduce Olivia to all the Cornish women. Olivia nodded and smiled, but her mind focused on Lester as he stacked kindling in the corner wood box. He'd yet to return one packet of school work that Olivia had created for him.

She would speak to Judith. These orphans were not the mine's property, to be told when to come and when to go. They were children who deserved to learn to read and write fluently, to play, and to have friends. Little Lydia came near, reaching for Bonita and Esther's hands. Sweetly, she pulled them to a side rug left of the wide banister, where Judith knelt playing blocks with the small children. Olivia felt a stab of insecurity. She was wearing one of Judith's dresses; she still hadn't gone in to Grass Valley to find things for herself. The other women, obviously well acquainted, were all talking amongst themselves.

"Please, Miss Bradstreet. You must come." Mrs. Kitt smiled, pulling a large quilt from her basket.

Olivia turned back to the parlor's occupants and smiled. What were they saying?

"Our men have worked close to all day and night." Mrs. Hocking added. "The St. Piran's Day may have to be just one evening, but it's better than nothing."

"I agree." Another woman nodded. Belly swollen with child, her sewing basket rested upon her round bump like an impromptu shelf. Clipping the threads against what appeared to be a baby gown, she looked up. "I'll be bringing my mother's pastry dish."

"I'll have the spiced cider ready then," Doretha added, and all the women yelped and cooed. "We want our men awake!" they laughed.

"At least able to dance," another said over the laughter.

Olivia observed their camaraderie, flavored perfectly with matching Cornish accents. She felt like a left shoe on the right foot. They all had such familiar ties, and for some reason she wished she'd stayed back in the quiet of the guest cottage. Katy walked into the middle of the chatter, setting a plate of cookies on a side table. "Help yourself, Miss Bradstreet." Without any sewing, Olivia didn't want to sit in the sewing circle with nothing to do. Lester came from the butler's pantry so she stopped him.

"Lester, how are you doing? I thought you were going to bring me your school work from last week."

"That's a bit my fault." Judith rose and straightened her peach gown trimmed with brown piping. "When Katy has no need of him, he's been joining Maxwell at the mining office. He's been adding and tallying the sums." Judith patted his shoulder. "He's been making wonderful use of his arithmetic skills and running messages back and forth for Mr. Wright, saving him time from going from one end of the mine to the other."

Olivia pursed her lips, feeling an iron rod stiffen up her back. "Judith, I'm at a loss. Truly, I don't want to be perceived as cross or difficult, but it feels I've lost all guardianship of the children. The needs of the mine have dictated their every move."

"I know." Judith touched her sleeve and sighed. "Thank you, Lester." She let him go and spoke softly. "Ian is trying so hard to keep it all afloat."

"And what does that have to do with the children? Will *I* be asked to run errands or drill for gold next?" She drew in a shaky breath. Never had she addressed this benevolent woman in such a manner. Now she was angry at herself. "Maybe it's best I take the girls and go."

"No, please." Judith pulled her into the dining area. "Everyone has been short-sighted. I don't even think I've asked you about the fearful night of the fire you all suffered through." Judith rubbed her back, but Olivia could feel no warmth. "Please forgive me, Olivia." Judith frowned. "Ian makes a plan and everyone jumps to carry out his intentions."

Olivia held her tongue though her body, stiffened anew. *Jump was right.* A wave of the Cornish women's laughter rolled into the dining room and Olivia's shoulders slumped with the opposite feeling. "I don't mean to sound ungrateful. You took Dr. Hastings and me in. You opened your arms to the orphans. It is *your* home in Sacramento that is gone forever." The pounding in her heart lessened. "I'm...I can't even say what it is." She pulled her hand down her face. "I want to blame it on Ian's return, or on being back in Grass Valley, or no one having any time. I'm just so…so…perplexed and misplaced here."

Judith tightened an arm around Olivia's as they turned toward the sound coming from the parlor. *"Come Thou Fount of every blessing, tune my heart to sing Thy grace."* The women's soft, heartfelt singing captured Olivia's attention. *"Streams of mercy, never ceasing, call for songs of loudest praise."* The little children meandered to their mothers, leaning on their laps and holding their skirts. Olivia noticed Esther and Bonita sitting alone, and her throat constricted. How could she complain? Hadn't her heart been full enough to care and love those who God had given her? Sitting with them on the rug, she pulled them close. *"Praise the mount. I'm fixed upon it, Mount of God's unchanging love."* Her voice and spirit joined in the lovely melody, feeling the voices of praise breaking through her dark shell.

An hour later, like sunshine through the shadows, Olivia had Mary Ellen, Lester, Esther, and Bonita all singing the silly farmyard song she had taught them for the Sisters of Charity fundraiser. Lester, the only boy present to sing his part, did so with vigor, and all the Cornish women and children clapped as they bowed at the end of the performance.

Lester bowed again, and Olivia couldn't help but ruffle his hair. He loved the attention, and Katy waited on the side with open arms to wrap a thick hug of approval around him and Mary Ellen.

"We must have this song for our St. Piran's party," Mrs. Kitt exclaimed, and all the women agreed. "And maybe another, makin' it slow and romantic." The expectant younger woman piped in, nodding to Olivia.

"I'm a thinkin' you've had enough of that, young lady." Doretha snickered.

"I was only askin' for poor Mr. Beckner. To keep his heart hopeful after what the wretched woman did to him. Promise to marry him. *Tisk, tisk.* And then after he pined for her our whole trip, she breaks it off with him his first day back to humiliate the poor man. I don't think that would be allowed in Cornwall.

Breaking his heart like that, back home, his fiancée might trip in the dark of night and have a long fall into the ocean."

The women covered their snickers and Olivia caught Mary Ellen's shocked expression.

"We were taught that gossip is a sin." The teen's brow crossed before her bottom lip popped out.

"'Cause she's standing right there." Lester frowned as he pointed to Olivia. "That's not nice to talk about Miss Bradstreet that way."

Olivia tried to silence them with her wide eyes. But all her desperate gestures didn't connect.

"You?" Camille spoke, but all the Cornish women echoed with wide, shocked eyes. "You were his fiancée?"

"No, no." Olivia held her hand up. "That is not me. That was someone else."

"Oh." Mary Ellen giggled. "That makes sense. You are his *new* fiancée."

Lester nodded. "I was wondering why you were all talking about her, with her standing right here." He looked around the circle, and Olivia's breathing had ceased. "Yep, Miss Bradstreet is the *new* fiancée."

Like a shadow, she felt her hand reaching to clamp over his mouth, yet her body stood frozen solid. *New fiancée*. Now it had been announced twice. With every feminine eye glued to her, her body began to waver. "The children have, ah…" She searched from orphan to orphan. Why were her fingers tingling?

"Lester." Esther glared at him. "Mr. Beckner told us not to talk about it. See, look at her." She pointed to Olivia. "She's starting to get all white and clammy again."

Mrs. Kitt dropped her quilt to the floor and took Olivia's arm. "Come now, dearie, and sit here. You do look a little pale." Another woman poured her some water and held it out. "They were probably not wanting the news out just yet, seein' how Mr. Beckner had just lost the other engagement."

Olivia sipped her water, wondering if fainting would be a better move than enduring these speculations.

"It's no shame, Miss," a kind voice said to her left. "All these ladies know I was engaged to a man who broke it off with me and then married my cousin two weeks later. But I showed him. I married his brother three weeks after that. Always liked him better, and now four tykes later, I'm glad I did."

"Blessing from above," another woman agreed.

Olivia hadn't raised her eyes above the water in her glass.

"And that Mr. Beckner, he's the best kind of catch. That other gal, to her the loss." Mrs. Kitt nodded once and patted her back while the others chimed in.

"He's the best kind o' man—one not taken to drink. He *is* a hard worker."

Olivia took another sip. She didn't want to mention she'd been caught by him already one night when he'd had too much liquor.

"Handsome." Agreement and giggles crackled around the sewing circle.

"Faithful. Never did chase skirts like those other men on the ship."

"True, true."

"Man of his word."

"That's important."

"White, straight teeth."

"Um-hum, fetching smile." They agreed.

"Ladies." Judith's voice rang out. "I've so enjoyed having you all; shall we sing one last hymn before we leave." Clearing her throat, she started to sing gently and the others joined in.

Just as I am, without one plea, But that Thy blood was shed for me, And that Thou bid'st me come to Thee , O Lamb of God, I come, I come...

Olivia sat back with red flushed cheeks and a pasted-on smile. She couldn't make eye contact with Judith. The woman sang with a gracious fervor, but likely she was ready for the morning to end. The gossip had turned to her son and Olivia had done nothing to right the wrong. The sweet voices sang around her, but only shallow, short breaths were entering her lungs.

Mind spinning, all she could do was breathe in and out and move her lips as if trying to sing along.

Another lie spun around her.

Nineteen

The next evening, with Maxwell at the big house, Olivia retired early. The girls slept on their pallets and she pulled her blanket close, listening to the rain patter on the window. When her heart had been lonesome after her mother's death, she would lay in bed and picture them back in the bright sunroom. Nibbling on their flaky croissants with peach marmalade, sipping tea from painted teacups. They could spend hours studying the latest details of the fashion magazines.

Yesterday, Judith had pulled her aside and congratulated her on her engagement, saying she understood why they hadn't wanted to make an announcement. It seemed Judith and Dr. Hastings had a similar predicament. But she was glad they could talk freely. She'd wanted Olivia to know Judith had found a special connection with the doctor who'd found his place at Empire Mine.

Shocked by their secret, yet excited to have the focus off of her, she excused herself, needing to ready the girls for lunch with a promise they would talk soon. At least one budding romance was genuine. She'd wondered about all the time Maxwell had spent with Judith, and understood how an attachment more than friendship could present itself.

A quick tap repeated lightly at her window and Olivia rose and peeked from the side of the curtain—a man with dark hair, blurred through the thick shadowy pane.

"Ian?" She shook her head, and cracked open the front door. "What are you doing?" she whispered.

"You were supposed to open your window." Water dripped from his hair and face.

"Why?"

"Your reputation, Miss Bradstreet."

"Oh, that?" She huffed and opened the door to let him in. "The children are asleep, and Dr. Hastings is not here."

Ian looked puzzled, noting the boys asleep near the fire. "Where is he?"

"I think you'd better talk to your mother about that." Olivia stepped quietly to the kitchen and grabbed a towel. Before she realized it, she'd reached up to pat his face dry. When his eyes simmered on hers, she caught her mistake. "Here." She handed the towel to him.

"Now I've felt your gentle touch once more and witnessed you in your night clothes for the second time." His whisper was soft, his eyes teasing. He stepped closer, cupping her elbow while she gripped her gown at the neck. "We must still the vicious rumors and announce the engagement that you fantasize." The man was impossible, mocking her distress.

"How would I know your past engagement would be the talk of the women's sewing circle?" she whispered hoarsely as she inched to the side. He smelled like soap and rainwater, and was far too close. "It's disconcerting how those women know your every detail. Spouting all your fine qualities. *Straight teeth*," she mumbled, rolling her eyes. Ian smiled and nodded his approval. Olivia huffed. "Then every eye was on me. I'm the *new* fiancée? The replacement? Ack." She sneered. "The innocent children again exposed to confusion."

"No more than I." His shoulder rose and fell. "To be congratulated by the workers for my upcoming nuptials? What was I to say? It was all a farce to protect Miss Bradstreet's reputation? Wouldn't that still leave you a liar?"

Olivia clenched her jaw. Ian Beckner was overdue for a good scolding. This was all his fault. If he had never tried to shield her from the cold with his very own body! Her mouth flew open then snapped closed, not wanting to wake the children. "Why are you here?" she hissed. "I haven't seen you for over a week, and you come tapping on my window just to harass me?"

"No, I didn't come *just* for that." Amusement flashed in his eyes, and he fingered his wet hair back. "I wanted you to drive with me Monday. I'll take you to Sacramento and you can visit Sister Patricia while I drive on to San Francisco. My business won't take long, and I'll come back for you. It's a lot of time in the buggy. But I need to get straight back to the mine—if you are willing."

Olivia hesitated, weighing her irritation. Everything was about the mine. But there were so many things they would have time to talk about. Maybe they could even find a solution to break off these circulating falsehoods. And seeing Sister Patricia...By the grace of God, could another home have opened up?

"What of the children?"

"The Hockings would like to keep the boys, and I can ask Katy to watch over the girls."

"That's another thing I have to talk to you about, Ian."

"We will, I promise." They both turned toward the front door as it opened. Ian tapped her chin before he dashed out the back door.

"Maxwell." Flustered, Olivia grabbed the towel and began to fold it. "How was your evening?" *Ian Beckner has the nerve of a fox.* Drops of his wet steps shone on the floor.

"Well, thank you." He slipped his coat off. "I understand Judith told you of our courtship?" Shaking his head, he lifted a winsome grin. "Is that even the word at our age?"

With all the distractions, Olivia wondered how she felt. Of course, he deserved to be happy. "I suppose it could look like whatever you want it to. She's a lovely lady, and you've been a great help to her and the mine." Her words sounded sincere, but a piece of her heart sank. *More changes.* Her stomach pinched.

"You saw her the night she stopped wearing black." Maxwell stepped carefully around the sleeping boys and added a small log to the fire. "I asked for her hand that night, but we wanted to keep it a secret. We've been waiting, but Ian is in and out of cordiality with me." He exhaled, his tone tightened. "I don't think he would approve."

"Ian is not her keeper." The words came out terse. Most likely it was how she personally felt about him.

"Well, as he's Judith's son and is carrying the weight around here, neither of us wants to do anything that would make him feel unconsidered."

"No, of course not. And what of your son, Morgan? What do you think he will say?" Olivia wondered.

"I think he will be happy. I want to travel back to Auburn soon." Maxwell sat and unlaced his boots. "But with so much going on at the mine, we've all been working harder than ever."

"Speaking of travel, Mr. Beckner asked me to travel with him on Monday to Sacramento. I've letters to mail to the Sisters of Charity but now I'll be able to see them in person. Perhaps there's news awaiting of another position or possible home for the orphans." Her optimism faded. "But I must realize the sisters can run things without me. I was only given the position in the Oak Street Home because of Mrs. Beckner."

"So, if another opportunity would arise, you would gather the children and go back to Sacramento?"

"In a heartbeat." Olivia hadn't meant to sound so desperate. Didn't she just sit with the girls at the sewing circle and tell herself to be thankful? "Now that you will be starting a new Chapter, I suppose I should find my own way." She meant her smile to encourage him, but he frowned and leaned on the table.

"Is it just a rumor then? That you and Ian are engaged?"

Olivia felt her insides crumble. "It is a rumor started by me." She rolled her eyes. "And I fully regret it. Ian Beckner has not asked me to be his wife, and I highly doubt he ever will." She sat at the small table. "The night of the fire, we all slept huddled in the barn. I don't remember how the confusion started, but in thinking I was *protecting* young minds, I mentioned the reason

Mr. Beckner and I could sleep close was that we were engaged."
She dropped her forehead on the palm of her head. "I actually
believed they would forget. Of course, I didn't know six of them
would be living with me here at Empire Mine. Mary Ellen and
Lester let the news out Thursday at the sewing circle. It was so
awful, and they were all staring at me. I couldn't tell the truth. I
let them believe the lie. Just like everything else." She sighed,
dropping her eyes. "I'm a coward, and I know it."

Maxwell tucked his chin down. "And your other secret? Have
you shared it with anyone?"

"Oh no, Maxwell." She grasped his arm. "You are the only
one who knows my true beginnings. Will you keep my horrid
secret to the grave?"

"If you promise to hold your head high all your days." He
nodded once.

Olivia couldn't find the words. She'd never lie to him. He'd
been the only secure arm she'd known. "How do I do that when
they all think I'm a real Bradstreet?" She rubbed her brows.
"Even in Sacramento, people came to me at the fundraiser,
offering invitations because I was a Bradstreet. Now I'm starting
to wonder if lying pumps through my blood."

"Let them all think what they want." He huffed. "You were
loved and raised as a Bradstreet, and that is the truth. But now
you are in a new place, a brand new state. Just as Judith and I
have left our social expectations aside, wanting to move forward,
you will too." He patted her arm. "Maybe on Monday you and
Ian can figure out a solution for this *misunderstanding*." He
stood, looking down. "I've a difficult task ahead myself. Judith
has asked us to Sunday luncheon. We want to make our
announcement with Ian present and set a date."

"And I have to be there?" Olivia offered a crooked frown.
Trying to lighten the moment, she smiled and bid Maxwell
goodnight. Straightening against the chair, she wondered if
faking a previous engagement was in order.

That was going to be one interesting meal.

Twenty

Olivia fidgeted in her chair at the Beckners' fine table on Sunday afternoon, nervously awaiting Ian's arrival. She would speak first; that would help her heart rate return to normal. She'd break the ice by coming clean with Judith; in all the myriad of confessions, her falsehoods from Thursday's sewing circle had not been cleaned up. Maxwell removed his hand from Judith's back as he pulled her chair out. The admiration on Judith's face made her look like a young woman again. That is how two people in love should look, Olivia mused. Mary Ellen came in in her maid apron and sat a basket of rolls on the table.

"Thank you, Mary Ellen. Where is Lester?" Olivia asked.

"In the barn." She turned to leave.

"Judith, I must speak to Katy. I still have not seen any school work from Lester. I try each night to work with Thomas and Milton, but you should see them. They fall asleep with pencils in their hands." She knew frustration peppered her words.

Judith was about to respond when a heavy weight landed on Olivia's shoulder, and she jumped, spinning to see Ian. "You scared me." Her eyes closed and she clenched her teeth. Could he be any more thoughtless, she'd almost come off her seat.

"Good day, Miss Bradstreet." He walked around the table and took his chair. "You were deep in conversation. I'm sorry I interrupted."

Olivia didn't trust his words. There was a bit of sarcasm always lurking to be discovered. She nodded but could not return a greeting, now vexed he looked so handsome in a starched gray shirt and woolen vest.

"Please carry on." He took the glass pitcher and poured his water.

At least he was not reaching for liquor. Or maybe he should? Olivia wanted desperately to remove the weight in her gut. "I want to say a few things first." She blurted out the words, causing Mary Ellen to freeze and stare at her. When Olivia stared back without speaking, Mary Ellen set another dish down and scurried from the dining room.

"So, this is more than a friendly brunch?" Ian cocked his head, wide-eyed.

"Ian, just let me say it." Olivia sucked in needed air.

"Yes, please do." He sat back and tapped his fingers into the tablecloth.

"Judith." Olivia leaned her head, not able to make eye contact. "Thursday, with the sewing circle. I didn't correct them, and I should have with you first-hand. But Ian and I are not..." She peeked to the kitchen door seeing no one. "We are not engaged. It was a story I made up the night of—"

"Morning." Ian piped in.

"Yes, fine—the morning after the fire." She repressed her irritation at him. "It was quite innocent, but in the flurry of everything, Ian and I slept in the barn surrounded by children. And I...I...panicked and told them it was permissible because we were engaged. But we're not." Her jaw hung open a minute, and the room was too quiet. "It's a bit humorous, or naïve, on my part, because I was sure they would all forget."

Judith blinked, her expression stoic.

"I'm so sorry." Olivia felt deep regret. "I can see I've upset you. I will tell each of the Cornish women the truth."

"I'm just...sad." Judith murmured. "After Ian said he would have nothing to do with you because of your family money, I thought the tide had turned. My heart desired to have you as a daughter-in-law." Her lips wrinkled into a frown.

Olivia's eyes whipped from mother to son. *Nothing to do?* Olivia mouthed across the table, her angry expression burning a hole on the rake's face.

Ian scratched the back of his head. "Now that that's over, can we eat?" He reached for the tureen.

"So, this bride that comes with an inheritance discussion—I would like to know more." Olivia leaned forward, feeling prickles all over her body. Grateful he was not privy to her disinheritance—only two at the table knew there was no dowry. "Is the Bradstreet money not good enough to help the mine? Because, unfortunately, it comes with me." Her round eyes widened. "Nothing *to do*—Please elaborate, Mr. Beckner."

"No, nope, nope." Ian shook his head and scooped the cooked greens into his bowl. "That was never said. And my mother's words were taken out of context." He picked up his fork to eat and set it back down. "Excuse me." He lifted the tureen and handed it to her. "Olivia?"

Olivia didn't move a muscle, except for the flames of anger coming off her skin and her tongue running over her front teeth.

"Dr. Hastings." Ian shifted the white bowl to the man.

"Thank you, Ian." Maxwell took it and scooped his serving. "Olivia, I don't want to interrupt, was there anything else you wanted to say?"

Olivia had a line of unsuitable words that were fit only for frustrated teamsters on the wagon trail west. Thankfully, she had enough pride left to keep her mouth shut. "I just wanted to make my apologies to Judith."

"Very well." Maxwell rocked forward in his seat and then stood and came to Judith's chair. Touching her shoulder, she reached up to grasp his hand.

Olivia almost enjoyed seeing the way Ian's eyes narrowed, and his jaw twitched.

"I've asked your mother to marry me." Maxwell's voice was so dry that Olivia felt for him. "And she has graciously agreed."

"Really?" Stunned, Ian's face flushed red. "My mother has not finished a year of mourning, sir."

Judith squeezed Maxwell's hand. "Son, things are different here."

"Not so different that the man could show a thread of proper respect," Ian said sharply.

"We know our youth is over; neither of us knows how many years we have left." Judith said. "We've both loved and mourned the loss of our spouses." She bravely smiled up at Maxwell. "We will marry in a month. We'd like your blessing."

"A month?" Ian's chest thrust forward. "Have you even thought this through, Mother?"

"We've been serious about more than a friendship before today," Maxwell spoke up. "I find your mother kind and gracious. It would be a high honor to have her by my side and care for her as my own." Maxwell glanced at Olivia and she smiled back.

Beautifully said. Olivia felt her chin quiver. Maxwell deserved every—

"You." Ian's coarse tone turned on her, and she jumped in her chair for the second time. "You've known about this?" His eyes turned dark gray.

Every fiber in Olivia froze. "Yes?"

"That's rich!" He stood, pulling his chair backward. "While I'm out working day and night, chipping away at any sediment that might keep this place from going under, the three of you are planning wedding wreaths and ribbons. Grand. Just grand." He stalked around the table. "Is this what you've always been after, Dr. Hastings? 'Just to help,' you said. 'Just an investor.' My father agreed." His face waxed as cold as his voice. "I don't care." He turned his back to them, grabbed the banister, and pulled. "You can have it all."

Olivia rolled her lips together and glanced at Maxwell and Judith. Their silence echoed her own discord. Judith stood, and Maxwell took her in his arms. "I'm sorry, love, I'd hoped that would go better."

Olivia dropped her eyes away from their embrace, their intimacy so tender her chest squeezed.

"He'll need time." Judith sighed, resting her head on Maxwell's shoulder. "He's been working without a break. I know Monday he will feel better, taking a payment to San Francisco."

Olivia stood slowly, dropping her napkin on the table. Like everyone else, her appetite was gone. Monday, his late-night invitation to her, was all about business. She, on the other hand, just wanted time to talk to him and have him listen to her. Maybe focus on the things she needed. Drawing her fingers down over her mouth, she pushed on her lips, repressing a groan. Foolishness and disappointment riddled her being. Now, with that betrayal in his eyes, likely the offer to take her to Sacramento was over. "I'm sorry for my part in this mess. I...I...will walk back to the guest cottage."

Maxwell turned, "I can walk you back."

"No, please. You two talk and make your plans. It will be a glorious union." She forced her face to brighten. "I'm sure of it." Olivia took her cape from the hall tree and let herself out the front door. Stepping onto the gravel walk, she heard an unclear noise and looked up to the second-story windows. Finally, it registered. The faint sounds were the strumming of a guitar. Frowning and drained of this place, she walked away.

Twenty-One

The next morning, a low fog lay settled on the grounds of the Empire Mine. The boys finished their oatmeal and bread. Olivia met them at the door. Buttoning up their coats, she realized they didn't need her help, but found little else to care for. She missed them so.

"See you at supper." She plopped their felt hats on, and they left. Beyond the path to the large house, Mary Ellen jogged toward the guest cottage with arms loaded.

"What do we have?" Olivia let her in and closed the door behind her.

"Mr. Beckner said he would pick you up in fifteen minutes," she panted. "This is Mrs. Beckner's wool coat and gloves for your trip."

Still in her robe, Olivia pulled back, surprised. Ian planned on taking her to Sacramento after all? He likely planned to leave her there, she mused.

Mary Ellen met the girls at the table. "You two are with me today, so finish up."

Bonita and Esther took their bowls to the sink, and Bonita pulled on Olivia's robe. "You coming back, right?"

Olivia knelt. Had the child heard her thoughts? "Yes, my dear. But it will be late, so you and Esther will stay with Katy today." She brushed her wispy dark hair back and glanced up at Esther. "You both will be good helpers, yes?"

"Yes, ma'am." They grabbed their coats and followed Mary Ellen to the door.

"The boys will need supper if I'm not back." Olivia stood, feeling unprepared. "Check with Dr. Hastings?"

"Got that." Mary Ellen smiled and left with the girls in tow.

Olivia turned in the small cottage; it was so quiet, so peculiar. Without any children to take care of, she stared unencumbered out the window. The girls jogged back down the path, and her heart felt neither excited nor hopeful. The fog brought a strange, ghost-like mood to the morning. A strange ache she'd never experienced before filled her bones. The opportunity was hers, she'd wanted a break from all things Empire Mine, but now, when given it, she suddenly missed the children. *Peanuts for brains,* she huffed and started the dishes.

What had Mary Ellen said? *Fifteen minutes.* The thought propelled her from dirty dishes to quick morning preparations.

A sleek black mare pulling a matching covered buggy slowed in front of the guest cottage. Olivia checked the fire and grabbed Judith's coat and her small reticule. Maxwell had insisted on giving her money for any needed things from Sacramento. Thankfulness collided with her pride. All the money she'd carefully saved from her position as headmistress had burnt in the fire. A loud knock caused her to take a deep breath.

"Good morning," Olivia greeted while stepping out. Ian nodded and held his hand out to help her up. Though he was dressed in a dark suit, he'd not shaven, and his eyes seemed tired. He entered the comfortable buggy from the other side and drove the horse around and out of Empire Mine property.

The horse picked up to a steady trot, and Olivia looked out to the side. So much of Grass Valley had been green and lush; when had the winter come and stripped it so damp and bare? Without turning, she knew Ian held the reins tight and his body even tighter. What a long, frozen journey this would be. And *frozen* in more ways than one. She found her handkerchief and dabbed the moisture from the corner of her eye. Without any desire to speak first, she leaned against the buggy's tufted seat and decided to weather the trip as best as she could.

The cold air blew harder as they took turned onto a wider road, and she dabbed her nose and eyes.

"Are you crying?" He broke the silence.

"No, the cool air makes my eyes water."

He clicked his tongue and pulled the horse back to a slower trot. Could that question and gentler pace be laced with friendly concern? She thought about his questioning tone. *Definitely not.*

"Are you cold?" Steel gray-blue eyes narrowed on hers as he broke the silence again.

"Not really. Your mother was kind to lend me a coat and gloves."

"Humph. That coat was a gift from my father, three Christmases ago." His broad shoulders rose stiffly. "I'm sure, like everything else, she'd freely give it away." He exhaled.

"Please, Ian, you shouldn't work so hard to hold back your bitterness," she mocked. She knew it sounded brash, but Olivia was tired of him rattling her goodwill at his every convenience. She could play the antagonist just as well.

"Bitterness, really?" He shook his head, and the buggy wheel hit a rut in the road. Olivia had to grip the bench seat to keep the bone-jarring dip from knocking her around.

Like it was nothing, he continued at a clipping pace. "What I wouldn't give to know the date Dr. Hastings found out about my father's passing. How sudden was his decision to come to California? That could leave a bitter taste, you're right."

Olivia knew enough to know Ian was a smart, logical man. "You traveled from California to England and back to California by ship?" she asked.

"Yes, you know that." He leveled his gaze on her.

"How was the delivery of correspondence all those months?"

"Nigh to nothing."

"I can tell you for a fact that Dr. Hastings was mourning the loss of a son to the Mexican-American War, and another who lived through it but had no desire to return home. After waiting for weeks, he got word that Morgan had settled in California to mine gold. When we arrived in Auburn, Morgan had no knowledge of our arrival. If the correspondence was that poor between them, do you really think he had knowledge of what happened at Empire Mine?

"He talked about meeting your father many times on our trip here. I assure you, you are mistaken." She dabbed a cold tear from her cheek. "He's never been waiting in the wings to come in and take over. If you had enough fortitude to get to know him." Olivia gripped the seat as Ian snapped the horse back into a faster trot. His jaw hardened, her own bias was sounding a bit ugly.

"Bitter and cowardly." He nodded, staring forward. "Funny, I work daily around hard, prideful men whose opinions I can take or brush off when needed. But for the first time in a long time, I cared what someone's perception of me was." He glanced at her, eyes narrowing. "Yours, Miss Bradstreet. Thank you for setting me straight, you've been clear and to the point of your opinion of me."

Olivia wilted. Not a bone in her body wanted to make him feel worse. "Ian, I don't think you bitter or a coward. I...I can imagine that one thing after another has burdened you greatly." She wanted to rest her gloved hand on his arm, but the way his eyes steeled forward, she thought better of it. "This mine was your family's dream, their existence." She dabbed her wet nose. "I don't know, maybe you gave up your own dreams to partner with your father, to make the trip to Cornwall."

"Empire Mine was always my dream as much as my father's."

"Then to come back and find him gone. I know you were honoring your mother in accepting help from Dr. Hastings, but if you'd asked us to leave, we'd have been gone."

"And now that is too late."

"What if they were to leave? Do you want your mother to move on with Dr. Hastings?"

"Don't be ridiculous. The Empire home, the cottage, the grounds, gardens, and fountains are all her creation, her...I thought her *only love*."

Olivia dabbed the drips from running down her cheeks. "If you could remove the belief that he was here maliciously, if you could believe that he was just a local doctor who made a social connection with her, would you still reject him?"

"I don't know." He shrugged uneasily. "Why do you press me with questions when you know I'm inconsolable?" He finally looked at her, possibly searching for a sliver of true empathy.

Olivia felt her hand reach toward his sleeve. When she looked closer, his face was drawn, and an apology formed on her lips. She settled her hand in her lap as he turned and led the buggy over a small bridge. Maxwell had proven his ability to be patient, never asking her for any help to win over Ian Beckner. Why would she try now?

After miles of cold silence, she hoped the air would clear a bit. "What is this business in San Francisco? Your mother said something about a payment. Does this have anything to do with the workload at the mine?"

"Yes, everything." He rocked forward, stretching his back. "I'm meeting with a lawyer to secure payments to another investor, Mr. Grant. He is threatening to put a lean on the mine and shut us down until his loan is paid in full."

"Oh, Ian, I'm sorry." That was the pressure lurking under his skin his mother alluded to. "You have no Sacramento house to sell. In all the changes, I didn't put all these things together. I apologize I've been so focused on the children."

"As you should." His tone was lighter than any other time the entire morning. Olivia wondered if he could tolerate what she needed to express.

"Speaking of the children, you know Mrs. Hocking and her daughter-in-law came for a visit."

His eyes met hers and he nodded.

"If I understand her correctly, they would like to take on Milton and Thomas. To adopt them?"

"I told them to talk to you."

Olivia pressed her gloved hand to her cold cheek, waiting for the right words. "I'm not sure of the impression you are giving. But these boys are not joining a family to bring wages to the home. Thomas reported being lowered into a deep shaft to secure some…something. Children and mining should not be combined. I don't even know how it happened, but they should be in school, not hauling rock or being dropped into the earth."

His jaw stiffened into a frown and he nodded.

"Just like Mary Ellen and Lester." She continued. "I do appreciate all that Katy is offering. But are these orphans just Empire house staff now?"

"I'm sorry we aren't the Oak Street Orphanage. You told me yourself, each of the children helped out with chores and duties."

"They did." She answered, trying to lower her tone. "And Sister Patricia and I oversaw each one. We decided when and where and how, knowing that each of them—"

"Wait." Ian quickly gripped the reins with one fist and held his hand up. "This is about others stepping in? You don't like that *you* don't have the say?"

Olivia huffed. "Exactly. I don't." Her voice was dismayed. "These children are not just recipes I can exchange with the other women here!" *Why not just get it all out?* "We had a horrific fire, and we had nothing. Again, I've told your mother how thankful for her generosity I am, but I've been waiting patiently to go into Grass Valley." She sucked in a quick breath. "I've wanted to talk to Father Dalton. He might have connections. Even today, a home might have opened up back in Sacramento."

Ian tilted his head back and released a full laugh.

Agitated, she squinted at his strange behavior. Impossible, unpredictable man, what was so funny?

Twenty-Two

"You don't see it? Really?" Ian shook his head, still amused. "I would think you, Miss Bradstreet, would recognize we suffer from the same malady."

Olivia huffed and stared out the side of the buggy. Far off beyond a field of cows, a lazy stream of smoke rose in the air. The faint smell of burning brush distracted her. What was he talking about? The man went from brooding to laughing in no time. She turned to him. "No, for the life of me. I have no idea what you're talking about or what you find so amusing. Perhaps you would be so kind as to let me in on the joke."

"I was about to tell you about the Hockings." His fingers ran through his dark hair, exposing the untrimmed curls at his collar. "They are good people and even better parents. I stood by their side as their child, already gone with the angels, was lowered into the sea." He paused, swallowing an unrestricted groan from escaping his throat. "They pulled together and they let the others hold them and help them. I feel they have mended as best as one can." His words were guarded. "These boys would never be used for labor or seen as hired help, they would be family. I want you to believe what I'm saying." He pulled the reins back, and the horse slowed. "Now do you see it?"

Olivia studied him closely still confused. What was she missing?

"I want you to believe me. I *know them*, Olivia." Ian's eyes held hers steady. "I *know* they wouldn't do anything malicious."

"Oh." She thought a moment. "Are you trying to prove to me their character is trustworthy as I've tried to convince you of Dr. Hastings?"

He nodded his head toward his shoulder. "Don't you find it a bit ironic?"

"That we both feel so strongly?" Olivia sighed. They stared ahead in silence for a moment. "That we both want our good recommendations to be seen and received by each other? Certainly, I want you to heed my counsel." Olivia wiggled back in her seat. *Truly, her point about Dr. Hastings was more valid than his. Wasn't it?*

Olivia rubbed her temple with her finger, but after a few minutes of considerations a dull pain landed in her gut. Her convictions could hardly be compared to those of the driven Ian Beckner. *Could they?* Olivia's testimony flowed from a much purer and…and…holy…she frowned. Ian, however, was far too confident, just like now, trying to take her away from the point she was trying to make.

"If we were to follow this road of thought you so brazenly put us together in, then answer me this," she countered. "What is your fear of allowing Dr. Hastings a place in your family, your work, the mine's future?"

"And should I answer," His eyes narrowed. "I will be allowed to ask you the same question."

"Yes, of course." Olivia would think of a rebuttal attesting to her justification when the time came.

Ian's jaw shifted, and his lips tightened. One shoulder rose and fell quickly. "I don't really fear anything." Olivia opened her mouth, but he held a finger up to stop her. "But, I would say…" He pinched his nose, and his brows crinkled. "Any man must take his rightful place to *be* a man. To own his God-given existence, to carry his place with honor, what his Creator created him to be. I've only seen myself in the role of owner and leader of the Empire Mine. And the only one I was willing to share that with was my father."

Olivia tried to understand his point. Without being a man, she'd little scope. *Maybe a son who wants to honor his father?* She spoke carefully. "Sharing your home and business with your father didn't compromise who you are?"

"Exactly. It would be a natural ebb and flow of decisions, of managing."

Olivia chewed on the corner of her lip. There was no doubt that Ian Beckner carried the weight of all decisions on his own shoulders. Then why could he not see that Dr. Hastings could be of help? "I've heard Dr. Hastings say he doesn't want to lead or take over the mine. Though he is invested, I think he has shown you that he doesn't want to push you or the mining business around." Olivia pulled a loose strand of golden hair back and tucked it behind her ear.

Ian shook his head. "Marriage is a legal contract, Olivia. My mother has no titles to hold land or business, but he will."

Olivia was positive the union wasn't about business. It was a fool who did not see how they cared for one another. "Can you talk to him?" she asked. "You have a lawyer in San Francisco. What if it was written that you would be the sole proprietor of the mine, *only* you?"

"Why would Dr. Hastings agree to that? There's no future for him, for his investment?"

"Maxwell has his own money, Ian. I believe the only future he wants is to be closer to his remaining son, and now to love a wonderful woman like your mother."

They rode a while without speaking. "A house divided is no home at all, Olivia said. "Even if you own it all and struggle with these bloody knuckles to make it go." She tapped his hand holding the reins. "When they stroll arm and arm in the gardens. I think you'll still be miserable."

"I would have to move out," he said, clipped. "Can you make room for me in the guest cottage?" He bumped her shoulder. "You've lent your room before."

"I've seen you do well enough in a barn." Olivia bumped him back, enjoying the change in their banter. The tension seemed to disappear as they rode awhile in silence.

"Now, what was that question you asked me?" Ian sat straighter. "Umm, oh, yes. Olivia, without talking of all their needs, tell me what is *your fear* of letting go of the orphans."

"Oh, drat." It slipped out unbridled, and Ian laughed.

"I can't say fear, maybe it's what I dread."

"Close enough, Miss Bradstreet."

Olivia sucked in a deep breath. "This will sound terribly selfish, but I dread being afloat without work or purpose or…oh, I don't know." She sighed. "You said something a while back how the matrons in my pedigree don't work, and that was truly how I was raised. I planned to marry Ronald and make a fine home for him and our children. And I believe that is a worthy calling." She tilted her head back and watched the tops of the trees go by. "I wanted to volunteer at the orphanage, but your mother insisted the work demanded a fair wage." She squeezed her reticule, sitting on her lap. "The work gave me a responsibility and firm foundation to thrive upon…It didn't ever feel like work; it felt like godly service. Each day was my reason to rise, my position made me come alive." She shook her head. "Now I feel I'm being ambiguous and rambling nonsense."

"No," Ian spoke up. "You're not, keep going."

She dipped her head. "So, every time another decision about the children is made without me, it's like a part of my reason for living is taken too. I feel afloat again, unanchored." *There. Enough baring of one's soul. Wasn't this supposed to be just a simple ride to see Sister Patricia?*

"So, help me with this question." He pulled the horse back as the wide countryside gave way to the clustered Sutter's Fort. "Wasn't the point of your job to find homes for the children?"

Olivia rubbed the crease between her eyes. "Yes." She sighed. "But I guess I figured there would always be more orphans than homes."

"I see." Ian's tone sounded genuine. "And this was your secure place? Your work, the Oak Street Home?"

"Yes. After so much tossing around, I thought that was where I belonged." She murmured.

Ian nodded and pulled the buggy down the street toward the church grounds. He seemed deep in thought. "What about being a teacher? You are smart enough and have the disposition."

"I've never trained as a teacher."

"It seems a bit below your family's station, but the miners' children and those of Grass Valley would—"

"Please." She stopped him. "I shouldn't have told you those things." It was too close to her heart. *If he only knew the origins of her birth mother's work.* "I know you are trying to help me as a friend. But honestly, most days, I feel there is no hope for me. I am eternally fickle." She lifted a crooked smile.

Ian stopped the buggy and set the brake. The simple mission-style church rectory and a few other small structures stood, held together with thick gray mortar filled with straw. Olivia struggled to move. What if Sister Patricia had been assigned another mission? Would the day here just add to the melancholy story she had just told? Gripping her skirt layers, she took Ian's hand as he came around the buggy and helped her down. "You said something." He still held her hand in his. "That I only wanted to help as a friend?"

She nodded, watching the tenderness in his blue-gray eyes capture hers.

"Thank you for knowing that." He nodded once and brought her gloved hand to his lips and kissed it. "I will see you in a few hours." Ian circled back around the buggy and jumped in. Olivia's heart thudded in her chest, and her hand still hovered in front of her as she watched the rig pull down the road.

Twenty-Three

Watching the different people cross the wide dirt road in front of him, Ian slowed the buggy through the center of an open market of vendors. A whiff of burning oil and Mexican spices entered the buggy before he turned toward the open road to San Francisco. Every creek, river, and piece of land had changed in his months at sea. The gold rush had brought thousands of people from every country, every culture, and every background creating boomtowns overnight. Funny, he'd been the one to bring over twenty from Cornwall to reside in Grass Valley.

A random thought nettled him. He could bring men from Cornwall, but he could find *no* tolerance for Dr. Hastings from Chicago? And yet, he could give all day to the beautiful Miss Bradstreet. She was an immigrant to be enjoyed from the eastern sunrise to the western ocean's sunset.

Miss Olivia Bradstreet had an endearing heart, and it was one of the many things he admired. His own parents had generously wanted the Oak Street Home available to help the disadvantaged, but maybe his mother had made an error. Putting Olivia in that position had created a young woman who, far from home and family, had lent her very soul to the home's needs. By her own confession, without it, she had now lost her way.

Watching the road, he remembered her pure voice the night of the fundraiser. Besides being a natural headmistress, her songs could fill music halls. He shook his head, wishing he could help her, but singing would not be a respectable vocation. Ian tapped the reins and rubbed his chin against his coat sleeve. The reasonable solution to her feelings of being afloat was obvious to him.

His chest squeezed and he cleared his throat, as if someone was judging his thoughts. Olivia Bradstreet should marry him. Empire Mine would be their home, their passion. His lips tightened, and he glanced left to right over the fields. She'd never said the mine was her passion. But today they hadn't spoken of how to divert their engagement either. Maybe secretly she'd hoped it was real? Right now, that thought seemed idiotic. Hadn't he been the one who'd prayed for the mine to be saved? He had little energy for anything else.

He shouldn't have invited her today; it really was only to appease his mother, who'd said Olivia wasn't adjusting well. After the shocking announcement of his mother's engagement to Dr. Hastings, *he* was not doing that well either. The plan had been to drive her to Sacramento, not exchange outlooks and motives or try to analyze each other. Blast it.

She pulled his heart like a string around a top. He was all wound up, with no level surface to play on. The possibility of what could be was painfully real. Beyond all his protective stances to goad her and stay distant, moments like this morning, where he'd felt safe enough to open his heart, were his undoing. He did want to protect her and make her happy, hold her and watch her smile and laugh, take her in his arms and allow his fingers freedom to run through those soft golden locks. He glanced down. Cringing, he hoped his touch had not marred her beautiful creamy skin. His hands were callused and nicked from all the chipping he'd done in the new shaft. He was infatuated or…or was it something more?

It mattered little.

Ian stretched his neck and blew out a long breath. What mattered was that he'd mined enough gold to make the next payment to Mr. Grant. Thankfully he would not have to see the

Grants himself, and with any luck, the entire Lesandra debacle would keep his rambling imagination off beautiful women, *and* the law off his land.

Steam rose from the church's outdoor kitchen and Olivia strained to see past the flutter of black habits until the face she sought found hers.

"Olivia!" Sister Patricia dried her hands on her apron and then wrapped them tightly around her shoulders. Pulling back, she blinked with a wide grin. "I'm so glad to see you again. Let's step away so you can tell me everything." Sister Patricia looked around. "No children with you?"

"No, they are all being cared for at the mine."

Sister Patricia found a bench under a tree. "Let's sit."

"Everyone looks so busy. How are the remaining Oak Street children?" Olivia sat.

"Crowded." Sister Patricia grinned. "We had six new children brought in yesterday." She touched her shoulders and forehead in the sign of the cross. "Parents both dead. The oldest speaks a bit of English mixed with Spanish. She said her mother had a fever and could not get air."

Olivia's faced lined with pity. "And their father?"

"Killed in a knife fight in front of his claim."

"Oh, dear Lord, poor things." Olivia sighed.

"The youngest two are sick with fever and sore throats. No rash yet, so we are praying it is not contagious."

"Yes, I will be praying also." Olivia's conscience bit at her. This was the real work of these saints. She was the outsider, foreign to the dirt and grit these people faced each day.

"And how are the other children in Grass Valley faring?" Sister Patricia asked.

"Well, I suppose healthy, no sickness." Olivia found herself torn. She'd wanted to speak to Sister Patricia, but now her worries felt trivial. "And we are to have a wedding."

Sister Patricia lowed her chin with wide-brown eyes.

"Judith Beckner has agreed to marry Dr. Hastings."

"Ahh." Sister Patricia smiled and patted her leg. "I see. This is wonderful news."

Olivia feigned half a smile.

"I can tell you want to speak, and please speak freely." The intuitive Sister Patricia waited.

Olivia straightened her back. How did she say things were moving forward everywhere—at the Empire mine, with the nun's work here in Sacramento—without sounding resentful? There were obviously no other homes available for the orphans here, or Sister Patricia would've mentioned it. She sighed. "I'd hoped maybe another home had opened up. That maybe I and the children could come back."

"That would be a blessed miracle." Sister Patricia's eyes brightened. "The Beckners, have they spoke of helping us again?"

"No." Olivia frowned. "They're having problems at the mine." Pulling her chin to the side, she huffed. "In fact, I need your advice. Milton and Thomas have been helping at the mine. A mother from the Cornish women has shown interest in adopting them. I really don't know her, but Mr. Beckner speaks highly of her and her husband. I'm bothered that the boys will only know mining and neglect their schooling. Even Mary Ellen and Lester have gone to work in the Empire house."

Sister Patricia sat back and held a finger to her chin. "The children's arrival has caused an effect on the Beckners' household?"

"Yes, more mouths to feed, and those staying in the little cottage went from one to six. But they have been so giving and have never caused any of us feel like a burden. Mr. Beckner was kind enough to bring me here today on his way to San Francisco."

"You don't want to see things change? You were content in the past. If there was another way to gather the chicks back, you would?"

Olivia nodded her head, looking at the ground.

"Do you remember how we prayed when we heard that the home was to be sold?"

"Yes," Olivia whispered. *But could the answer from God leave her heart so bereft? Surely, her faith could be stronger than the downcast face her mirror showed her?* "You think I should be thankful and allow these things, these changes to go forward."

"Pray to the Lord, beautiful child," The wise nun tipped up Olivia's lowered chin. "He will speak to your heart and give you peace in the storm."

"I suppose prayer would be helpful since I'm a hapless guardian."

"Oh, no, no." Sister Patricia crooned. "But since I've never seen your cooking skills, I'm going to teach you to make bread." She jumped up, pulling Olivia to standing. "So much to be done here, and now God, in His care for us, has sent two extra hands." Sister Patricia wrapped a tight embrace around Olivia's back as they headed to the kitchen.

Twenty-Four

In the cool of the late afternoon, Ian pulled the buggy to a stop in front of the church grounds. He pinched the top button of his collar back in place. A strange nervous energy pulsed from him. The charming Miss Olivia Bradstreet was his to share a buggy ride home with. Just the two of them, uninterrupted and alone. Considering the morning had started with his justified contempt for her collaboration with Dr. Hastings and the engagement with his mother, now anticipation spiked in him and he felt quite the opposite.

An elderly priest walked toward him, and Ian shook his hand. "Father Gilbert, if I remember correctly?"

"Yes, Mr. Beckner." Father Gilbert bowed slightly. "I'm thankful to have an opportunity to tell you in person how sorry I am about the fire at the Oak Street Home." He shook his head, frowning. "Thankfully you were there, and not one child was harmed."

"Yes, I couldn't agree more." Ian walked with him over the churchyard to a small adobe structure.

"Olivia has reported that the six children who joined you in Grass Valley are faring well."

"Yes, we are managing." Ian wanted to correct the word *we*; he'd had little oversight of the children. "She was excited to have time here today."

"And it has been our pleasure to have her. I will be corresponding with Father Dalton in Grass Valley. He is new to the work there, but I think Olivia would be a wonderful help."

Before they could reach the door of the small mud and straw room, Ian could hear her voice. Bright and engaging, she was singing the tale about the farmer whose cow got out. Not wanting to interrupt, he stood to the side. It appeared that a few of the dark-haired children were sick in their beds. Olivia sat near them, holding their hands as they fought to keep their eyes open. Sister Patricia looked over, saw him, and came to the door.

"Thank you, Mr. Beckner, for bringing her today. It has been a balm to my soul to see her." She smiled. "Six new orphans came in just yesterday."

"Are they in need of a doctor?" Ian asked.

"Miss Bradstreet asked the same thing, volunteering Dr. Hastings to come to us. But the man from Sutter's Fort said he would look in on them tomorrow." She clutched her chest. "We'd take an abundance of prayer."

"Yes, of course." Ian observed Olivia brush the children's hairline and squeeze their hands as she rose. Her care and love for orphans was a sight to behold. Reaching out, she said her goodbyes, hugging the priest and the beloved Sister Patricia. Still filled with hushed awe, Ian offered his elbow, and she took it. As they walked in silence, part of him felt like he was taking a mother from her children. A small, content smile rose on her lips as he helped her into the buggy. She'd spent a good day here.

"Oh." She tapped her forehead.

"What? What did you forget? The buggy rocked as Ian stepped in on the other side and sat.

"It's nothing." She shook her head quickly.

"No, tell me. Is there something you need?"

"I…" She held her reticule up. "I forgot to go shopping." She plopped it on her lap. "But I'm fine. I know we both need to get back."

"No, it's all right. To a ladies' shop?" Of course. Since the fire, she'd been at the mine in nothing but extras from his mother.

"Ian, it's all right. Really." She gazed over her shoulder as they pulled away from the church.

"I know just the place." He avoided Oak Street as he led the buggy closer to Main Street. "How was your visit?"

"Wonderful. To see the others from Oak Street doing well. And…I now know how to make bread." A small dimple appeared when she smiled just so. "The new children, poor little angels, sick and misplaced, know very little English."

"And yet you found your songs would reach them."

"The gift of song and touch." She pressed her hand over her cheek. "I pray they found some comfort."

"After the Cornish women congratulated me for finding a wife," he said, looking to her with wide eyes, "they wanted me to ask you to sing at their St. Piran celebration."

"And what did you say?"

"I said it would be up to you."

"I'm sure they swooned anew over that—a man so handsome and generous."

Ian stopped the buggy in front of a large wooden sidewalk where there were different wide-windowed shops. It was happening again. Without trying, she could have him believing that pleasing swirl in his gut was akin to love. But hadn't he thought that before with Lesandra? Had Lesandra ever said a kind word about him? He came around and offered his arm. As soon as she pressed her fingers into the crook of his elbow, it felt more right, more natural than anything he'd ever felt before.

"Olivia, I want you to get whatever you need." He caught her eyes. "I mean it, I will pay." He reached for his billfold.

Her hand slipped from his arm, and she turned to look in a display window. "Dr. Hastings gave me money." She turned back to him. "I won't be long, I promise." She stepped inside, and he scanned up and down the sidewalk, replacing his billfold. *Dr. Hastings again.*

Ian waited for a wagon to pass and stepped across the street. A new café looked promising, and his stomach growled with the thought of a warm meal. Finding a nearby bench under a tree, he stretched his legs out. Truth be told, the name Maxwell Hastings did not sting as it once had. The lawyer who helped him make payments to the Grant dowry had said he would draw up the paperwork for the mine to be in Ian's and his mother's names only. It brought a slice of comfort, yet he worried what his mother would think.

After Ian had watched people come and go for thirty minutes, Olivia appeared with packages in her arms from the front of the lady's store. He cleared the street and reached out to help her.

"I took too long. I'm sorry." She transferred the bundles to him.

"I will forgive you if you will join me for supper at that café." Ian pointed across the street.

"What of the time?" Her bottom lip frowned to the side. "The children?"

"They are all well taken care of." He placed a hand on her back as they walked across the street. "Miss Bradstreet, I'm asking you to step out with me."

Olivia affected a shocked expression. "Haven't you heard, sir? I am previously spoken for. It was a whirlwind courtship." She walked through the door Ian held open. "You probably didn't know. It wasn't in the papers or discussed by our parents. It was a matter of a certain party's reputation being exposed as suspicious—it's been quite the invention." A woman in a white ruffled apron showed them a table. "But, if you promise never to ask me again…" Ian held the seat out for her, and she sat. "Then I can be agreeable to this scandalous meal with you." With a proud grin, she tipped her head once.

"You are in quite the mood, Miss Bradstreet." Ian took his seat. "I'm not sure what to think of you, just now."

"Shopping." She lifted her shoulders. "I do dearly love to shop."

"I will take note of that." Ian watched the waitress pour their coffee.

"And spending the day away." She nodded a smile at the waitress. "Away from the mine and all that goes on there. I spoke with Father Gilbert about new work in Grass Valley."

Ian forged a smile, sure she would elaborate on all the pleasures of shopping, but the passionate woman had found her calling and seemed fixated on it. He ordered two plates of beef and vegetables and tried to listen as she related more details of what she would discuss with Father Dalton. One thing was clear as day: the mine would never be her passion *unless it housed orphans.*

"Just please tell me you aren't going to become a nun." His eyes narrowed on hers. "That would likely ruin the wedding we haven't planned." Ian took a full breath. He wouldn't allow her to pull his emotions back and forth; better to keep the banter light. "Not to mention, completely ruin the wedding night." He leaned back as the waitress lowered two plates of steaming food to the table.

"We wouldn't want that." She rolled her eyes as she picked up her fork. "This looks delicious."

Ian tried to move his food around, but her last quick retort felt like a punch to his stomach. His teasing had bitten him back. If the stunning Miss Bradstreet were his wife, how many candlelit moments would they have in each other's arms? Would he ever be able to sleep without thinking of her in his bed?

"And of your business in San Francisco?" Olivia dabbed the napkin on the corners of her mouth. "Did it go satisfactorily?"

Ian took a gulp of coffee. "Yes, thank you."

"Since we have the time, and I'm a bit curious, how did you meet your real fiancée?"

"*Former* fiancée." Ian frowned as he chewed. "A family connection," he murmured.

Olivia tilted her chin with wide eyes. "You can do better. I want the details. The first meeting, the courtship. Did she cry when you told her you would be gone to England over a year?"

Ian took another bite and chewed carefully. He'd rather talk about shopping then Lesandra.

An older woman in a pale blue dress and matching feathered hat stopped at their table.

"Miss Bradstreet. I thought that was you."

Olivia's eyes widened, and she stood and took the woman's hand. "Mrs. Newcomb. How lovely to see you again."

Ian stood and nodded.

"This is my husband, Rockford Newcomb."

Ian shook his hand. "Pleasure to meet you, sir. Ian Beckner."

"Oh, the Mr. Beckner, the owner of the Oak Street Home?" Mrs. Newcomb's head tilted to the side. "I work with Miss Bradstreet in the Ladies' Protection and Relief Society."

Ian nodded back.

"We offer our condolences for the loss of such a lovely home. I pray you will rebuild soon and give our destitute youngsters a safe place to live."

Ian gave her a half smile. He would make no promises of rebuilding. Making the mistake of looking at Olivia, her downcast eyes seemed to know that already.

"We'll let you two get back to your meal." Mrs. Newcomb bowed slightly. "Olivia, I'll see you at our meeting in December." She patted her arm. "We have many lovely ideas I know you will enjoy participating in for the holidays."

"Mrs. Newcomb, thank you." Olivia's tone wavered. "In all the rush of taking care of the children, I should've written my formal resignation as Secretary."

"Oh, no, dear." Mrs. Newcomb frowned.

"Thanks to the generosity of the Empire Mine," Olivia swallowed. "The matron, Mrs. Beckner, has allowed six of the displaced children and me to have the guest cottage."

Mrs. Newcomb's eyes traveled to Ian and back to Olivia. "So, you reside in Grass Valley now?"

Olivia nodded. "It has been a pleasure to work with such fine Christian women, but I live there now, and well, you see…um…yes, that's where I am for now."

Ian didn't like the last flash of Mrs. Newcomb's narrow eyes on him. For the second time, he felt a stab of remorse. Blast it all, should he say he didn't start the fire that upended her life here…but he *had* been going to sell the house out from under her.

As soon as the well-dressed couple moved on, he sat and took a deep breath. The Newcombs, in their life of leisure, hadn't read the headlines of late; life was hard everywhere. Ian swallowed his uncivil attitude; the food needed to be finished before it was cold.

Twenty-Five

The next morning, Olivia awoke to faint streams of light, and rolled over in her warm bed in the cottage. Esther and Bonita slept soundly, and she relished a few moments to herself. Yesterday had been a much-needed reprieve. A day to be free from the restraints of her new life at the mine. Oh, the joy to be back alongside Sister Patricia! The woman's faith seemed to infect Olivia whenever they were together.

Olivia recalled the quaint ladies' store where she'd shopped for the items she needed as another blessing. She ran her hand down her new nightgown. It smelled fresh and new. A smile crept up on her unawares, remembering the supper alone with Ian Beckner. She nestled into her pillow. It was almost reminiscent of the untainted young lady she'd been in Chicago. But as she tried to picture those days in her mind, they seemed like another lifetime ago. Likely she and Ian had both needed a break from the heavy load that had come upon them of late.

Thinking back to the buggy ride home, Olivia's unanswered questions remained. She'd wanted to see if she could press Ian past his deep thoughts. A wariness had shifted within him after the Newcombs had come to the table, so she'd questioned him for more details of Lesandra Grant.

Most everything he recounted had to do with how naïve he was—a clod who'd believed that after a year at sea Lesandra would have waited for him. He seemed to blame himself for not seeing her true colors, blinded by his own expectations. With few details of their actual courtship, he began talking about the trip to England and meeting the Cornish families.

He hadn't seemed to notice that he'd talked for an hour nonstop about their lives and how they'd helped him find his own compass. The Cornish men lived and breathed generations of mining, and the more they laid plans for the Empire Mine, the more he grew in excitement and strength. He confessed he'd always been a driven person, but with this new passion for the mine, his life finally felt like a river that could flow without restraints. He regretted not sharing the work with his father.

Olivia sighed and turned to her other side. Ian Beckner was all fortitude with a side of charm, and when he wasn't trying to goad her, he was very sincere and likable.

She blinked her eyes closed. What a silly scene she'd made at the cottage door last night. He'd helped her with her packages, but when she'd peeked in the window and saw Maxwell reading, she'd taken them from him, set them back down on the buggy seat, and given him a hug. The words *thank you* came out clear, but then why had she risen on her toes and given him a kiss on the cheek? He'd smiled, but instantly she'd felt ridiculous, like a child who was thankful for a kitten.

Olivia rubbed her neck. In all the talking, they had never spoken of how to dissolve their fake engagement. He was probably waiting for her to decide, since she had been the one to make up the tale.

Maybe they could meet later, after his work, when the children were asleep. They could meet at the garden bench. Olivia could hear Maxwell in the small kitchen, starting the morning coffee. She rose, flinging back her covers. That would be the worst place. No, she needed to find a solution, and not in a place that would give way to more speculation. The truth needed to be told, and soon.

Olivia smiled at the sleepy faces waking up. "Good morning, girls." She sat on the edge of the bed and opened her arms.

The tangled-haired girls came close for a warm embrace, and Olivia pulled them back with her on the bed. A few tickles had them giggling. "Yes, I missed you both."

The following Thursday, Katy made a special hot cider and brought out the Beckner's fancy goblets. The Cornish women set their sewing aside as Katy asked them to hold their glasses up for a toast.

Katy pulled Judith into the center. "Mrs. Beckner has given me permission to announce that the Empire Mine will have its first wedding in two weeks."

The women oohed and aahed, looking back and forth between Judith and Olivia. "Raise your glasses, ladies," Katy finished, "Mrs. Judith Beckner will be marring Dr. Hastings."

A loud gasp rose from the circle of women, interspersed with cheers. Standing, everyone took their turn to clink glasses with Judith.

"And here we thought this was about you!" Mrs. Kitt touched Olivia's glass.

"No, no, no date set." Olivia turned, taking a sip, and quickly found Mrs. Hocking extending her glass. "Thank you for letting the boys stay Monday," she said. "We wanted to see about the next weekend, if you don't mind?"

The spiced cider caught in Olivia's throat. "I…I…they reported enjoying time with your family. I'm sure the weekend would be fine."

Mrs. Hocking turned. "Ladies, let us ask. Would the Beckners be so kind as to let us use our ideas for St. Piran's Day and host a party?"

Judith smiled brightly at Olivia. "The wedding ceremony will be here in the parlor with our family, and then after…I suppose… thank you." Judith nodded. "We would love to celebrate with you all. But promise, there will be no fuss."

"Oh, no," the elder Mrs. Hocking mocked. "No fuss for the family who gave our men jobs and our families a place to live. Nah, no fuss." The Cornish women laughed, chiming in with excitement and touching their glasses again.

"Katy started all this." Judith said to Olivia with a bright grin. "Although I suppose Maxwell and I had a measure to do with it." She beamed. "Say, I was wondering if you would be so kind as to stand with me at the ceremony?"

Olivia felt an instant tingling in her nose. "Judith, I would be honored."

Judith set a hand on her back and moved them from the center of the room. "I don't know what you said to Ian, but I know some of the load he's been carrying was lighter after traveling with you to San Francisco. I imagine you might have swung his opinion as well. He sat down with Maxwell and me last week and apologized for his poor behavior. Eventually, I slipped from the room as they talked about the ownership and future of the mine. You can imagine my feeling that my prayers had been answered, to have my son and new husband in agreement. I shouldn't be so blessed when others have so little." Judith gazed tenderly at the Cornish women as they began singing a hymn.

"Judith." Olivia set her glass on the dining room table and put both of her hands on her arms. "You are one of the loveliest-hearted women I know." Olivia squeezed. "You can do whatever you wish in this life. Your creation of beautiful gardens and lands are a testament to that. And yes, you should be blessed, because you go beyond that and help those in need. And my favorite thing about you is how you walk with so much grace through it all. You're blessed as a child of God and blessed as a mother and now blessed to love again. And..." Olivia looked back to all the women singing. "You are a blessing to all of us."

Judith's chin quivered and her eyes filled. "And I am blessed to have you," her voice cracked, and she gave Olivia a hug.

"Maxwell has received a post from his son in Auburn. Morgan will be here to stand with him. What a joy it will be to meet him." Her eyes crinkled with delight. "And for you to see him again. His letter alluded to some good news of his own." Judith laughed and wiped her face dry as they hugged again.

"A God of miracles, He is."

Twenty-Six

Olivia sat at the guest cottage table, sipping a fresh cup of tea. Esther and Bonita sat close with their needlepoint hoops in hand.

"Miss Bradstreet, do I come up with this stitch or go down?"

Olivia pulled her attention from what she held in her hand after reading it for the tenth time.

"Let me see." Olivia took Esther's hoop; the embroidery thread was caught around the hoop. "I suppose we should take this out and start again." Olivia pulled the long needle free and pulled the green thread back through the fabric. "So, start again from the back and go up. Your leaves are coming along nicely." She reached for the pattern, a small card with a large scripted B on the front.

"What about mine?" Bonita lifted her hoop.

"Yes, dear." Olivia wasn't sure what happened to the simple row of cross-stitches. "That is coming along nicely, also," she hedged.

"I want to give it to Mrs. Beckner for her wedding," Bonita said.

"Oh." Olivia caught her first thought before it left her mouth. "How thoughtful." Taking a small sip of hot tea, she reread the note that Thomas had brought the night before from Ian Buckner.

My Dearest, Beloved Olivia, or, My Dearest, Eternally Fickle Olivia. (This is a two-part note to read as you wish.)

'No words can express the turmoil I feel when the days go by without seeing you, OR, I feel bad I have not been free to see you, but the mine is my priority.' Olivia shook her head. Clever. The man was far too clever.

'I constantly reminisce of our outing together. Your words, your touch, the time spent with you made my heart beat anew, OR, I'm glad you came. It was nice to have someone to talk to.' Olivia pressed her lips together. Though she fought it, each time she read it, his jesting made her smile. *'Because you are the wisest woman I know, I have heeded your every word and found common ground with Dr. Hastings, OR, that was kind of you to offer a room for me in the guest cottage, but I think now I can share a breakfast table with the man as long as those two behave themselves.*

'All I wanted to ask (before this nonsense) is if you would be so kind as to save me a dance after the ceremony. It's difficult being the lone bachelor, and you are the only woman (I will apologize to Mary Ellen and Katy) who can tolerate me. If Thomas or Milton gets to you first, I will be irrevocably jealous.

'Because it is late and I've worked underground twelve hours, I can't keep this game up, so in truth, my fickle darling...

'I look forward to seeing you on Saturday.

'Yours Truly, Ian'

Exhaling with a small smile, Olivia watched the girls work on their needlepoint and felt a strange tingle in her stomach. The man was saying *something* without saying it. Was their connection hidden in there between the lines? *Oh, this rogue who had kissed her before he even knew her.* The silly note in his beautiful handwriting demanded to be read one more time.

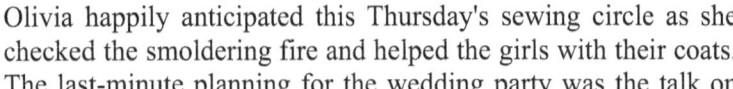

Olivia happily anticipated this Thursday's sewing circle as she checked the smoldering fire and helped the girls with their coats. The last-minute planning for the wedding party was the talk on every woman's lips. Judith had been so kind as to allow the ladies free rein to celebrate the couple however they wanted. Ready to leave, Olivia opened the cottage door and jumped back.

"Morgan!" She squealed and threw her arms around the tall man. He picked her up off her feet easily and finally set her down.

"Olivia. Wonderful to see you."

His smile was like being back a hundred years; he was Ronald's little brother, and he'd changed little. Without her realizing it, her hand rose and touched his scarred cheek. "What a delight to see you!" she exclaimed, breathless with happiness. "Your father said you would be here to stand up with him." She stepped back. "Let me take your coat. You must tell me everything."

He nodded, slipped his coat off, and glanced around the small guest cottage.

"Oh, forgive me." Olivia pressed her hands together. "These little peanuts are Bonita and Esther, my charges from the Oak Street Orphanage. May I offer you something hot? Coffee or tea?"

Morgan nodded with a warm grin at the girls. "My father wrote of the fire. I'm so glad you were all safe." He paused. "I feel as if you were all about to go out?"

"Just the women's sewing circle at the Empire Home. Have you seen your father yet?"

"No, I had hoped to find him."

"We could walk together?" Olivia felt a flutter of excitement to see Morgan Hastings standing in the small guest cottage. A piece of her past stood mirrored in the tall, handsome man. "Or, please, if you would like to rest, I could make you something to eat."

"You cook?" He notched his chin down.

"Morgan, I would need a week to tell you how much I've changed." She shook her head. "But you aren't here to see me. Your father has found a lovely lady to marry." Olivia held her hand over her heart. "They're so happy together."

"Then let's walk together." Morgan slipped his jacket back on. "You can point out where I might find my father, and tonight we'll meet again so you can tell me about the new you."

Olivia's brows rose. "And you. I want to hear how you've been." She gathered the girls as Morgan held the door open. Her throat tightened with joy to be walking alongside him. In truth, he'd always been like a brother to her. She placed her hand in his elbow. Now it was funny to think that when she first arrived in California she'd wondered if they would find any basis for courtship. It hadn't been hard to move on to Grass Valley, and the man clearly wasn't interested in her for his future.

"How is Carlotta?" She asked.

"She is well, slow, and sassy as ever." Morgan declared.

"And Emery, do you ever hear of her?"

He tilted his head side to side, unsuccessfully holding back a smile.

"Morgan," she crooned. "What are you not saying?" She pulled on his arm.

"I've asked her to marry me, and she has said yes."

"What!" Olivia jumped a little, her throat constricting further. "Does your father know?" Her tone was hoarse with shock. She'd wondered if the young woman with the sweet baby had feelings for Morgan, but before Olivia could get to know her Emery had left for her home on Eureka Creek.

"I will speak to him when the time is right. Like you said, this is my father and Judith's time. Emery and I will be inviting everyone soon enough."

"Oh, Morgan, I am so happy for you." She bounced up, pulled him close, and kissed his cheek. "You deserve all the happiness."

Morgan caught her and gave her a quick embrace. "Thank you, Olivia, that means a lot from you."

Olivia smiled at the girls as they walked toward the Empire home.

Standing over his desk in his room, Ian gripped the new shaft map he'd worked on late last night. Dirty from head to toe, he tried to figure the best way from his room without disturbing the large group of women in the front parlor. Glancing out his window, he saw Olivia and the girls came up the path with a tall, dark-haired young man. She had to know the man, from the way she clung to him. Ian stepped back from his window, but his curiosity pulled him back to the scene at hand. As soon as he did he wished he hadn't, Olivia jumped into the stranger's arms and kissed him!

Lesandra.

Ian pressed against his bedroom wall, red-faced and feeling the fool. Half of him felt a fool for accusing Olivia. They had no real commitment, and she was free to flaunt her charms to her heart's content. The other half of him felt foolish for allowing his own feelings to be pulled around like a ring through a pig's snout. He pushed off the wall and headed back down the back stairs. What had he expected? He whisked past Katy and out the back door. He'd offered his best natural charm, yet cowardly kept her at arms distance. The only moment he'd taken what he wanted had been the kiss in the garden. Women and their emotions were too much trouble, and clearly, his weak attempts were not worth the effort. Her affections for this stranger were quick and to the point. Everything he was not.

Twenty-Seven

Judith told Maxwell to spend the evening at the little cottage with his son. The three of them would need to catch up, and, to Olivia's delight, Katy had brought over a stuffed chicken and mashed potatoes. Thankfully, she wouldn't have to reveal her incapability of working the stove. The four children played in front of the fire while the small band from Chicago found themselves reminiscing of days gone by.

"Oh, how I wish Ronald was here." Olivia finished drying the dishes. Both the remaining Hastings men nodded. "He would have been delighted to see his father marry and find renewed happiness." Her smile was sincere, and it didn't hurt to talk of Ronald as it once had.

"I think you are right, Olivia." Maxwell reached out to squeeze her hand. Morgan scratched his head, leaning back in his chair. "The loss was devastating to all of us, but think of where we are today—sitting here in Grass Valley. For me, I could not return home without him, so I joined a ragtag group of soldiers and came out west to find gold." He huffed. "And because of them, I met Emery." Morgan's eyes glowed with the thought of his wife-to-be.

Maxwell rubbed his dark brows. "And I could find no reason why I needed a large home and staff with no one to share it. So, without my sons returning to practice medicine, I decided to come west." Maxwell took in a deep breath. "And now I live and work at Empire Mine and will be married in two days."

Morgan clapped his father on his back. "I'm thinking of that verse—God works all things out for our good." Fresh wonder and appreciation shone on their faces, and Olivia had to turn away to set the dishes on the shelf. She was eternally thankful for these men and how they had found the good in their lives. But she could not add her story into the mix. Because of Ronald, she'd had the nerve to ask Dr. Hastings for help and, fortunately, he'd agreed. But losing the truth of who she'd thought herself to be, a real Bradstreet, held no blessing. An entire life, a lie.

"Children." Olivia swallowed the tightness in her chest before moving around the small table. "If you gentlemen will excuse me, I will get the children ready for bed and retire myself." Olivia stepped into the front room and asked the boys to unravel their bedding.

"Thank you for everything, Olivia." Maxwell stood. "I'll be taking Judith on a surprise trip after the festivities, and then I will move into the big house." He turned to Thomas and Milton. "You two can have my room."

The boys had little response as Olivia helped them open their blankets. They'd been moved around so much, a room to themselves was no attraction. Would they soon move into the shanties with the Hockings? Olivia took in a deep breath and knelt with the four children on the boy's bedding. They all held their hands together in front and prayed.

"Father, We thank thee for the night,
And for the pleasant morning light;
For rest and food and loving care,
And all that makes the day so fair.
Help us please You as we should,
To be to others kind and good;
In all we do, in work or play,
To grow more loving every day.
Amen."

Olivia quickly kissed the boys' cheeks before they lay down, and the girls went into their room. A wave of dizziness overcame her as she stood, and she gripped the back of the settee. She was overtired and emotional, having Morgan here.

"Goodnight, gentlemen." She smiled at the men before she joined the girls.

The next morning Olivia awoke with a pounding headache. She'd tossed and turned and had awoken from too many strange dreams drenched in sweat. A cup of hot coffee often settled her. Blowing out a long breath, she hesitated, a bit lightheaded. She dressed slowly, hoping some food would give her the strength for all that needed to be done today.

With all the food preparations and time working with the Cornish women, it was late afternoon before Olivia found Maxwell in the kitchen.

"I'm so sorry." Her body was riddled with fatigue. "Will you ask Judith to forgive me for not attending the family dinner tonight?"

"Are you all right?" Maxwell touched her elbow.

"It's nothing. I woke up with a headache, then realized I hadn't eaten any lunch. I'm just going to eat something at the cottage and go to bed."

"Of course." He nodded. "I will check on you later."

"No, no, please. I will get the children settled and be fine. Tomorrow is a big day, and I want to be my best." She feigned a smile before she went out the back door.

If he only knew how badly she wanted to be there. She hadn't seen Ian Beckner all week. A hundred times, she'd tried to write a clever note back to him, but all her attempts seemed silly. Like a school girl passing notes to get a boy's attention. And truth be told, he could've knocked on her door any night. But he hadn't. Olivia rubbed her forehead, each step toward the guest cottage pounding up her limbs and into her head.

To her dismay, Olivia overslept the morning of the Hastings/Beckner wedding. When she woke up, the girls were already gone from their pallets. She fell back into bed. After a night of hot and cold sweats, she'd have to start the day with a bath. If only she could find the strength. She took a long look at her rose velvet jacket and ruffled burgundy gown. It was the nicest gown she owned, and perfect to stand up with Judith today. Who knew leaving it here at Empire Mine would save it from becoming ash? After the bath, a simple work dress would do as they finished the last touches for the party. Ian would close the mine at two, giving the workers and their families time to enjoy the reception that afternoon.

Esther opened the door a crack and peeked in. "Are you up, Miss Bradstreet?"

"Barely." Olivia held her throat, her voice only a croak. "Sweet Esther, could you pour me a cup of coffee or tea? Whatever there is?" She tried to clear her throat, but it felt and sounded like it had after the Oak Street fire. With labored and careful movements, Olivia slowly rose and began her morning ablutions. This day was far too special to lay abed.

Ian Beckner walked by the newest mine shaft, fighting the urge to go below and check on the progress. His mother had asked him to stay above the earth today. He couldn't blame her. For some reason, he felt a sense of nerves or discontent he couldn't pinpoint.

When he entered the mine office, Maxwell was missing at his desk, and the small room felt hollow. The dinner with his son Morgan last night had been tolerable. Ian sat and rifled through his paperwork to find this week's earnings. Of course, the son had known Olivia many years, and Maxwell had told them that Morgan would be getting married soon. A young woman from the mining camps around Eureka Creek. He was happy for him but irritated that he'd felt such a strange surge of jealousy seeing Morgan with Olivia. Why jealousy? And what of her absence last night? Had she made excuses to give them time alone? Did she not realize she was more family than guest? Likely, it was because every meal they shared at that very table ended dreadfully. But it didn't change how badly he wanted to see her.

Miss Olivia Bradstreet had belonged and literally glowed at past Empire dinners. She'd stolen the self-reliance from his heart the minute he'd seen her across the flickering lights and table settings so many months ago. And beyond all reason, his desire to see her was stronger, possibly deeper entrenched, than he wanted to admit. While everyone had laughed and shared stories last night, he'd found it difficult to focus.

Ian tapped another note he'd started to her. How did one say, without being to forward? 'I missed you last night. I hope you are feeling well? Your absence pained me, body, and soul.' He groaned in frustration and pushed the note aside. It was time to get ready and look forward to her attention for the evening.

Twenty-Eight

Breathe, Olivia reminded herself with each faint, quivering breath. *Forget it all. This stupid corset.* She felt the pressure squeezing against her ribs. Today of all days, why did she think her vanity mattered when she'd asked Esther to pull the strings taut with all her might? Her hands began to sweat as the Reverend read the vows for Maxwell and Judith to repeat. Carefully dabbing her hands with her handkerchief, she made the mistake of glancing at Ian and then quickly to Morgan. Ian looked cross at her, like she'd a bug on her nose. Morgan smiled while listening to his father pledge his everlasting honor and goodly world or…what did he say? *Worldly goods? Just breathe, Olivia, in and out.*

"Till death do us part." Judith's smile trembled. The woman stood poised and beautiful in her ivory satin, bead-trimmed gown. Her hair was carefully styled, with a matching beaded comb and soft ringlets atop her head.

"Let us pray."

Olivia closed her eyes, swallowed, and held back a painful groan. *Not her throat too.*

Opening her eyes, she just caught the reverend pronouncing them husband and wife. Maxwell held Judith's chin and placed a sweet kiss on her waiting lips. It was so personal, so touching, that it was no wonder Olivia felt like swooning. The small party of well-dressed friends stood and formed a line across the foyer to congratulate the couple. Olivia saw Katy out of the corner of her eye and stepped over to the butler's pantry.

"I need water." Olivia croaked. "And possibly a chair away from it all."

"You go right ahead." Katy never took her admiring gaze from the parlor of wedding well-wishers. Olivia carefully navigated her way through the kitchen and between the Cornish women taking trays of food from the back door. Sipping a cool dipper of water, she found the hallway back to Katy's room. She opened the door, the room's cool air bolstering her with fresh resilience. Just a few minutes to sit and rest. That would be the ticket.

Ian made his way past the garden area and back around to the guest cottage. Leaning in the small cottage door and calling Olivia's name, he realized she was not there. An hour ago, after greeting everyone and seeing the line for food start, he had been determined to find the missing maid of honor. She seemed to have disappeared from the afternoon. Now, walking back in the dusk of night, he was starting to worry. A large bonfire was roaring with the night chill coming on. The simple music had started, and the Cornish men were dancing with their women as the children giggled and danced around in their own circles.

"Mr. Beckner." Doretha Hocking stopped him as he approached. "Have you tried my whiskey cake yet?" She held the tray inches from him.

"I had one incredible piece, and will have to try one more." He took the square off the plate and ate it in three bites. The rich, sugary flavors melted in his mouth. A large purple bell skirt swished in the corner of his eye. *Finally.* He watched Olivia wave off the children trying to pull her into a circle to dance. The night shadows and the bright yellow and orange from the fire highlighted her face, and he could only stare. Olivia Bradstreet was stunning, and his heart finally felt the rest from worry. He stepped up behind her, his right hand boldly sliding around her waist, just under the opening of her velvet jacket.

"Oh, Ian." She smiled at him over her shoulder and rested her fingers over his. "If you've come to be my strength, I'll take it."

Was he dreaming, or did she lean closer into him? Standing in the intimate pose behind her with their right arms touching, the tenderness of their embrace nearly scattered his brain and body in desire. Careful not to disrupt the warm, yielding weight of her body, he touched a golden tress with his free hand from where it brushed her soft cheek. His fingers joined in the liberties he was taking, running down her soft neck. "Your skin is hot," he murmured into her ear.

"I should stand back," she whispered. "The fire is overwhelming."

They stepped back in unison, moving further into the darkness. His pulse quickened, like the jumping beat of the music. "You said you would save me a dance."

Olivia sighed, still leaning back against his frame. "I cannot." Her head tilted forward, looking closer. "Is that man playing your guitar?"

"It's his," he countered. "With all the long months at sea, he taught me a few chords. It was all in an attempt to impress Lesandra." Olivia smelled like flowers. His left hand inched in and around her waist.

"Of course." Olivia still melted like soft butter in his arms, and he wondered if she'd had too much whiskey cake. "Don't worry, it worked on me." Her voice was low and husky.

Ian held her, vacillating between shock and delight. She'd kissed his cheek weeks ago. Was it his note? Did she read it as a love letter or a declaration? Did all women become pliable romantics at weddings? Finally, when he could inch back from where she rested on him, he turned to face her. "Olivia, are you feeling all right?"

"Oh." Her head tilted from side to side. "All the wedding details, and having Morgan here…" She clutched her hand to her throat. "I think the coffee this morning must have scalded my throat. It's so painful to swallow."

Ian set the back of his hand on her forehead. "Olivia, you're burning up. This is more than the heat from the fire." He looked closer. Her dark lashes surrounded eyes with a strange glossy blue. "Where were you this afternoon, during the party?"

"I...I...went to rest in Katy's chair just for a moment and woke up hours later." She sniffled, a frown crossing her face. "I'm upset at myself, a remiss maid of honor I've been...re...miss..." She groaned, her body drooping against his.

"Good night, woman. You're sick and should be in bed." He scooped her up and turned toward the Empire home. The full layers of her dress made this same young lady he'd carried before twice as heavy. He turned on the path for the guest cottage. Grateful, it held no stairs. "Olivia, keep your arm around my neck."

She pulled it closer. "Yes, my neck, it's on fire. The fire has taken my voice too. Don't let the fire take me." She gasped.

Instinctively he knew that she was more than tired, and Ian was no doctor... "Milton!" He saw the boy playing in between the trees and shadows. "Get Dr. Hastings to the guest cottage!"

"Yes, sir." Milton ran off, and Ian struggled with the cottage door. "I have to put your feet down, I can't find the handle with your dress...Olivia, can you stand?"

"Yes," she whispered, clasping her arms around him, her face buried into his suit coat. "You smell so good."

Ian gave her a half-smile, grasping the handle to open the door. "And you smell wonderful as well." Not wanting to risk her falling, he caught her back up and carefully laid her on her bed. Striking a match, he lit her lantern and set it on its hook. Her face was pale, and he tried to remove her velvet jacket. "Olivia, have you been ill all day? You didn't look right at the ceremony." After her arms were freed, the crooked hair decoration came off next.

"I'm just tired. I need to sleep." Her eyes drifted closed.

He flung her jacket on her chair and glanced up to see Morgan Hastings in her door frame. "Where is your father?" he said, irritated. "I need Dr. Hastings. Olivia is burning with fever. We need him now."

Morgan went to her washbowl and washed his hands. Ian had heard at dinner the son had also been a doctor, but the scars on his hands had made the work too difficult.

Morgan came close and laid his hand along her cheek. "They just left, I can help. Olivia, what is wrong?"

"She's burning up with fever." Ian snapped. "I'll send a friend after them."

Before he could step away, Morgan rolled her to the side and began to unclasp the long line of buttons down her back.

"What are you doing?" Ian said appalled.

"We need to get this heavy dress off." Morgan worked the buttons down the center of her back.

"Sir, you will go for Katy or Mary Ellen at once." Ian stood back in shock as Morgan continued until he jerked the dress from her body and tossed it on the floor.

"I need cold water and rags." Morgan walked away. "Her lips are turning blue, get her corset off." Morgan left her room, and Ian shook his head. "Olivia, you will never forgive me for this." He undid the top strings and pulled the stiff garment off. "I'm sure he's like a brother to you, but I am surely not."

Morgan returned with a pan of clean water and began to dab at her skin. "It's a high fever." He set the rag over her forehead, and she twisted, her chemise falling loose around her shoulders.

"What ails her?" Ian swallowed, his heart racing.

Morgan searched along her collarbone, neck, and under her arms. "I don't see the scarlet rash."

"You mean scarlet fever?" Ian raked both hands through his hair and stepped to the end of the bed.

"Who else has been ill?" Morgan continued to lay the compresses around her skin. "Usually, it attacks the children first."

Ian huffed and paced in a circle. "I...I...know of no sick children. You were at the party tonight. That was all the families and children we have."

Morgan nodded to the pallets on the floor. "None of the children in this cottage have been ill?"

"I..." Ian ran his hand down his face. "I've been busy at the mine, but I don't think so."

They both watched as Olivia began to shake, the shivers making her chin quake. Morgan unhooked her boots and pulled the blanket out from under her, carefully covering her.

Ian squeezed his forehead. "Wait! Two weeks ago, we were in Sacramento. There were sick children at the mission. Olivia sat with them and sang to them."

"How are they faring now?" Morgan asked.

Olivia released a short whimper. "I'm so sorry, Judith." Her low, gravelly voice brought them back to her attention. "I can't sing, my thro...at..." she tilted her head up, straining for air.

Morgan groaned and put his hand under her neck to support it. "I think it's diphtheria," he mumbled. "Just rest now, Olivia, you don't need to sing for anyone."

Ian had often heard the word diphtheria used when an epidemic was reported in the papers, but it couldn't be true. "What can we do? Please, there must be something," he pleaded.

"Come support her neck while I get my father's medical bag." Ian did as he was told. Her neck felt like fire, and he felt shame run cold down to his toes. What a dolt. Could he have been any more stupid? He brushed the damp hair stuck to her cheek. "Olivia, I'm sorry," he whispered. He'd hoped her soft, tender stance tonight had been a woman yielding to his touch. *That he alone held the power to seduce the fair Miss Bradstreet.* Once again, he played the fool. This time, all by himself. The poor woman, he should've known by her expression at the wedding that she was riddled with sickness.

"Oh, forgive me," he whispered, taking the cloth to dab her face.

Twenty-Nine

A rattle at the door brought both men to attention. The children shoved through the door, laughing, then stopped suddenly.

"What's wrong with Miss Bradstreet?" Esther inhaled quickly, with wide eyes.

"Children, get back." Ian panicked. "Your mistress is very sick."

Bonita's face began to crumble, and Ian knew he'd seen this before. "It's going to be alright, child, Dr. Hastings's son is a…."

Bonita's mouth popped open, and a large bellowing sob filled the room.

"The fire!" Olivia's eyes flew open, and she gasped for air. "Ian. Get the children!"

"Ain't no fire, Miss Bradstreet." Thomas frowned, about to cry himself. "We all safe now."

Bonita went to shriek again when Morgan scooped her up in his arms. "Miss Bradstreet needs to rest." He patted Bonita's back. "Be a good girl, and don't wake her."

"What's wrong with her voice?" Milton frowned. "She doesn't sound right."

"Should I take them all to the main house?" Ian pulled the children out to the front room, and Morgan stood, holding the sniveling Bonita.

"I would say no." He sighed. "They've all been in the house with her. It could be the beginning of an outbreak, but we won't know until we keep them here and see how they fare."

Ian nodded. Olivia had been with his mother daily, Katy, Mary Ellen, and the other Cornish women. Closing his eyes, he gritted his teeth. A sickness like this could take out their entire mining community.

"Children, do what you do for bed." Ian looked around, trying not to lose control of the situation. "Girls, bring your things out here. I will keep watch with Miss Bradstreet."

They took a few minutes to get the children settled. Ian saw Esther nudge the others up on their knees with their hands clasped in front. The power of childlike faith. He paused and listened, feeling the desperation in his bones. Before they said amen, he prayed for mercy and healing. *Please, God.*

Ian walked back into Olivia's room while Morgan used a strange wooden tube to listen to Olivia's chest. Morgan laid it back into his father's bag. "Her lungs sound clear, but her breathing is more labored by the hour."

"What does that mean?"

Olivia shoved the blanket off of herself, her chemise and pantaloons damp like she'd come up from a bath. Wringing the rag out, Ian began to cool her face and neck.

Morgan walked around the room, stretching his fingers out and then curling them into a fist. "With diphtheria, a false membrane can form in the throat and swell to the point that the stricken dies of suffocation."

"What?" Ian froze. "What, what can you do?" His eyes pierced Morgan's. "You said at one time you were a surgeon; can you remove it?"

Morgan blew out a held breath. "I cannot." Running his hand down his own throat, Morgan shook his head. "It's beyond reach." He refused to meet Ian's gaze, his eyes sinking to the floor.

Taken aback, Ian stood and shook his head. "No." His chest squeezed, and his eyes filled. "Go now and find your father." He pointed to the door, his chin quivering from a mixture of shock, anger, and pain. "I...cannot...lose...her." His chest rose and fell with the clipped words. "Surely your father can do it." The statement came out desperate, but not as desperate as he felt. His chest cracked with pain; every ounce of his being was in love with Olivia Bradstreet. He would give his own life if only she would live. He sat on the edge of the bed and took her hand in his, bringing it to his leg. Stabbed with emotion, Ian leaned forward and grasped his head with his other hand. *Please, God, please God.* Two tears escaped, dripping onto his lap.

Morgan took the items from his father's bag, surveying the contents. "It's too risky."

"What?" Ian's head popped up. "What is risky?"

"The high fever speaks to the infection." Morgan rubbed his furrowed brow and chewed on the side of his lip. "I'm not sure."

"Just say it." Ian ground out.

"There is an airway, an opening. Just above the trachea." Morgan touched the spot on his throat and scowled. "I can make an opening that will get the air into her lungs."

"Yes, yes!" Ian sat up.

"But there is nothing in my father's bag. The procedure requires something to keep the incision open."

Ian blinked. A hole in her throat was far beyond what he could imagine. "What do you need? I will find it."

Morgan rubbed his scarred hand and drew in a ragged breath. "In worst cases, I've heard of the hollow of an eagle feather or a reed from a river bank being used."

Olivia gasped and tilted her head back, struggling for air. Ian held her head. "Stay with us. Olivia, please," he whispered. "We're going to help you." Her lips were turning blue again.

Ian faced Morgan. "Tell me." His pulse pounded in his ears. "You are describing something with a hollow center. Something that would not collapse, but allow the air to flow through." Ian's mind raced, he'd seen no reeds on the property.

"Yes, that is the idea. It has to be small, but not too small." Morgan pulled on his chin.

The room grew silent except for Olivia's ragged breathing.

"I'm going to the main house. There must be a quill or something." Ian stood, taking a long glance at Olivia, wishing his will was enough to force her to stay with him.

Running toward the large stone house, Ian could see the small embers of the night's bonfire. Everyone was gone. Entering the house he found a candle and lit it. Running up the stairs, he went to his desk. His quill was solid through the center with dried ink, and he tossed it on the desk and ran into his mother's room. Her quills were long wood, nothing that would work. Frustrated, he looked around upstairs; nothing but furniture, paintings, and rugs. Dropping down the stairs, he opened the cupboards in the dining room. The serving dishes and silver were of no help. Ian pounded his fist against his forehead. *Please Lord, what, what—* Ian took the candle into the kitchen and opened every cupboard and drawer.

Katy peeked around the corner in her nightcap. "What're you looking for at this time of night?"

"Something hollow, long…I don't have time to explain."

Katy scratched behind her ear and reached up to a set of bowls sitting on a top shelf. "Something like this?" She pulled out a white ironstone gravy boat with a long, narrow spout. "I don't use it often, because the gravy comes out so slow."

Ian grabbed it from her hand. The long spout was slender. This might work." He turned in a circle. "Where is your saw you use on meat?"

Katy reached in a drawer to her left and pulled it out. Ian took a cutting board and a dish towel, and laid the gravy boat on its side. "I just need the spout." Pulling the candle closer, he sucked in a deep breath. *Please, God, I don't want it to break to pieces.* Focusing on the cut, he set the saw to where the spout attached to the ironstone boat. Hands trembling, he began to saw, and the spout snapped off. Blowing any shards away, he bid his thanks to Katy and ran from the kitchen.

Quietly entering the guest cottage, Ian found Morgan leaning over Olivia.

"What of this?" He held the long narrow piece up. Morgan closed one eye to see through the thin cylinder.

"I don't think she'll last another hour. I need to try." Morgan stood and signaled Ian to hold her head back. Morgan went to his father's instruments and shuffled the small knife back and forth in his hands. Rolling his eyes to the sky, he took the damp rag and held it to her throat. "Can you hold her down in case she awakens?"

Ian saw the blade coming closer to Olivia's neck and moved to trade places with Morgan. Closing his eyes, he took her hands and leaned over her. "I've got her."

His eyes closed, muttering fraught prayers under his breath, Ian didn't know how long it took, but Olivia never moved a muscle. Afraid she'd stopped breathing, he finally looked up. The strange spout protruded from a hole in her throat, and Morgan gently dabbed at the blood pooling on her chest. His own breathing labored, Ian finally loosened his hold and asked, "Did it work?"

"I think so, but we must stay with her if she gets agitated or knocks it out—"

"I'll be right here. I can't sleep." Ian swallowed. "You sleep for now."

Morgan went back to the basin to wash his hands. His lips tightened with something unsaid as he dried them on a towel. "I wish I could give you hope, but I can't." Morgan touched his tongue to his upper lip. "Olivia has been like a sister to me." He stepped toward the door. "Keep cooling her skin and...pray."

Thirty

Eyelids heavy with fatigue, Ian started the simple pattern again. Rinsing the rag with cool water, he took her hand and began at her fingers. He gently set the cloth to each finger. Olivia Bradstreet had slim, ladylike fingers, matching the slender young woman asleep in bed. He turned her hand over and dabbed at her palm, then moving up and around her wrist. He had her limp arm memorized by now; he hoped his treatments were cooling her fiery skin. A rounded white shoulder next, pressing the cloth over the three faint moles that made a triangle. Next, he checked her skin as he had each time: no sign of bumps or rash. Ever so carefully, he laid the cool cloth under her ear and up along her cheek. Carefully avoiding the strange object protruding from her throat, her only access to the air she needed to live, he set the cloth on her forehead and whispered another round of jumbled prayers. God had heard them each time, but the...words...came...his head fell forward then violently jerked upward, awakening him.

Ian stood and set the rag back in the water. Raking his fingers through his hair, he stared out the window. No sign of the sunrise, but it had to be somewhat soon. He paced to keep himself awake and turned to watch Olivia from the same glow of the lantern. Her fingers twitched, and he stepped closer just in time to catch her hand rising in the air. Holding it firm, he pressed it against his chest and sat down as her eyes opened, rolled, and then closed again. She tried to turn onto her side, but he was able to gently hold her in place. Her other arm rose and he held it as it sagged back. Her heavy lids strained to open, and he grinned, hovering only inches away.

"Olivia, beloved, I'm right here. Please rest."

Her lips began to move, and he saw her face tense with pain.

"You can't talk." He brushed his fingers into her damp hairline. "Don't try."

Her glossy eyes creased shut as her head rolled back and forth.

"Be still, sweetheart, go back to sleep." Ian stretched his arm across her waist, holding his hand over her arm. Carefully he rested his head on his arm, using his other hand to keep her head still and body at bay. "You will live and not die." He whispered. "But sleep…now…"

A small tap upon his shoulder brought his heavy eyes open. Thomas stood stoic, eyes narrowing on Olivia. "Miss Bradstreet has an arrow stuck in her throat, and now she is going to die." Ian could not get his thick throat to refute those words. Thomas glanced back at him. "My ma was kind, with yellow hair, just like her. There's nothing you can do. Everything I love dies."

Ian awoke to someone moving in the room. Had he dreamt that Thomas had been there?

"Sorry I did not relieve you earlier." Morgan rubbed at tired eyes.

Ian sat up, shocked he'd allowed himself to sleep draped across Olivia. A faint line of light creased across the once dark room. They both stared at the sleeping woman.

"Her color looks better." Morgan laid the back of his hand to her cheek. "Skin's cooler to the touch."

Ian stood, feeling himself waver. The night, all their efforts—had it been just a bad dream? "She woke. Tried to move." His voice sounded like he'd been tarred and feathered.

"Go sleep on my father's bed." Morgan nodded to the door. "I will watch and pray."

Ian walked with heavy feet into the living room. The children still slept; he counted three heads as he found Dr. Hastings' room. Falling like a limb onto the forest floor, his body buckled onto the bed.

Muffled sounds woke him, and Ian opened his eyes, scanning the room. *Where was he?* The guest cottage. Blinking, he sat up in bed. *Olivia.* He pulled in a deep breath and stood. He reached for the door handle and stopped. What if she was gone? What if he'd promised to be with her and...and...? Rubbing his face, he listened to the faint voices coming from the other side of the door. The children talked, but there was no crying.

Ian shook the foreboding from his mind and opened the door. The girls and Milton sat at the table. Blinking, he searched the small cottage. "Where is the other boy? Thomas?" he asked as he went to Olivia's door.

"He was gone early. I think he thought it was a work day." Milton shrugged.

"Go after him. It's Sunday and I gave everyone the day off." Ian stopped. "But don't enter anyone's home or go by the big house. Just find him and come straight back."

"Yes, sir," Milton said sheepishly.

Ian wondered what he was missing. Possibly the three wide-eyed children sitting at an empty table without fire or food or Miss Bradstreet's care?

"We will eat when you return." Ian nodded as the boy took his coat and left. Turning the knob carefully, Ian walked into the sunlit bedroom. Olivia rested there, pale and still, as he'd left her last night.

"My father kept a bit of laudanum in his bag." Morgan rose from the chair. "I've given her a few drops to keep her asleep. I can't tell if the swelling in her throat has lessened. But for now, the extra airway is keeping her alive."

Ian felt his face flush. "This is good? What can I do?" He would do this man's bidding all year if it kept Olivia alive.

"Do you cook, make coffee?" Morgan asked.

"I...I...don't. But it can't be that hard." Ian scrutinized him. "Do you?"

Morgan crooked a sad grin. "I have a Mexican woman that does, Carlotta."

"You continue to doctor." Ian nodded. "I will figure out the other things." The words sounded confident, but once again, he was at a loss.

He stepped from the room and spied the girls. "Miss Bradstreet is doing better." He eyed Bonita, praying there'd be no tirade this morning.

"What does Miss Bradstreet do first?" Frustration set his voice sharper than usual.

"The stove is cold." Esther frowned.

"So, we need a fire." Ian looked around. "Where is the kindling?"

"The boys are supposed to bring it in before they leave for the mine." The girl dropped her chin onto her upraised palm.

Ian checked over his shoulder; the tinder box by the fireplace was empty. He would never take a pot of hot coffee for granted again. Stepping out the door, he found the ax and woodpile.

Thirty minutes later, Ian entered Olivia's room and handed Morgan a hot cup of coffee. "There are flapjacks on the table." His tone was flat. "The girls said they taste like flour and water. I told the boys to come straight back. I fear they may be sitting at Katy's kitchen table this very moment."

Morgan nodded his thanks and sipped the coffee. "You said she was around some ill children, maybe two weeks ago?"

"Yes, in Sacramento."

"I need to ask something." Morgan ran his fingers across the scars on his cheek. "It's of a personal nature, but I ask from a medical standpoint."

"Anything." Ian straightened.

"You have shown a tender care for Olivia." Morgan took another sip, watching from the top of his cup, then lowered it slowly. "Do you care for her? Have you kissed her?"

Ian opened his mouth, but the torrent of defenses he planned would not pass his lips. "Not…recently." It slipped out, the recollection of holding her at the wedding celebration still fresh and intimate to him. He'd grazed his fingers over her heated skin, longing to show her his affections were real. He closed his eyes. *What was the question?* Had Morgan seen them and judged him? "The kiss. It was months ago, before the trip to Sacramento," he said quickly.

Morgan's brow's furrowed.

"I had just returned from months at sea. I'd thought she was with your father." Ian heard the explanation come from his mouth before he could stop his loose lips. "I apologize, I've only had a few hours of sleep." He huffed. "That makes no sense."

"You thought Olivia and my father were a couple?" Morgan's eyes grew wide.

The air creaked from Ian's mouth. "I did." He walked closer to the bed. "She had no problem putting me in my place. And…then one strange thing after another happened—I've found her heart to be filled with compassion, fortitude, wit, and beauty." He remembered her radiant smile after her time shopping, the way they talked on the drive home. She was so much more than his equal—a young lady any man would want for his own. The room stilled with the outlandish conversation. "I believe her first love is the orphans." His voice was thick with sincerity. "And she would say my only love is the mine."

Morgan nodded.

"If you would excuse me for a moment." Ian leaned to look out the window. "I suppose I should find the boys. I understand you are trying to keep this sickness at bay?"

"Yes," Morgan sighed.

My only love is the mine. Ian stepped past the door, trying to ignore the gnawing pain in his gut.

Thirty-One

Ian jogged to the big house and stopped when he saw Milton from the corner of his eye.

"Where is Thomas?" The annoyance in his voice rang across the yard. "I told you to come straight back."

"I can't find him, sir." Huffing, Milton flopped down cross legged on the ground. "I've called for him from one end of this place to the other.

Ian watched the boy's chest rise and fall from running. "Did you check all around the mine?"

"Yes, sir. No one is around like you said, they all took the day off."

Ian's eyes roved the grounds left to right. It was unusually quiet. "What about the Hockings? Did you see or ask them?"

"I caught the girl going to the outhouse, she said he wasn't at their place."

Thomas was trouble, and Ian had no tolerance for it. First the fire at the Oak Street house and now this escapade. "You can't think of anything? When he runs off, how long until he usually comes back?"

Milton stood, twisting his hands in front of him. "I don't know. He gets upset easily. He and Joshua were better friends."

Ian looked around the area again and crossed his arms, digging his fingers into his jacket. He'd no time for this child's antics. He needed to be with Olivia. Just the sound of her name brought his thoughts to her. If she could speak, what would she want? Ian drew a long breath. She'd want all of Grass Valley up and looking for him.

"Come along," he said to Milton as he marched to the shanties.

A few minutes later, in the center area, Ian was regretting holding the cowbell in the air and giving it a good ring. Heads popped out of various doors, and men pulled their jackets on, followed by women wrapped in knitted shawls.

"No day off, boss?" someone yelled from his left.

"I apologize, I really do." He held his hand in the air. "There are two things…" Their trusting faces caught him off guard, and he had to swallow the emotion in his throat before he could talk. "There is sickness at the guest cottage." Many of the women's eyes widened with alarm. "Miss Bradstreet has a high fever, and by the grace of God, though Dr. Hastings is gone, his son, who's also a doctor, is assisting her." Ian took another deep breath to project the strength he did not feel. "He has been by her side and tending to her with great care. He suspects it might be diphtheria."

Gasps rolled through the group, and mothers clutched their children to their skirts. "Right now, only the children who live at the guest cottage, Morgan Hastings, and myself are to be secluded and watched." Ian held both hands out in front of himself. "If none of us become sick, then we have just one case. Miss Bradstreet was with some sick children a few weeks ago." Ian couldn't help notice that some of the men frowned, looking at their feet. "I would appreciate your prayers for her recovery."

Low murmurs rolled among them, and heads nodded in agreement.

"The second thing is the boy Thomas was missing this morning. Have any of you seen him?" The group shook their heads. "Milton has been looking and had no luck." Ian rubbed his forehead, his lips pressed thin. "I truly wanted all of you to have a day of rest. Your tireless sacrifice this last month has not gone unnoticed."

"You worked as hard as any of us," Joseph Turner yelled from the back. "What do ya need?"

"Could I ask this half of the group to span to the south?" Morgan pointed over the Empire property. "This half, will you take the north side of the property? We'll meet back here or ring the bell when he's found."

Heads nodded in agreement. Mrs. Hocking buried her face in her husband's shoulder. Walking with her toward Ian, the husband asked, "Do you think he's down with the sickness somewhere?"

"He was fine last night, so I can't say. But please do not touch him," Ian's voice rose to the crowd. "All of us at the cottage want to stay separate for a while."

"Got it, boss." The group began to split and search.

Ian turned to Milton. "Did you check the main house?"

"Yes, sir, but I didn't go in, like you said. Lester was going to milk the cow. He said he'd not seen Thomas."

Ian took Milton by the shoulder. "Is there any area you didn't search?" They walked on until Mr. Kitt jogged up to them.

"The bucket in shaft five is missing."

"What?" Ian turned, marching toward the mine.

"That's the one we used to put Thomas down." Mr. Kitt had to jog to keep up.

"Oh, good Lord." Ian stopped and rubbed his head. "When no one could reach the pick that fell in the coyote hole?"

"Yep. I gave the bucket rope a tug. It came right up. He might be down there." Mr. Kitt's shoulders stiffened. "I'll go down and look."

"No." Ian stood over the deep shaft. "In case he is sick, I need to be the one. Get the mule harnessed and lower me down."

Surges of fresh blood pumped hard in Ian's veins as the bucket lowered him into the deep pit. Each thud in his chest was fueled by anger and dread. The water level at the bottom of this mine was a constant problem, as they had tried to flood out the side rows of diggings they'd done.

"Thomas!" he yelled. Only cold air whiffed up from the bottom of the sheer drop. With a low, rusty creak, he locked the pulley in place at the first extension. Leaning past the lantern hanging from the bucket, Ian carefully hooked a leg into the hole before he released the bucket. Hunched over, he called for Thomas again. The small candle on his mining hat was his only light to see forward. If the boy had lost his light, the child's fear could overwhelm him. Ian called his name again, and taking a few more steps, found the end of the tunnel. The stony damp air penetrating through his jacket, he returned to the bucket and hoisted the rope and pulley to the next fissure on the right.

"Thomas!" Ian listened to the silence and wiped the perspiration from his forehead. The next extension was low and short, taking only a few minutes to crawl in and back out. "I'll hang you from your toenails," Ian murmured, thinking of the boy asleep under a tree somewhere.

The next tunnel Ian took only revealed two dead rats and some spat-out tobacco. By the time he crawled into the fourth and lowest tunnel, he could almost find a true breath. The boy was not here. Taking a handful of rocks, Ian dropped them into the bottom of the shaft and listened. Why had the sound not sounded like drops into the water? He took another handful and dropped them again. Strange. The miners had sent wood down to shore up the sides, but the last report had said the water table stopped them from working any further.

Ian looked up to the sliver of waiting light and fresh air. Biting tersely into his bottom lip, he pulled the mining hat on tighter and lowered himself down. The boy was not here, he was sure of it. But he had come this far, and he might as well inspect the depths while he was here. Looking over the bucket, Ian's light reflected off of something strange. His head shot back so fast it slammed against the stiff pulley ropes.

Holding his breath, he looked again. The faint light shimmered with the same fear radiating from his body. Brown fabric and a patch of yellow hair, floating face down.

He had found Thomas.

Mr. Kitt and a few others clutched their foreheads as the bucket came to daylight. "Oh, bless'd Jesus." The groans revealed what Ian hadn't yet said. The wet child hanging over his shoulder was dead. The men secured the bucket and reached to help Ian.

"Don't touch him," Ian growled and stepped away, holding Thomas. "Call off the others." Ian's eyes stung from the light and his own inward pain. The mine had taken a child. He felt it like shards of glass slicing his insides. He knew, just like the men, the dangers of the work, but a *child*. It was his fault for putting them to work. With the lifeless boy flung over his shoulder, he forced each weighty step to the big house. The cowbell rang out across the grounds.

Olivia would never forgive him.

Ian pushed open the front door and laid Thomas on the dining room table. The white tablecloth still remained on it from the wedding. Before he could remove his wet jacket, Katy bustled from the kitchen and covered a screech with her hand.

"Stay back." His voice broke. Knowing the other children would come any minute and see their lifeless friend, he wrapped Thomas in the white tablecloth. "He drowned in the bottom of a shaft."

"Oh no, oh no." Katy wept. "Oh, the poor child."

Some of the miners stood at the front door. Mr. Hocking's face paled, and yet Ian could not move. "He was at the bottom."

Mr. Hocking's mouth hung open, the shock evident. "I'll go now and be with the missus."

"Please." Ian's throat wouldn't work, the guilt squeezing it shut. "Please." He wiped his face with his sleeve. "Please, tell...tell her how sorry I am."

As soon as Mr. Hocking left, Ian saw the pale face of Milton standing in the empty space. "Come here, boy."

Ian lowered to a knee and held the boy to his chest. The small body trembled and gasped against Ian's shoulder. "I should've found him," Milton wept.

"No." Ian pulled him away, piercing him with his eyes. "This was my fault. You did everything you could." Ian kept his hand firm on Milton's back as he rose. Sniffles and sobs turned his attention toward the kitchen door, where Katy held Mary Ellen and Lester. His eyes wandered back to Thomas, but he couldn't seem to think or move.

"We'll dig a nice spot for him, boss," one of the men said at the door.

Ian pulled in a pained breath. "Yes, thank you. But I know where he's to go." Ian wrung his hands in front of himself. "About a half a mile straight past this house. You'll see my father's grave. He'll lie next to him."

Thirty-Two

Ian held the door open for Milton at the small guest cottage. He knew the importance of speaking to the children, but the need to talk to Morgan weighed on his beaten shoulders. He carefully entered Olivia's room. The small pipe still protruded from her throat, but her skin had returned to a better hue.

"What happened?" Morgan winced at the sight of Ian's haggard face. "Are you sick?

"No." Ian shook his head. "The missing boy. I found him at the bottom of one of the mine shafts."

Morgan's lanky frame stiffened.

"I believe he drowned." Ian sank into the chair, suddenly exhausted. "We did our best to stay clear of everyone." Facing the ground, he squeezed his forehead. "The miner families, they…they did the burial, just a few minutes ago."

Morgan paced in a circle. "I'm so sorry. I can't imagine…now this too." He drew his hand down his face. "One day a wedding, one day a funeral," he whispered. "Thankfully, the girls have been fine today. No complaints."

"I don't know what to tell you," Ian said, dazed. "Was he sick? Milton said he runs off when he's upset," Sighing, with closed eyes, he stood. "But why go into a mine shaft?" Immeasurable confusion inundated his brain, and Ian leaned his arm into the wall, dropping his forehead. "I am responsible. Olivia never wanted the children around the mine."

"I've been all over these boomtowns. Accidents happen all the time, to adults and children." Morgan squeezed his shoulder. "You could never have known that was where he'd go."

The uncomfortable silence lingered until Ian spoke. "And Olivia?" He turned. "Please tell me some good news." He paused, stepping closer to her bed. "She looks better."

Morgan nodded. "With the reduction of the fever, I want to ensure the infection dissipates. I believe we should try to take out the pipe. She'll awaken soon and need water."

"All right. I need to speak to the girls, and then I will be back to help." Ian walked out, heading for the small kitchen for water. Three sets of eyes followed his every move from where they sat on the settee. They knew something was wrong, and he knew nothing about talking to children.

"Bonita, I need to say something hard, and I know you are going to want to cry." He poured water into a cup, taking a long drink to calm his nerves.

Her alarmed brown eyes filled fast. He'd just shot himself in the foot. "But I don't want us to wake Miss Bradstreet."

Her quivering chin bounced up and down.

Milton moved away, crouching down to poke a stick in the small fire. *What could he say to spare them more pain?*

"Thomas is no longer with us."

The girls frowned. "Where did he go?" Esther asked.

"He's dead, Esther," Milton growled, throwing the stick into the fire.

Bonita's face turned red, and she ran to her bedding and burrowed in as far as she could. Ian could see her feet kicking and hear her muffled sobs.

Ian felt worthless. The discomfort in the room was like the days on the ship with grieving parents. He sank into the kitchen chair, and Esther walked to him and leaned into his chest. Feeling awkward as she began to cry, Ian pulled her onto his leg, and she melted into him, wrapping her arms around his waist.

Bonita stood up and took a deep gulp of air before she walked near and climbed onto his other knee. Without much choice, he held her wet face on his other shoulder. Maybe it was this simple. They just wanted to be held. Milton's eyes met his, and he nodded for him to come too. The boy had no problem bumping Bonita closer to Ian and finding comfort in the mass of thick arms and girls' tears.

"He always wanted to be with his ma." Esther's watery eyes sadly peeked up at his, her cheeks wet.

Ian gently kissed her temple. "I'm sure they are together at this moment." Esther sucked in a gulp and nestled back into his chest. Ian blinked. Their little hands clutched his arms and torso, and he felt something grueling yet tender at the same time. *Orphans.*

Never had he really taken the time to wonder how a child would go through life without a mother or father to call their own. He pulled Bonita closer and kissed her soft hairline. No wonder the child raged at every difficulty. Though he could feel her cries next to his chest, she held back her usual screams. Miss Bradstreet was the protective hen who gathered the chicks, something he had not been able to understand—not until this moment. Comfort was a powerful thing. All that he had given to them was a chest and two arms, and for the first time all day, his life had an inch of calm.

He likely needed this moment as badly as the children. After a difficult year at sea, and then losing his father, Ian felt the warmth of their bodies surrounding him like a balm. With Lesandra's betrayal and the money needed to keep the mine afloat, he'd carried so much of an uncontrollable load on his own shoulders. And now the loss of Thomas. As if reading his mind, Bonita's small hand patted his cheek.

He pulled in a quick breath and took her hand in his. "Though these have been hard days," he whispered, "we will stay together and help each other. Yes?"

The children sniffled and wiped their faces. "Yes, Mr. Beckner."

Ian closed his eyes, holding them one more minute. How easy it had been to ramble to Olivia of the Hockings' resilience after losing their child. Had he ever really felt someone's pain other than his own? He'd found his own comfort satisfied in profitable mining reports or a pick in his hand. But something had speared his heart. *Nothing matters without the people you love by your side.* Being able to hold them and comfort them was a valuable treasure he'd never known before. *Had he ever really known what love is?*

A soft knock at the door made Milton rise.

"We must not invite anyone in." Ian reminded him as the girls scooted off his knees.

Milton smiled. "Katy is walking away. It looks to be a box of food."

Ian was dazed by those welcome words. "God bless her."

As soon as Morgan ate and the children were fed and settled into bed, Ian washed his hands as he'd seen Morgan do.

Morgan lit another lantern and set it on the chair. "I'm going to remove it and stitch the hole up. I want her to feel the pain."

Ian looked wary.

"I want her to come out of her sleep and breathe again with her nose and mouth. But you must hold her down. I can't do the stitching if she is thrashing." Morgan prepared the thread and needle.

Ian pinched the bridge of his nose. He felt aged far past his twenty-seven years. "Hold her still. That is my job." He gritted his teeth.

"Yes. Tell me when you're ready." Morgan waited.

Ian reached in to grasp her head, but could not keep his arms settled on her arms at the same time. Fighting the knot in his stomach, he climbed on the bed and straddled her hips. Keeping each of his knees pressed on her hands, he held her head still with sweaty hands and closed his eyes.

Without looking, he could tell that this time she felt everything. Her short gasps of air and the jerking of her limbs rocked them both.

"Keep her still," Morgan whispered. "Just a few more ties."

Go ahead and fight me, Olivia. Any movement meant she had strength left in her. She squealed weakly again, and Ian could tell Morgan had pulled back. Opening his eyes, he saw watery blue daggers locked on him. "Breathe, girl, and I'll let you go." Like a duckling coming up for water, she sucked in air and tried to raise her head. Her lips moved, but no sound came out. Ian moved his knees off her hands and took them in his. "Don't touch your throat." He swung to sit on the side of the bed. "Olivia, you're okay. Morgan needed to help you breathe." She twisted her head, still gasping and muddled. "Slow it down." Ian pressed on her chest, and she stared wide-eyed at his hand, pressing on her skin.

"Dr. Morgan, you may need to speak to her. I think I'm upsetting her." Did anyone realize that over and over, he was far from his abilities or sensibilities?

Morgan set his father's bag on the floor and took a cup of water. "Upsetting is good." Morgan stood next to the bed. "Olivia, please don't try to speak. I'm going to hold this cup to your lips. Take a few small drinks and swallow gently."

Olivia's eyes followed Morgan's hand, and she took a small sip. Like she was seeing a ghost, she glared at Ian.

"You've been very sick." Ian pressed her hands in his. 'If I let go, you cannot touch your throat." Little black threads covered the incision.

Her eyes drooped, and she nodded.

Ian let go, and his eyes roved over her frail features. Touching her hair where it lay along the pillow, he wondered if he could survive her disappointment in him. His neglect of Thomas would surely seal her opinion of him forever.

Her light breathing seemed to even out.

Morgan stepped back. "I'd like to get some sleep. Call for me if anything changes."

"Thank you." Ian nodded and set his elbows on his knees. He dropped his head to his fists, his shoulders sagging. The agony and chaos of the day tried to steal the thankful moment he wanted to have. Laying right here, breathing on her own, Olivia seemed to be improving. Thoughts of the past ten hours wrestled in his gut until soft fingers rose and held his wrist. Without looking, slowly, he opened his hand, and slender warm fingers intertwined with his. Keeping their connection, he slipped to the floor and rested his head on the side of her bed. He was so tired and numb, but shouldn't he do something for her? Tell her of Thomas? A feathery, feminine touch gingerly caressed his hair in what must be a dream. Feeling peace down to his soul, he allowed the dream to continue.

Thirty-Three

Ian grimaced from the painful position he'd slept in and glanced up to see Olivia's door crack open. Esther peeked in while he tried to raise his stiff bones from the hard floor.

"Yes," he croaked.

"Miss Katy brought a box for breakfast."

Ian rubbed his eyes and ran his fingers through his hair. A cloudy light poured across the bed. Olivia seemed to be sleeping soundly.

"Go ahead and help the children eat." He rose slowly, feeling every joint and muscle creak with stiffness.

Stretching side to side, he stood at the door and watched as the children quietly placed the items on the table. Thomas was missing, and it was his fault. His stomach growled with hunger—and something else. Looking back at Olivia and her fragile state, he sighed. Her greatest need was for rest, solace, and peace. He ran his hands over his stubbled jaw and pinched his eyes closed, realizing the closeness they'd shared would never be his to enjoy again.

Later in the morning, after Morgan had propped up her pillows and helped her drink some water and broth, she lifted a wary smile at both of them.

The clarity in her eyes spoke of her recovery, and Ian desperately wanted to celebrate and give God thanks, but instead, he walked in a slow circle. The intolerable silence had lingered long enough. "Olivia, I have to tell you something." Ian sat on the corner of her bed. "I know you still can't talk, so I will try and tell you everything as best I can." He took a deep breath and scratched the back of his neck, finally letting his eyes rest on hers.

"We were at the bonfire when you became sick. Do you remember this?"

She nodded, her eyes narrowing.

"That night you became ill and developed a rapid infection that...that almost kept you from breathing. Thankfully..." Ian glanced up at Morgan. "Morgan knew what to do." He tried to collect his thoughts. He was sure she thought he was only going to explain why her condition was the way it was. "He did a procedure that put a hole in your throat. It allowed the air to bypass the infection and get into your lungs."

Morgan stood a few feet away. "I think it will be a week or two until your throat heals, and your voice returns."

Olivia's eyes warmed on Morgan, and she mouthed 'thank you.'

Ian cracked the tension in his jaw and forced the rest of the story to come out. "Sometime in the night or early morning..." He cleared his throat, feeling weaker than he had even when the two children had died on the ship. "I believe Thomas was upset. There was a lot going on, and he ran away."

Face constricted, Olivia shook her head and winced as she tried to sit up.

He was doing a pitiful job; this was not about a runaway child. "Olivia, I have to speak to you about a tragedy." His words caught, fighting to continue. Despite her fragile state, she strained to speak, the confusion filling her eyes with alarm. "While everyone at the Empire Mine was searching," he said, lowering his voice, "I found Thomas. I found him in the water at the bottom of mine shaft five."

A faint squeal escaped her, and she rose off the pillows.

"The child, Thomas, he drowned."

Olivia whimpered and sunk back into the pillows, turning away.

Ian reached out to touch her shoulder, but found his hand couldn't finish the connection. Did he not remember that she would find him the devil? "The Cornish families performed his service and I've told the other children." Holding his mouth in a tight frown, he needed something of comfort to come out. "And…and I wish to everything in heaven and above…I wasn't saying this to you. You've been the perfect caregiver, governess, mother and…"

Her hand swung back, batting him off the bed while her back trembled with faint, broken cries. He stood, watching her fist pound and twist into her blankets.

"I'm sorry. I blame myself." He closed his water-filled eyes and swiped his sleeve across damp cheeks. Helpless again to right any wrongs. The recurring fear of failure that had come to make a home in him returned. *When would it ever leave?*

Morgan stood silent in the corner and nodded to Ian. He appreciated something about the man's presence.

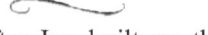

Later in the afternoon, after Ian built up the fire in the small cottage, he sat staring at the crackling flames.

Morgan walked in and looked out the front window. "I think Olivia is going to be fine. But with these dark clouds, I'd like to make it back to my place before dark."

His words seemed to knock Ian from his stupor. Of course, the man wanted to get back to his home, his mining claim. "Yes." Ian stood.

"My father and Judith should arrive home anytime." Morgan lightly rubbed the scarring on his cheek. "I don't worry about my father. He has built up an immunity to many things. My concern is for your mother."

Ian gripped his neck and squeezed. "What should we do?"

"They should stay at the big house. Keep Olivia away from others for another week." Morgan kneaded his hands together.

"All right." Ian swallowed hard, realizing without Morgan, he would be Olivia's inept caretaker. "What else?"

"Keep Olivia sipping water and broth, and I don't expect her voice to return for a few weeks. In some cases, it never does." Morgan appeared worried as he scanned the small cottage. "Keep yourself and the children in for another week. Just keep doing what you've been doing."

Another week? In all the commotion, Ian hadn't thought about the mine. With all the increased work needing to get done, how could he be away another week? How could he possibly make the payment to Mr. Grant? Despite all his feeble attempts, along with the fire destroying the home, this escalated the inevitable quicker than he could have imagined.

"I'm going to say something." Morgan pushed his hands into his pockets. "And I am not the one who should preach this, believe me. But I can tell by the alarm in your eyes, Ian, you carry a lot of weight. Maybe for one week, because you care about the people on this land. For one week, you can put the mine in the hands of God and let go." Morgan nodded toward Olivia's door. "You are the only one who can care for her." His voice lowered. "You are good at it…and you have little choice."

It was the truth surrounded by a soft reprimand. He could not work shoulder to shoulder with the men knowing he might get the Cornish people sick. Mr. Wright knew the daily workings of the mine. *Let go and put the mine in the hands of God.* The words sounded worthy.

"I don't expect Olivia will welcome my help." Ian wondered if that wasn't what he needed to pray for right now.

Morgan nodded slightly. "I've told her I need to get home, and she also has little choice." He stared out the window. "Since I've known Emery, my wife-to-be has needed many weeks of healing. The heart and the body do not always heal in any predictable order." Morgan sighed and walked past Ian. "Looking back, I wish I'd trusted God more."

Ian pondered those words as Morgan went into his father's room to gather his things. *A week. Had he ever been still for an hour?* He glanced at the children at the table, looking down at their slates. "Milton, did Thomas have a slate?" Milton rose and pulled it from Thomas's things and handed it to him.

"Miss Bradstreet has to rest her voice. But we can ask her to write about what she needs."

Bonita sat straighter. "And if I don't know the words, can Esther read it to me?"

"Yes, of course." Ian lifted a small smile to Esther.

Morgan entered with his coat and bag and patted the children goodbye. "Here are the directions to my place." He set a paper on the table. "If something happens and my father is not here, don't hesitate to send someone for me."

"Thank you." Ian extended his hand. "I don't want to think of where we'd be if you had not been here." They shook firmly, and Ian held the door as the tall young man left. Ian turned and stared at Olivia's door. Nodding at the children's watchful expressions, he took Thomas's slate and chalk and knocked. After a moment, he let himself enter. The room was cool, and Olivia lay on her side wrapped in a ball around her pillow. Leaving the door open, he walked around the bed and found her awake, tears rolling across her nose and onto the pillow.

"Olivia," he said softly. "Morgan has left, but I will be here to see to you and the children." Her watery blue eyes stared stoically at the wall.

"I have an idea. With the slate, you can write what you need." She seemed locked away somewhere as he set the slate in front of her. "I hold no skill in nursing. You have to tell me how to help you." He heard something and turned to see the children at the door. "The children have prayed, and bravely held back their fears. Would you like a moment with them?"

Pulling her hand from under the pillow, Olivia pushed the slate and chalk off the edge of the bed. The thread of peace unraveled as Thomas's slate rattled against the hard floor. There was no need for her to write a word. Her frozen, lifeless stare said it all.

Thirty-Four

The misty winter morning brought rain off and on. Ian stood at the door, watching Mary Ellen run back to the big house with her jacket held over her head. He pulled the box inside, the sausage and eggs scent wafting up his nostrils. While he set the box on the table, the children gathered with plates and cups, ready to eat their breakfast. Ian removed a wrapped package from the box to find a clean set of clothes and his razor and soap. Another of Katy's blessings. Under the packages was a letter from the Hockings for Milton and a report from Mr. Wright. Even with all the misspelled words, Ian could grasp the work that was progressing at the mine without him.

Esther walked past him with a plate of food for Olivia. Even if she could, he doubted Olivia would speak to him, but at least she'd warmed to seeing the children. The woman was amazing— in between napping, she'd written out their simple lessons from her bed, giving them something to do as they sat at the table throughout the day. Often, to curb his own boredom, he sat and went over sums with them and found himself staring at their faces as they worked. If one of them became sick, he would be at the end of his rope. By the grace of God, they all seemed to be in good health. A knock at the door made him drop the mine reports. The children stopped eating to watch. He slowly opened the door to find a large black umbrella.

"Son!" His mother called out as the umbrella rose. "I can't believe what has happened. I'm desperate to come inside and hold each one of you."

"But we won't," Maxwell said quietly from where he stood beside her. "I understand Morgan has gone, and you all have been isolated here."

"Yes." Ian nodded gravely. Seeing their concerned faces, his battling emotions overcame him. "I would imagine about another four days. Thank God the children have been well."

"This is good news." Maxwell squeezed his arm around Ian's mother's shoulders. "The children usually lack the fortitude to recover. And how is Olivia?"

"Better each day." His voice lowered. "The loss of Thomas has made her own ailment worse." He looked to the ground. "But I believe her health is improving."

"Oh, son," Judith exclaimed, holding her hand over her mouth. "I can't imagine all this, these trials, and here we are, kept at arm's length. After Katy told us everything, Maxwell and I spoke. He can return to the cottage for any doctoring that is needed."

"Trust me, I will call for you if anything changes. For now, we must wait and pray no one else becomes sick."

"Yes, of course," they said in unison as his mother laid her head on Maxwell's shoulder. The concern in their eyes seemed to be blanketed in strength, support. Their clear love for each other and those inside the guest cottage made his chest hurt.

"After here, I will go to each home and check on the workers," Maxwell offered.

"Thank you, that would mean a lot to me."

"And what else can we do?" His mother piped up.

Esther and Bonita snuck around his sides, and he placed his hands on their shoulders.

"Girls. So good to see you." His mother smiled. "I know for a fact that Katy has two apple pies in the oven, and one is coming over here with your supper." The girls nodded as they leaned against his side, and their warmth brought a strange, touching contrast to the cool air of the winter morning.

"Thomas wanted to be with his ma," Bonita said, matter-of-fact. "Now they are both in heaven."

"Yes." Judith's face grew heavy. "They are together now." Her eyes locked with Ian's. "I know this is strange and difficult for you—to be removed from the mine while helping with Olivia and the children." She shook her head. "We are praying." Her voice caught, and she quickly caught a tear from the corner of her eye. "Please tell us if there is anything you need."

"I will." He backed the children up and said his goodbyes. Seeing his mother held by Maxwell as they walked away was strange, yet comforting at the same time. He didn't want her alone in all this mess, especially when they'd lost the mine and the house. He slowly closed the door.

As the girls went back to the table, Ian peeked into the crack of Olivia's door. She stood in her gown and robe, watching out her window while holding on the bed frame. Though her eyes were dark with pain and she appeared feeble in body and soul, he risked a step through her door.

"You heard. My parents are back."

Her face narrowed, confusion in her eyes. She tried to produce a sound, but it was so faint that Ian handed her the slate.

"Parents?" she wrote, her hand trembling.

Ian pulled back, catching his mistake. "My mother and Maxwell." He lifted a half-smile while instinctively taking her elbow. "Would you like to come out and sit by the fire?"

Olivia nodded, and Ian carefully walked her out to the small front room. Pulling a footstool in front of the settee, she sat and let Ian prop her feet up while reaching for a blanket. Kneeling to wrap her feet and legs, he looked up to see her watching him. He froze as a powerful wave of desire overcame him. Not as a man desires a woman but as a sinner desires forgiveness. Her hair hung messy and loose, her neck wrapped in a cloth. Somehow, they were both helpless, poor, and needy.

"Olivia," he whispered. "I am truly sorry." Their eyes locked, and her chin began to quiver, her tongue touching her top lip. Finally, she glanced away, holding her hand over her mouth.

"Miss Bradstreet, look." Bonita came close with her slate. "I already did my letters this morning."

Olivia dabbed the back of her hand over her wet face and took the slate. A feeble smile rose as she nodded her approval to the little girl.

Ian walked to the kitchen and poured hot water over the tea strainer. Taking a sip of the steaming tea, he added some cold water to temper it. Carefully bringing it to Olivia, she pointed to the side table, and he set it down.

"How are you feeling?" Ian grimaced, remembering she could barely talk. He went into her room for the slate and chalk and handed it to her. This time she took the chalk and carefully wrote a few words before handing it back to him.

"Like a wagon and six horses ran me over," it said.

"Yes." Ian released a short chuckle then sobered. "You heard me at the door."

Olivia nodded.

"We are all stuck here together. And what is worse is that I am daily acting as your nurse." He blew out a breath, setting the slate on her lap. "But, thankfully, not the cook." He grinned. "I've figured how to make coffee and tea."

Olivia took the warm cup and brought it to her lips, taking a sip. She carefully set it down and mouthed *thank you*. Taking the slate, she wrote, "The mine? How can you be gone?"

Ian felt a surge of delight. She was talking to him. Could Miss Bradstreet, who didn't have to—might she have found some forbearance for his irrevocable mistakes?

"I have Mr. Wright, and he puts the mine reports in with the breakfast box each morning."

"I got a letter from the Hockings." Milton came around and sat next to her. "Let me read it to you."

Ian could see the displeasure in Olivia's eyes, yet she nodded to the boy.

"*Dear Milton,*

We think of you each day and pray that you remain in good health. Though we are sad and broken in heart over the loss of Thomas, we just wanted you to know that when everyone is feeling well, we would like to have you over again. Mr. Hocking has a couple of good branches he has made into fishing poles. That would be a fun outing and good for supper.

"Write to us about how you are doing. Best regards, The Hockings." Milton smiled at Olivia. "I'm writing them back," he said, returning to the table.

Olivia's shoulders slumped, and she took the slate, erasing it with her hand before she wrote, "He will NOT go near the mine."

"No. I understand." Ian nodded as he placed another log on the fire. "It was short-sighted of me to let the boys work. I didn't realize the obvious dangers. It will never happen again."

Olivia erased her words and wrote. "Tell the Hockings he will not work." She flipped the slate up for him to read and then erased it. "Then see if they still want him."

"Olivia." Ian frowned and lowered his voice so Milton would not hear what he desired to say. He wanted to defend his friends, but this was not the right time or place to convince her of anything. She was severely pained from the loss of Thomas. "We'll all have to wait and see."

He wanted to change the subject. "Morgan Hastings was a godsend." He took a seat across from her. "I can see why this family is special to you. They are calm under pressure." He tilted his head to the side and sucked in a quick breath. "Unlike me." The fire popped, and he wondered if she remembered him holding her down. "Morgan even offered advice on something I should've done all along. He admonished me and told me to trust God with the mine." Pressing his lips into a thin line, he hesitated. "I feel the need to do just that. I want to change, Olivia, I do." He rubbed the stubble on his jaw. "Seeing you on the brink of death and relinquishing poor Thomas to the angels has made me realize I can no longer live life with my feeble attempts and failures. I need to place the mine in God's hands and trust for His direction and help." Ian leaned forward, pressing his elbows into his legs.

"I have to trust God in all things," he said, looking through his eyelashes to meet hers.

"I have to."

Thirty-Five

The next morning, Ian awoke to the sounds of children whispering and the occasional giggle. It was so foreign, this strange routine of leisure. Yesterday, Olivia had just sat and read, napping throughout the day in a soft chair. Just like five birds caring for the nest and each other, this tiny home and its simplicity had its benefits.

Ian had been raised a gentleman, but found purpose for his life when he was sweating and laboring with hard-working men. Honestly, he'd always thought a day without mining was like a retreat from battle. Maybe God had set him aside to show him how unimportant his efforts really were. The miners continued to mine from the earth, and yet, no matter the profit, he'd no way to get to San Francisco. Should he warn Mr. Wright of the likelihood of the mine being closed? How long without a payment would Mr. Grant wait?

Ian pulled on his clothes. *Wasn't it just yesterday he'd told Olivia he would have to trust God with the mine?* Anxious to see to her, he finished tucking his shirt in and stepped from Maxwell's room. Maybe today more of her voice would return.

Olivia sat at the kitchen table in her nightgown and robe as the children ate oatmeal and bread. She looked up with fearful eyes and handed him a note. Ian braced himself. *What had gone wrong now?* After reading it, he reached out and touched her shoulder. "Maxwell will come this morning to take your stitches out. This is good," Ian tried to reassure her, but her body seemed to crumble as she held the side of her neck.

"And how is your voice? Can you say my name?"

Olivia struggled two or three times to get the word past the soft feather of air that came forth. Frustrated, she tried to stand and swayed to the right. Ian caught her in his arms and gently held her. Embracing each other had seemed to work with the children, and they continued to eat like him holding Olivia was nothing out of the ordinary. He pressed a soft kiss above her ear. "Do you remember asking me to be your strength?"

She lightly shook her head no against his chest.

"It doesn't matter," he whispered. "Please allow me." He rubbed light circles around her back and felt her frame shudder in his arms. Slowly, her arms came to rest on his back, and for a fleeting moment every misfortune fell away. This is what he saw in his mother and Maxwell, and this was everything he wanted. Olivia's hand pressed gently against his chest as she moved back, her eyes and head swinging toward the children. Miss Bradstreet was proper. She was perfectly suited to be in his arms, yet her respectability was her foremost concern. "We *are* engaged," he whispered in her ear before he released her.

Her mouth opened, and one eye narrowed at him.

"You really don't need a voice, Olivia. I'm learning to read your expressions quite well."

A soft knock at the door brought a sad squeak from the back of her throat.

"It will be fine." Ian turned to open the door and greet Maxwell. "Much simpler than what happened to open your airway." He hesitated, taking Maxwell's coat. "Right?"

"Yes, this is simple. Let me get my bag." Maxwell walked past the group and into his room.

Ian led Olivia into her room, where she reluctantly laid down.

"I'm happy to report that all the Cornish workers seem to be in good health." Maxwell entered and pulled tweezers from his bag. Ian came around the other side of the bed and took her hands in his. "Just look at me."

Her eyes slanted on Ian, and her jaw flexed as Maxwell tugged on the little back threads.

"The incision looks healed, and there is no infection that I can see." He tugged three more stitches out. "How is swallowing?"

Olivia's face pinched as he pulled the last one out. Nodding with watery eyes, she lifted a slight smile.

"That would mean all right, but not great." Ian released her hands.

Maxwell placed a light bandage around her neck and tied a knot. "You can bathe as long as the water is clean. Try to eat more food than you feel like, and if you see any redness or seeping, come for me."

Maxwell dropped his doctoring things back in his bag, and Ian remembered how Morgan washed his hands before and after every treatment. Olivia lightly touched the bandage.

"Thank you," she said faintly as she tried to sit up.

Maxwell squeezed her leg. "Let's wait two more days, then release Ian from his post here at the guest cottage." He smiled and gestured to Ian. "Could I speak to you outside for a moment?"

Ian inhaled. "Yes. Excuse us, Olivia." His back stiffened as he followed Maxwell out the front door.

Maxwell chewed on the side of his lip and looked out along the wet path. "I did something." He slipped his coat back on. "It was something your mother and I talked about at length." He cleared his throat. "And it may gravely offend you."

Ian froze. Just when he found Maxwell trustworthy—

"On our honeymoon trip, we went to San Francisco, and I met with your lawyer."

Ian felt his stomach slam into his shoes. How could his mother ever agree to give Maxwell the mine? Was he a manipulating snake, come to steal everything the Beckners had worked for? They should never have trusted him.

Maxwell pressed his fingers along his brow. "I paid off the money owed to Mr. Grant. I want you and the mine free from this tyrant holding the family and the mineworkers hostage to his threats." He held his hand up. "I know I was to stay clear. I know you would've met the burden yourself, I believe that." Maxwell shook his head, looking to the ground. "I guess I excused my interference with how much your mother worried."

Ian jerked back. "You paid off what I owe, Mr. Grant?" *This was the man he had just deemed a liar and cheat?*

"Here." Maxwell took Ian's hand and slapped a piece of paper into it. "You are a solid, hardworking man of pride and principle. This is the receipt. The debt is paid in full, and because I know you, I have made a reasonable quarterly return payment schedule. Look it over. I'm flexible in how you pay it back."

Ian knew his mouth hung open. "I will… look it over," he mumbled. Before he could find another rational word, Maxwell squeezed his shoulder and turned to leave. "And besides your mother," he nodded back, "we keep this between us." He waved and walked down the path.

"Wait," Ian called after him. "I…I…just… thank you." The words came out sounding like his voice, but was he dreaming?

Maxwell stopped and turned. Ian noted a shifting in his step-father's jaw. Struggling to speak, he said, "Thank you, Ian, for your care for Olivia. She's been through a lot." Something protective simmered in his eyes. "She's like a daughter to me."

Ian could only nod, the shock still pulsing in his body. Maxwell walked down the path, and Ian went inside the cottage.

Olivia sat at the table with the children and flipped the slate for him to read. "Is everything all right? What happened?"

Ian stood silent for a long time. He was so sure the scoundrel had come to take advantage of the mine and him once again. Yet Ian had said he would leave the mine in God's hands. He scanned the paper Maxwell had drawn up. The amounts and payments were all much more reasonable. The workers could go back to having Sundays off. Dazed, he smiled in disbelief at Olivia.

"My new step-father has taken great care to help with the mine while I've been here." He saw the cautious, wary look in her eyes. "And I count it a blessing from God." The words felt true down to his bones. "A very large burden is off my shoulders." Ian saw the faces of the children watching him. "Did any of you leave me some apple pie?"

Esther rose and brought the dish to the table. Lifting the cloth, he saw there was more than half left.

"Perfect, because I'm having pie for breakfast."

Thirty-Six

The next day, Olivia gripped the back of the kitchen chair, waiting for another pot of water to warm. Esther had helped her with the tub in her room, and Ian had taken the other children out to the garden for a walk. Fighting the heavy melancholy, she prayed a hot bath would help. Tomorrow was their last day of confinement together, and Ian would move back to his own room. Would the gray cloud around her heart fade or grow worse? With Maxwell gone, then Thomas, and now Ian, would the little cottage quietly ache with their absence? Without a voice, would she be able to keep up, even have the stamina to help the children with their lessons?

"I'll get this last pot." Esther carefully put the hot pads around the handle and carried it to Olivia's room.

"Thank you," she tried to say, but only broken groans of air would be heard. Like she was addled in the brain, she often went to talk to Ian or the children before she remembered her voice was only wisps of air.

Esther emptied the pot and swirled a finger around in the tub. "Feels good." Quickly the girl turned her back. "Get in, and I can help you with your hair."

Olivia wanted to protest that she would manage somehow, but in this last week of convalescing, she'd learned to be thankful for the help offered. Dropping her things in a pile at her feet, she gingerly stepped in. Her toes and legs tingled as she curled into a ball in the tub. Closing her eyes, she felt the warmth wrap her in delightful bliss, and she let her hair sink lower. Esther lathered up the soap and ran her fingers through Olivia's hair. It felt like a lifetime ago that she'd last had help.

It had been Mrs. Torres, who had traveled with them across the prairies. She'd often helped Olivia with their limited bathing in creeks or lakes. Olivia closed her eyes as Esther rinsed out her long tresses. Nothing compared to the large tubs at her home in Chicago. A maid had always been at her disposal, bathing her, into her teens. Olivia brushed the old memories aside and finished washing. Sweet Esther stood holding the towel with her eyes closed. Olivia dried herself while Esther set out her clean things. Gathering her gown and robe, she dropped them in the warm, sudsy water and listlessly dressed in a simple gray skirt and cream blouse.

Reaching for her slate, she wrote. "Go join Mr. Beckner on the outing. I will finish my washing and dry my hair by the fire."

"Thank you, Miss Bradstreet." Esther smiled. "I think I will."

Olivia stripped her sheets and scrubbed them with her other things. As she began to wring the fabric out, her arms began to ache, and a wave of dizziness overcame her. She stepped back and sat on the bed, her heart beating rapidly. The last thing she needed was for Ian to find her passed out on the floor. Waiting another minute, she took in deep breaths until the wavering passed.

Ian had been so patient and kind, and yet, like the black smoldering wood in the fireplace, her heart grieved and crumbled at his negligence of Thomas. It was unfair for the same man to hold two such dissimilar traits. She rose carefully, taking the comb from her basin table. Entering the small parlor, she pushed the footstool closer to the fire and sat to try to untangle the long lengths of wet hair.

Ian Beckner could be caring and protective, as an honorable brother should. Yet, he held her gaze with the confidence of a lover. All she had fought to protect, her responsible headmistress reputation, seemed long lost. They'd shared a cottage this last week. He'd seen her at her very worst and still offered her his gracious touch. Her arms tired again, and she let them rest on her knees. There were no positions available for a headmistress positions without a voice. There was no place for a woman holding a slate up at the Ladies' Protection and Relief Society. She rubbed her forehead, trying to remember that she should be thankful for her life. Thankful for the three children who needed her care. She raised the comb again. Funny how easily they'd let Ian take her place. With Maxwell settled with Judith, what future did this place hold for her?

She yanked at a knot in her hair, while a familiar gnawing grated in her chest. She was born into the world without belonging to anything stable; she was always at the mercy of someone else's provision. What if she'd died? Would Maxwell have insisted on notifying Wally Bradstreet, just so he could deny her existence in the family? The comb flipped from her hand onto the floor, and she held her head. How could anyone be so tired of being so tired?

Olivia rubbed her eyes. She possessed the strength of a newborn kitten. Grumbling what sounded like hissing air, she grabbed the blanket and curled into the soft chair. Setting her hair on the outside of the chair, she took slow breaths through her nose. Her chest rose and fell until her eyes slid closed.

Olivia straightened up at a pinch in her shoulder. She blinked back the fog to see Ian sitting across from her, holding a sleeping Bonita.

"She was going to read to me," he said, low. "But the running and fresh air must have—" He stopped as Olivia slowly knelt in front of him. Gripping his leg to hold herself steady, she set the back of her hand to the child's cheek.

"No, she has no fever." He took her hand in his and smiled. "You're dressed and…" He tilted his head to the side. "And it looks as though you threw the comb to the floor in defeat."

Olivia pulled her hand away and pushed back to her seat. Fingering her dried hair, she turned to see Esther and Milton playing at the table. She pointed her finger at them.

"Checkers." Ian's brows rose. "Mine from when I was a child. We find many gifts packed into our food box."

His gaze held hers and she wished she weren't so helpless.

"We could play later if you feel up to it. I could beat you." The faintest twinkle lit his eyes, and he winked. "I mean, teach you."

"I know checkers." A sound like words actually came out. Low and breathy, but enough that she heard it.

"Very good, Miss Bradstreet." His eyes widened. "Those were words coming forth."

Olivia wanted to feel happiness, but instead, she gently held her neck. She sounded like a creature with a bone lodged in its throat.

"Let me put her on your bed, and I will make you some tea." Ian rose and set Bonita on her bed. "I'm not sure about these things on the floor." He stepped from her room, holding the laundry she'd abandoned.

Embarrassed, Olivia rose and took them from him. "My washing." She should have been happy to have faint words coming forth, but she hated the low, prickly tone that was so different from her real voice. Turning, she found the drying rack and set it next to the fire. Pulling the fabric apart, her hands quaked, and tears swelled in her eyes. Would she sound like a feeble old recluse from now on? Would she ever sing again? She patted her wet cheeks quickly. How could she be feeling sorry for herself again? God had spared her life. Why could she not snap from her despair? Without looking, she could feel Ian's presence behind her, the man radiating strength and care. Obviously he wasn't a servant meant for childcare, laundry, and waiting on her with a cup of tea. Embarrassed, she took a deep breath and turned to take the cup. "Thank you."

"Tell me." He didn't move. "Why are you crying?"

Olivia shook her head and tried to look away. She reached for the cup, but he pulled it away. "Tell me." He held her warm drink hostage. "I can understand you."

"Too many things," she croaked and swiped away a runaway tear.

He carefully put the warm cup in her hands. "I wasn't sure when you would feel up to it. But we could walk to where Thomas is."

Olivia took a sip while the thought warmed her fragmented heart. "Yes." To pay her respects and have a moment would be difficult, but she needed it. "Yes, please," she whispered.

Minutes later, the five of them stood in their jackets and scarfs around the two wintery graves. The cold breeze whipped past their coats as Ian and Olivia stood shoulder to shoulder, the girls in front of them. Olivia heard the girls' sniffled cries, and she wrapped her arms around their shoulders, holding them close. Ian pulled Milton in front of him and did the same.

"I remember the words of comfort at my father's funeral." Ian exhaled, eyes rising above the tree line. "Jesus said he would prepare a place for us. It will be a mansion in heaven with many rooms and streets of gold." The children looked up at him. "Jesus would be there and those who we love who have left the earth will be there also. One day we'll be together."

"My ma and pa too." Bonita nodded quickly.

"Yes." Ian reached over and stroked her cheek.

Gently, Olivia felt his arm around her back, holding her. "Children, would you like to say anything?" he asked.

"We miss you." Milton nodded with his head down.

"Be good in heaven," Bonita sniffed. Esther turned and buried her face in Olivia's coat.

"God will bless you and keep you," Olivia whispered faintly. "Forevermore."

Olivia could feel the sway in her body, likely from the length of the walk or the emotion of the moment, but nothing would make her move. The huddle of arms and sniffles was like warm oil rubbed into her limbs, and she wanted to soak in these hallowed minutes. Earlier, she'd felt like an abandoned ship adrift, but at this moment, though she stood at the grave of dear Thomas, she felt surrounded by safety. *How could that be?* The cold wind pulled a strand of hair loose, and she pulled it back from her eyes. They all needed each other and shared the same grief. Holding each other tight seemed the only proper response.

What if Ian wasn't this kind of man? What if grief wasn't allowed to be shown and comforted?

"We love you!" A woman's voice rang out from behind them. Standing under a group of trees were Judith, Katy, the children, and the Cornish women. Olivia and her housemates turned to see them smiling and waving.

"So glad to have you back, Miss Bradstreet," Mrs. Kitt hollered and waved.

New tears sprang to Olivia's eyes, and her mouth hung open. Her eyes searched each face like she hadn't seen them in years, beautiful smiles radiating love and concern. Thankfully she really had no words. She waved back as the tears streaked down her face. Wondering if her heart would burst from within her chest, she stared at Ian. He nodded and smiled back at the well-wishers and then locked eyes with her.

A hundred feelings smoldered in between his dark lashes, and she could not look away. His jaw rocked to the side, and he swallowed his own emotion. Light raindrops began to fall, but he never broke his gaze.

"Olivia, I'm in love with you."

Thirty-Seven

B onita and Esther skipped back to the cottage as the light rain began to fall. Milton walked between them, and Ian knew he should take Olivia's arm. After waving to the women, she turned quickly and kept her eyes on the path, not slowing or showing any sign of needing his help. Had his declaration shocked her? She'd just given him a tender expression—had he just thought those words in his head? His mind, a nice safe place without speech—*evidently not.*

Olivia was obviously touched by the show of love from the women. Weren't his words just a natural extension of the warm sentiments? He went to reach past Olivia to open the door, but she pushed it open herself.

"I need to rest." Her faint words barely made a sound, but her closed bedroom door spoke loud enough. Just like the impulsive kiss when he barely knew her. He was an imbecile at the romantic arts. The woman was only a week out from her death bed. Ian hung up his coat and pressed his fingers through his damp hair. Couldn't he have waited a week or two to make a declaration like that? Shaking his head, he bent and added another log to the fire.

"Play checkers, Mr. Beckner?" Milton asked.

"Sure." Ian walked to the small kitchen table with him. Anything to keep his mind off what he'd just done.

Weak and shaking in the knees, Olivia laid her coat and scarf over her chair and sat on the edge of her bed. Was it the walk? Of course not. A driving energy surged within her, thrilling and erratic. She stood and paced in a small circle. Now to get her heart to stop pounding. Taking her towel, she lightly pressed the rain from her loose hair. Ian Beckner was in love with her? Her body swayed. She sat, pulling off her boots. Did she hear those words right? *He did say* my *name, didn't he?*

A strange impulse made her step to her bureau and pick up her hand mirror. Pulling her high collar down, she inspected the scar at her throat. Moving the mirror back, she noticed the dark circles under her eyes, looming above sunken cheeks. The unkempt hair lay loose around her shoulders. How could she have known that someone would see them at the gravesite and alert the others?

Going back to sit on the bed, she hunched over herself. What was wrong with Ian? He was in love with frail, speechless Olivia? She could barely have held his attention when he'd first came to Oak Street, but the night of the fire, he'd given her his shirt. A wispy groan escaped. *Any man would do that.* Their dinner in Sacramento had been special, although he'd talked over an hour about the mine and his plans for the future. Now he'd been away from his first love for a week. The driven man was homebound and addled by such tight quarters.

She grabbed the blanket and laid across her bed. Just like her, he was out of his normal routine, and with such unusual isolation, strange things could happen. She filled her lungs with a few deep breaths. Besides, he still thought the Bradstreet money would come with her hand in marriage. A novel way to help the Empire mine succeed. Without the Oak Street home to sell, it was the next rational means to his ends.

She had nothing to offer and no one but Maxwell knew she was not a true Bradstreet, with no dowry. She covered her face with her hands, trying to settle her hasty conclusions. Ian had said nothing about marriage. She was the one who'd duped everyone into thinking they were engaged.

Olivia released her face and dug her fingers into her scalp. In her heart, she truly cared for him and found him generous in comfort and care. When he touched her, warmth flooded over her being, feathery and stirring. The intense longing she saw beneath his long, dark lashes frightened her. Those piercing blue-gray eyes undid her at times, and she could get lost in them for days if she allowed herself the freedom. Gripping her fingers together, she bumped her knuckles against her forehead. *Stop now, stop now. This is no way to rest.*

"Mr. Beckner," Milton exclaimed. "This is the third game I've won." A light shone on the boy's face as he swiped Ian's last piece off the board, stacking his plunder proudly on top of the rest of the checkers.

Ian leaned back in his chair. "I'm suffering from lack of concentration." He dropped his hands onto the table. "I accept defeat." He stood and looked over the things he used to make Olivia tea. What was he to say next? A proposal seemed forced even in his eyes. Could he handle another rejection? He lifted the lid off a pot of stew that Mary Ellen had dropped by earlier. "I'm getting hungry," he said out loud as he added new wood to the cookstove. "Esther, could you peek in on Miss Bradstreet? See if she will join us?" He watched out of the corner of his eye as the girl opened the door slowly and then held it closed.

"I think she is sleeping."

"Well enough." Something unsettling clenched inside him. He'd opened the door to his feelings, taking a wild leap of faith. Even though they came straight from his heart to his mouth, they were as real and true as the sun in the sky and the stars at night. This powerful revelation was a lot to hear so he would practice patience and tolerance while he waited to hear her reaction to his declaration. If she would have him, he would love her without limits all his days. If she did not return his feelings… He held the lid and stirred the heating food. He…he…didn't know what he would do.

Olivia slept some, and as the afternoon flickered into low shadows, she could hear muffled talking at the table. Her stomach growled for food. She'd promised Maxwell she would eat. She rose and fingered at her hair, pulling the sides back with two combs. Maybe her stomach churned at the prospect of seeing Ian Beckner? This was their last night together to play house with their three children. She repressed a groan. Her own self-mocking did not help. Could they get through it with simple cordiality?

Breathing deep, she brushed the front of her skirt down and opened the door. The group at the table turned to her.

"Miss Bradstreet." Bonita popped off her chair. "We divided up the last of the apple pie, and we didn't eat your piece!" She took Olivia's hand and pulled her to the small table. Ian rose without looking at her and began to stir a pot on the stove.

"How are you feeling?" he asked, only turning for a second.

"Rested." Her voice was but a whisper. "Thank you."

"Please take my seat. I'm done." Ian scooped something warm into a bowl.

Olivia sat slowly. He seemed like the old Ian—postured, distant.

"Milton, could you get Miss Bradstreet what she wants to drink?"

Milton stood up. "What may I get you, Miss Bradstreet?"

"Water will be fine. Thank you, Milton." She rasped.

He poured her a glass and set it before her. "Mr. Beckner and I played checkers this afternoon." He smiled. "I beat him three games in a row."

"Truly?" Her brows rose as Ian brought a bowl for her.

Milton plopped back in his chair. "He said he was distracted."

Ian held the bowl an inch from the table while he closed his eyes, shook his head, and finally set it down.

"Possibly you were just superior at the game, Milton." Ian rubbed a spot between his eyebrows. "Children, let's let Miss Bradstreet eat in peace."

Olivia took a small bite of food to hide her smile.

"Can you play that music thing?" Bonita asked as they settled a few feet away, in the front room.

Ian grabbed the guitar and set it on his knee. Had the instrument been there all along, or did someone bring it today? She took another bite. The stew was warm and tasty. Ian strummed a few chords, and Olivia tried to face the kitchen. The gentle sound of him playing filled the small cottage with a dreamy lightness. It was impossible to ignore the river of delicate memories. Olivia let out a long breath. The peaceful music soothed her taut emotions. She took a long drink of water. Had he asked for the guitar on purpose? Did he know that this gentle, reflective side of him would melt her into a puddle?

Ian allowed each child to hold the guitar and put their fingers on the strings. Listening to the simple lessons and taking calming breathes between bites, Olivia finished her stew and rose to do the dishes. The thought of never being able to sing again went through her mind and her hands froze. Every gift that made her mother proud, she had lost. The tears rose quickly and she brushed her sleeve across her damp face. Before she could feel another wave of grief, the children's plucking distracted her. The playful voices suddenly broke out into several songs they had sung the night of the fundraiser in Sacramento. Making the farm animals sounds and a few added silly ones, their sweet, childish voices filled the small guest cottage. Olivia slowed her washing and drying, feeling as if God was nudging her to find rest for her soul. Whatever it was, it felt deep and gloriously intimate, similar to the feeling of love the women and children displayed this morning at the gravesite.

I have not left you, nor forsaken you.

Letting the words take residence in her mind, she took a steady breath and turned to smile at their delightful antics.

An hour later, the children said their prayers and laid down for the night on the floor. After kissing each one on the cheek, Olivia rose and went to the candle-lit kitchen to make a cup of hot tea. Ian sat at the table and rubbed his hand over the wood.

"You know I will return to the mine at daybreak." He looked up at her.

Olivia nodded, chewing on her bottom lip.

"Are you concerned?" He studied her. "I know my mother or Mary Ellen would like to come and stay with you."

Olivia shrugged. "I'll be fine," she whispered.

"You'll rest when you are tired?" He pulled the chair out for her to sit. "The girls are old enough to mind themselves."

She sat, her brows furrowed. When had he become the expert on little girls? "Where will Milton be?"

"With me or Mrs. Hocking."

Olivia slowly rotated the mug in her hand. "I don't know," she said, hushed.

"He'll not be put to work at the mine. I promised you that."

"The children..." Her words, her point sounded pathetic, coming from such a weak voice. "Need to be in school."

Ian leaned back. "Olivia, I know you come from wealth and privilege. It would be a grand benefit for all children to be educated as such, but I've helped Milton with the lessons you provided. He can read and do sums better than Mr. Wright." He ticked his jaw down, eyeing her. "That is a testament to the education you and Sister Patricia provided at the Oak Street Home. And..." He nodded back to where the children slept, his voice softening. "I think you should allow the Hockings to adopt Milton. He feels responsible for what happened to Thomas. He needs to know they still want him. They're good people, and they want to love him." A long silence hung in the thick air as he waited. "Will you allow that?"

Olivia stared at the stove, holding her fingers over her mouth while a hundred emotions pelted her. She could prove to the boy that her love was enough. What if she could find a large home where they would have beds instead of pallets on the floor? A loving schoolmarm to develop his intellect, and other children to be friends with? A chance to be something beside a miner?

The air now hung heavy over her shoulders.

God hadn't left her or forsaken her. She pinched her chin. But without a voice she would never return to the confident young headmistress she'd once been. The displaced children needed an advocate, and she couldn't communicate or procure the job. The double edged sword of heartache and disability sank deep into her marrow. As Ian reached for her arm, she allowed his comfort for a split second before she nodded once to him and moved to her room. The entire day and now evening had been overwhelming, and she didn't want to cry in front of Ian Beckner.

Thirty-Eight

Olivia laid in bed listening to a quiet rustling the next morning as the increasing rays of orange and blue came up over the Empire property. The front door clicked closed, and she rose to look out her window. Ian had a box of his things under one arm and the guitar in the other. Milton jogged alongside him like a boy wanting to keep up with his father. Except Ian Beckner wasn't his father. He was the sole owner and boss over the Empire Mine. Since the moment he'd arrived with the Cornish people, everything in her life had gone to shambles. Olivia leaned her head into the window frame. Unfortunately, *everything* included her heart.

The next three evenings at dusk, Ian walked Milton back to the guest cottage. He didn't try and talk to her or negotiate Milton moving in with the Hockings. Maybe he knew to leave well enough alone for now.

Katy had invited the Olivia and the girls to lunch in the kitchen today. It was wonderful to see how well the other children had fared in Katy's care. But after the children ran outside to play, Judith and Katy peppered her with questions of how she was doing, and soon her weak voice faded to a frog's croak. Embarrassed, she nodded or held her throat so they would hold the conversation without her.

Judith mentioned in passing that Milton had gone to Grass Valley with Ian today. Though he'd rarely spoken of the mine with her, at least he was keeping his promise to keep Milton from the danger. Fatigued from straining her voice, Olivia tried to gather Esther and Bonita, but they begged to stay a little longer, and Mary Ellen promised to walk them home. Olivia acquiesced and tucked her arms across her chest, walking down the path alone.

Hearing something, Olivia looked up and squinted. Was that Ian and his black buggy? But who was the man in the long dark cloak? Her heart jumped and her feet hurried—had something happened to Milton?

"Miss Bradstreet." Ian nodded as she approached. "This is Father Dalton, from the Grass Valley St. Patrick's church."

Olivia blinked at the short man of thirty or so and finally gave him a small curtsy.

"I had a minute to talk to him about your work at the Oak Street Home and your time with the Sisters of Charity." Ian eyed her. "Because conveying so much information would tax your throat, I told him of the work you did and your help in Sacramento. I mentioned the house fire and your recent illness. I hope you don't mind me speaking up about the care and effort you've given your work."

Olivia glanced back and forth at the two men, still confused. "A pleasure to meet you, sir," she whispered. He might as well know how poorly she sounded. "Where is Milton?" she asked Ian.

"He saw the other children in the big house. He's playing with them." The soft glimmer in Ian's eyes made her question what he was up to now.

"Can we go in and sit a moment?" Ian asked as he held the door open to the small cottage. She eyed him warily as she passed. Olivia suddenly noticed the blankets and empty cups, the evidence of her neglect of the messy little home. She quickly grabbed the items and tucked them next to the soft chair. Ian took her arm. "He knows you've been recently recovering. Give me your coat and come sit."

"I asked Father Dalton if he would share about the new work starting in Grass Valley." Ian waited to sit until Olivia and Father Dalton had.

Olivia, still confused at the reason for the visit, jumped up again. "Forgive me, may I provide some refreshments?" she rasped. "Tea or coffee?"

"No, thank you." Father Dalton nodded.

Why had Ian brought him here? She sat back down slowly, trying not to judge the situation. Why would this man want to hear her story and listen to her burdens? Did Ian want the children to go? They no longer felt like orphans in need. Did people think they were too much for her? She knew Ian didn't deserve to be thrust into sole guardianship and the role of her caregiver and nurse, but she was doing better now…

"So, as Mr. Beckner stated, I've been in Grass Valley for over a year," Father Dalton smiled and continued. "Bishop O'Connell heard reports of the mining accidents in our area. These mining towns have filled with people from faraway countries and cultures, yet, without their immediate family structures, many children are left fatherless or parentless. You know this well from your experience with the Sisters of Charity." His brow crinkled and Olivia felt her stomach clench. "St. Patrick's church is almost completed on South Street. That will allow us to begin on the rectory and a cottage for the nuns and children." Father Dalton glanced at Ian. "Mr. Beckner spoke to the wonderful work you did in Sacramento… and…"

Suddenly it hit her, and her alarmed thoughts drowned out Father Dalton's words. Ian was finding her a new position. He wanted her and the children out from underfoot. She hadn't returned his declaration of love and now she was a burden. With what had happened to Thomas, the children needed to be gone. Father Dalton continued to talk of the buildings and needs, but it all became so clear. How had she missed the glaring truth?

Her identity had been a lie for twenty-four years. Rules and decency were for a reason; even unknowingly, a lie could not marry a Hastings doctor. She could only remember Ronald in fading images. There could be no blessed union with a Bradstreet, because she was a false Bradstreet. Her brother had known the lie all along and he could no longer live with it. He'd had to kick her out. She'd had to leave her home and everything she'd ever known, traveling to the west. But it wasn't far enough to outrun her false identity.

She could never have kept her Oak Street position. She'd lived a lie as Headmistress Olivia Bradstreet. It also had to go. Why hadn't she changed her name? What would it be? Olivia Smith, or Olivia Johnson? But weren't those lies too? How would she ever live in truth without ever knowing her father's name—or even her mother's, for that matter?

"So, the first set of children were from Shasta County." Father Dalton was still speaking, but Olivia only heard pieces. "The most miserable little creatures—blind, lame, and poverty-stricken in the extreme."

Is that why she did not die from diphtheria? Had God spared her from hell? How could she enter the everlasting glory without her own identity? What did the Lord expect now? She would still never know her origin or where someone like her belonged. What did Father Dalton want her help for? She held back a whimper. A trapped animal panic gripped her body. She could not outlive her lie and she couldn't create a new one to cover the old. Where did that leave her?

"Olivia? Are you all right?" Ian's firm grip over her hand made her suck in a deep breath. "You seem upset."

She pulled her hand away, fighting to withhold pained tears. Everywhere she went, misfortune followed. Everywhere she found peace, she had to be pushed out. Ian Beckner was only the latest; he could no longer be with her. He was too good and kind… he deserved so much more.

"When do you want me to go?" she whispered, dashing the tears from her cheeks in an impatient motion.

"Whenever you want." Ian scowled at her, speaking slowly. "Only if you want to help."

Olivia reached for a cloth on the table and dabbed more embarrassing tears from the corner of her eyes.

Ian rolled his tongue against the inside of his cheek as he studied her. "Father Dalton, would you be so patient to give us a moment?" Ian rose and pulled Olivia's elbow up with him. "We will be back with you shortly." Holding her hand tight, he tugged her out the front door and closed it behind them.

"This isn't the first, nor likely the last." He sighed and closed his blue-gray eyes. "Really, with my whole heart, I thought I was doing something good, but I am obviously not." He huffed, scratching his chin. "I thought you would welcome a chance to help them."

Olivia's eyes fell, heavy, and then rose to see where the full blooming garden once was. How dare the sunshine break in this cold winter day. "They don't want my help," she whispered. "I can ask Maxwell. He'll help me find a new place to go." She swallowed the lump in her throat. *Far away from people.*

"What?" Ian tucked his chin. "You don't need to go anywhere." His warm hand rose and rested along her neck. His fingers lightly massaged her hairline. "Look at me." Ian gave her a concerned smile. "I think you misunderstood Father Dalton. He needs someone with connections. He's asking you about the fundraising you did in Sacramento. He needs help with provisions, blankets, and cots. Did you hear me tell him they could have the cookstove from the Oak Street home?"

Olivia chided herself, she'd been lost in her own thoughts. "How am I to help, when I can barely speak?"

Ian gently brushed his thumb along her damp cheek. "Can you write letters? Can you create your own Ladies' Protection and Relief Society here? I know my mother would be of help." The soft encouragement in his words nearly undid her.

Now she felt childish and foolish. "Of course."

"Only if you want to." Ian bit on his front lip. "Did I overstep? Is it asking too much with your recent recovery? You seemed upset."

Olivia's head fell to the side. "I didn't listen very well. I...I...thought you were finding me a job, wanting me to move on."

A strange sound came from the back of his throat, and his head bumped back. "Olivia." He brought his face in close to hers and gripped her arms until her shoulders rose. "That is the last thing I want."

She still could not look at him, and his kind reassurance didn't change the way her false identity came to interfere with her every step. "Let's go back in."

Excusing herself by saying she needed to take notes, Olivia asked Father Dalton to repeat the greatest of his needs and gathered the addresses of where people could send donations. They discussed a social celebration as soon as the church was completed. Bringing out the people in the new town of Grass Valley would bring awareness to the church's needs. They would meet at St. Patrick's in a week. Before Ian took Father Dalton home, they found Judith at the big stone house. She was able to donate six blankets and a box of food.

Needing to gather the children back to the cottage, Olivia couldn't help but watch Ian's buggy pull away. Like a bud of hope appearing from frozen ground, she realized not she, but the people and resources at Empire Mine, could be the greatest help in seeing Father Dalton's work grow and succeed.

Thirty-Nine

O livia fingered the stack of blank paper on the table. As the secretary for the Ladies' Protection and Relief Society, she'd taken pages of detailed notes. Every idea, person, or business of substance was on those notes. She shook her head. Every word, burnt to ash in the fire. Where could she possibly begin? Bonita sat at the table, reading her early reader book aloud to Esther. They'd all adapted, and she could either let discouragement win the day or just start over with the notes she'd received from Father Dalton. She could reward herself with a letter to Sister Patricia. She could spell out her ideas and ask her what she thought would work. Dropping the quill in the ink, she started with the most important things to go over with Father Dalton on Friday.

After an hour of working on her notes and letter to Sister Patricia, she stopped to fix the girls a simple lunch. They ate and chatted about going outside, but Olivia knew she had one more letter to write. Helping the girls with the water, Esther and Bonita wanted to do the dishes, so she sat back at the table and took a clean piece of paper.

Dearest Ian,

I can't explain the humble gratitude I feel for all you've done for me. A simple 'thank you' doesn't seem fitting for the measure of time and sacrifice you took to see me well. You are a man of great patience, and seeing to others' wellbeing above yourself is quite honorable. Olivia paused. He *was* noble in his care for her, just as he was for the needs of the mine, the children, or the Cornish people. It seemed to lessen the pressure of his love for her being his main interest. He took time and concern in everything he did. Taking a breath, she dipped her pen.

In light of the kindness you have shown me, I apologize for any difficulty I have caused you. I really do wish for the success of the mine. You were right about the Cornish people, they exhibit such stalwart strength.

Olivia dipped her chin. What she'd planned to be a simple thank you note was turning into a confessional. Should she say something about meeting with Mrs. Hocking today?

I pray in all things that you would prosper as your soul prospers.

That Bible passage sounded kind without personal emotions.

Respectfully,

The word was dull and lifeless. For heaven's sake, she'd allowed the man to kiss her. But *yours truly* sounded too forward, and she'd made no other mistakes to justify starting the letter over. Olivia huffed. It would have to do.

Olivia

"All right, girls, let's grab our coats and go for a walk." Olivia waited for the ink to dry before she folded it in fourths.

Milton ran up to the mine's office door and flung it open. Ian would have to ask the boy not to shake the walls just by entering.

"Mr. Beckner. Security Agent Milton reporting." Milton stood stiff and tall. "We have a strange sighting at the mine and I think you would want to know."

Ian stood, his chair scraping against the wood floor. What now? A strange sighting? It couldn't be animals, usually the noise of the stamp mill scared them away. Milton had a glimmer in his eye. What was the boy up to now? Just as Ian was about to ask, Milton was already running out the door.

Ian pulled on his jacket and glanced at Maxwell. They both looked curiously at each other before he went to see what all the commotion was about. As his hand griped the handle, his heart jumped from his chest. Through the thick glass, Olivia Bradstreet, in a full gray skirt, warm brown coat, and bonnet, walked his way, flanked by two girls and one excited boy. How could he blame Milton? It was indeed a sighting worth remarking upon. Ian brushed his fingers through his hair and stepped out, wishing his heart would stop pounding at his ribs.

"Olivia." Beyond her stunning beauty, just saying her name brought a sweet sensation. "What do we have here? An outing to the mine?"

"Just a delivery." She handed him a letter. "And then a stroll to see Mrs. Hocking."

"Mr. Beckner," Milton interrupted. "Can I show the girls the stamp mill?"

"I…" Ian glanced at Olivia. "If we walk behind them?"

"I suppose." She scanned the mine area. "Children." She lowered her gaze onto them. "You are to stay together and stay where we can see you at all times."

"Yes, Miss Bradstreet." They all nodded and linked arms.

"I work here. I do security," Milton explained as they walked away.

"And what is this letter?" Ian held it up. "An appeal to the mine owner? Perhaps for support of the new Grass Valley Ladies' Protection and Relief Society?" He offered his elbow, and she took it as they walked behind the children. Olivia had taken it upon herself to come to the mine office to see him. He wondered if anything could compare to this moment. Her skirts brushed his leg, and she lifted a coy smile.

"No, just a thank you note."

"For me?" His brows narrowed.

"Yes, for you." Olivia kneaded her fingers into his arm. She seemed nervous, or unsure. His own nerves gave way to silence while the mine buzzed all around them.

"Your voice seems stronger. You mentioned making a social call to Mrs. Hocking?" he asked.

She glanced up at him and then sighed, watching the children. "I had a talk with Milton last night—about his future," she said wistfully. "He said something, and I guess it is haunting me." She bit her lip.

"What is it?" Ian stopped and turned to look at her.

"Milton said he couldn't remember his parents' faces anymore." She fingered her jacket collar, tilting her head to the side. "It's not shocking, he was only four or five when they died." She pulled back close to his side, and they walked a few more steps. "I want the Hockings to adopt him, legally, so he will be Milton Hocking all his days. I want him to have names and faces he will always remember."

Ian met her eyes. Without him thinking, his elbow straightened, and his hand slipped down and over hers. He'd also grown attached to the boy, but believed it would serve him well to belong to their family. Slowly he raised their hands, watching her. Her arm was warm, tucked in with his, and he kissed the back of her hand. "I know this is difficult. Why don't I keep the children in the office while you two women speak?"

Olivia knew she should pull away. He stood there practically caressing her in front of a busy mine yard. Guilt riddled her for writing Ian such a lackluster, impersonal note. She should have a talk with him, but this sweet care was only making things harder. Her misfortune need not become his. Hadn't she just planned to deliver his letter and move to the Cornish shanties?

"Olivia?" His voice snapped her to attention. "I've wanted my actions to be appropriate and above board. It was hard for me to leave you and the children behind in the cottage alone, but I didn't want anyone seeing me coming and going, thinking ill of you or your reputation."

"Thank you," she mumbled, sensing there was more he wanted to say.

"Would Saturday evening work for you to come to dinner with me? We could dine at the big house. We can have Judith and Maxwell there too." He waited. "Or we could take supper in town?"

"I don't know." She turned to watch the children.

Ian dropped her hand and stiffened. "The day we walked to see the gravesite. I know it was impetuous, Olivia, but I hope you were listening, because I meant every word. I'm very much in love with you."

A tempered squeak escaped. Why was he bringing this up now? Her feet felt the urge to run, and run far. How could she explain to him that life was not going to allow her to live or love in a lie? She turned and gripped his thick upper arm. "Because I care about you, Ian..." Her hand brushed down his jacket sleeve. "I have to speak the truth." Swallowing hard, she pierced him with her eyes. "I am not who you think I am. No matter how much I care for you, I cannot lead you to believe we could have a future. After all the kindness and forbearance..." She tried to hold back the soft ache in her words. "After all you've done." She gave him a sad smile and touched his cheek. "I am not the woman for you."

"Look, Miss Bradstreet!" Bonita called out, running to them. "I think this might have gold in it." She shoved a rock up between them. "Mr. Beckner, can you put it on the big wheel, smash it and see?"

Ian stood back and blinked. "I think the stamp would crush it to powder."

She couldn't avert her eyes from his pained daze. In one quick drop now she'd crushed him. "I'm sorry. I never wanted to hurt you." She tried to breathe in. "I would hope we could continue as friends."

"I have enough friends." His face darkened. "And I certainly don't need the kind who tell me what is good for me."

"The girls are going to the shanties." Milton tugged on Ian's jacket. "Could I take a break and go too?"

His narrow, hawk-like expression finally turned down to the boy. "Yes, go ahead." Snorting something inaudible, he turned so quickly to leave Olivia could feel the cool air in his wake.

"Girls." Olivia reached out and held each one to her side. To make it to the shanties she would need their steady presence. How could she have said those words any different? It was the only right thing to do. He'd been led astray by Lesandra, but she would never do that. Was it naïve to think they could be friends, to be civil from a distance? She clutched the girls closer, for at any step she might just crumble into pieces.

Forty

Is mind whirling, Ian entered the mine office and tried to swallow the sand in his throat. *Women. Forget it all.* He was tired of being duped, over and over. He dropped a ledger on his desk harder than he realized.

"The stroll with Olivia didn't go well?" Maxwell asked.

Ian pulled her letter from his pocket and tossed it on top of the ledger. "You might as well know, I've fallen in love with your Miss Bradstreet." He moved some papers on his desk. "The woman is solely the most endearing, loving, beautiful woman, I know."

"Okay." Maxwell let the silence linger for a moment. "I'd wondered how false this engagement really was."

Ian didn't hear a word. "She claims she is *not* the woman for me. That she's not who she says she is." Cross, Ian turned a piercing gaze on Maxwell. "Maybe *you* could elaborate?" Before Maxwell could open his mouth, Ian started in. "Was she a circus performer in Chicago?" he mocked, shaking his head. "Did she lie about being engaged to your son? Is the name Olivia Bradstreet stolen from a scandalous theater actress?"

Maxwell rose and rubbed his finger across his ear. "Not exactly."

Ian stopped and searched his face. "What do you mean, 'not exactly'? I was being facetious. She is adamant about her reputation. The young lady would find an untied shoe socially unacceptable." He shook his head and searched out the front window. Of course, there was no sight of Olivia and her orphans. She'd plenty of love and forbearance for them and none for him?

"It's not my story or past to tell," Maxwell interrupted his justified anger. "But I will tell you, it wasn't of her choosing. It was done to her."

Ian turned and steeled his gaze on Maxwell. "Sweet heavens above, someone took advantage of her?"

"Not physically." Maxwell tapped his finger on his desk before sitting in his chair.

Ian felt his fiery ire leave his being. *Something was done to her?* Maybe it wasn't purely her rejecting him. Did she believe he deserved a wife of a higher standard? Somehow that seemed almost comical. It was clear for everyone to see that he was a lowly, struggling, inept mine owner. What if she revealed something from her past that he did not want to hear? Would it taint what he felt for her?

Quietly, he sat back at his desk and stared at the letter. Opening it, he read it over three times. She was clearly thankful and spoke to his qualities. With beautiful script, gracious but guarded, like someone handing you pyrite when you expected gold, her words were suitable but nothing of true value.

Ian dropped his elbows to his desk and rubbed at the tension between his eyes. Though she was friendly and cordial, maybe she could never love him after what happened with Thomas.

"I'd many a reason to stop pursuing your mother." Maxwell quickly tilted his head to the side. "You being at the top of the list."

Ian felt the barb.

"But I've never been so glad that I didn't give up." Maxwell looked down and took back up what he had been doing.

Funny how a few minutes ago his anger was all he wanted to feed on, but Maxwell had unassumingly brought a new view. What if there was some reason why she believed she wasn't right for him? Maybe he hadn't told her that as his wife she could work, volunteer. What if she thought he would never accept the girls? Had he told her both of them had wormed their way right into his heart? He'd be lying if he said the thought of becoming their father hadn't crossed his mind more than a few times.

Since the day he'd moved out of the guest cottage, the mine hadn't been enough anymore. He wanted the chatter, the entertainment of a family to come home to. Glancing over at Maxwell working, he realized he'd been a fool about many things. His mother was still young and wanted a companion. How could he not have seen how much Maxwell meant to her? Instead of harming the mine, Maxwell had only been a benefit, likely rescuing it from ruin.

Ian rubbed his hand over his face and sent up another pitiful prayer. Thankfully, the God of creation knew all about prodigals and tangled souls. *Help me find a way to Olivia. And give me patience when I don't understand.*

"You'd said you would take Olivia to Grass Valley on Friday?" Ian asked Maxwell, rubbing his jaw.

"Yes, but…am I too… busy?" Maxwell tempered a crooked smile.

"If you don't mind."

"Not at all. Your mother and I hoped that with Olivia's recovery, there would be no need to announce a broken engagement."

Ian tried to sort through those words. How do you announce a broken engagement if there never was a real one? He let out a long breath and wondered. With a little digging and more patience, would her feelings for him ever turn from pyrite to gold?

On Friday morning, Olivia walked the girls into the big house kitchen to find Katy cleaning and Mary Ellen churning butter.

"There they are." Katy turned to greet Esther and Bonita. "Two extra hands for the day." She smiled, taking the girls' coats.

"You stay as long as you need, Miss Bradstreet," Katy chuckled. "I got lots for these girls to do."

"I should be only an hour or so." Olivia felt a rattle of nerves. So many ideas to pass by Father Dalton. She hadn't listened very well last time, but she'd admonished herself to pay attention this time. She was excited to see the new church and meet the nuns who worked with him.

"Did you see Judith and Maxwell at breakfast?" Olivia asked. "Maxwell said he would drive me this morning."

Mary Ellen stopped pumping the handle up and down. "When I came in with the milk, someone was out in the barn pulling the buggy out."

"Thank you." Olivia smiled. "Girls, please be polite and obey." She kissed them on the forehead and walked out the back door.

Bending forward, a man finished hitching up the harness to the buggy. Olivia took in a fresh breath, the hay and new morning dew bringing a lightness to her step. As he straightened up and led the horse backward, Olivia froze.

"Ian?" She searched the area. Maxwell was nowhere in sight. "What are you doing?" They'd not spoken or seen each other since the day at the mine office a week ago.

"Maxwell had things to do this morning. So, I volunteered to take you to town."

Something did not feel right. He didn't sound overly enthused, but why should he? The joy of the morning quickly evaporated.

He came up next to her and offered his hand. "Are you ready?"

"Maybe I should wait until Maxwell is free. I know you must have other things you need to do more important than this."

"Must you tell me what I need and don't need?" His brows drew together. "Do I look that feeble-minded?"

Olivia felt her jaw start to clench.

"Just take my hand, Olivia."

Unsure, she slowly took his hand, and he helped her into the buggy's seat. As soon as he was sitting next to her, she was overly aware of his unreadable presence. He likely wanted this time to question her decision to keep him at arm's length. As the buggy pulled out of the driveway, her heart thudded. Right now, a friendship seemed highly unlikely.

"How have you been?" he asked, watching the road.

"Very well, thank you." She could play this game. The man knew he was imposing and impossible to ignore.

"You have some ideas for Father Dalton?"

"I do." Straightening her back, she clutched the papers on her lap.

"Do you want me to participate in the meeting?" he asked.

"I...I...don't see why. Do you want to?" Was this his attempt to be a friend? Somehow it didn't feel that way.

"No, I trust you will do better without me. It seemed the same way at the Oak Street home." He tapped the reins as they took a wider road.

Not a compliment, she guessed. "How are things at the mine?"

"Very well, thank you." He lifted a wry smile and she knew he was mimicking her.

She rolled her eyes to the left. Somehow, she liked his dark and surly side better than this.

"I know you are provoking me, Ian." *Oh, this man! Enough was enough.*

He jerked back. "What?"

"Was Maxwell really too busy?" She twirled a finger in front of his face. "I know when I left you last you were angry. In fact, you said you needed no friends like me. So, what are you doing now?" She unlocked her eyes from his as the small buildings of Grass Valley came into sight. Ian led the horse around another wagon turning into the side street.

The new wood-sided church with a door in the middle and two long glass windows on each side, came into view. Olivia almost forgot what she was saying as she noticed the small sign, *St. Patrick's Parish*, in front. "Goodness, the Empire Home is larger than this." Somehow it seemed too rustic, missing stained glass or a feeling of holiness. She swallowed as Ian set the brake. It just wasn't what she was expecting.

"Can I mention that when you are riled up…" He turned to her. "…your voice returns to its normal volume." He pressed a frown. "I was thinking all the yelling at me would be done on a slate in giant letters." He jumped off his side of the buggy before she could expel a gravelly groan. Coming to her side, he held out that brash hand that was attached to the brash rogue she knew he could be.

"Did you volunteer to drive just to unnerve me?" She stood, hands on her hips, waiting for a response. He grasped her waist with both his hands and tugged her forward.

Ian blinked. Looking up, his gaze held hers with sincerity. "No." He supported her weight as he lifted her from the buggy. *Why didn't he move away, blast it?* His piercing blue eyes and overt masculinity radiated from his close proximity.

"I wanted to talk about us." He nodded to the small church and finally relaxed his hold on her. The fresh-cut pine scent still carried on the light morning breeze. "I'll wait here until you are done."

His voice was so calm and serious all Olivia could do was nod once. Taking in a steady breath, she raised her skirts in one hand and her papers in the other. She wished she could say she was a stranger to the feeling swirling inside her as she walked to the little church, but once again, being anywhere near Ian Beckner undid her, leaving little solid ground under her steps.

Forty-One

An hour later, Olivia thanked Father Dalton. He'd given her a tour of all the land and places they planned to expand. He had great vision and was a generous man who appreciated her ideas and talent for reaching out to the budding gold town. They set dates for the Grass Valley community opening of the church and three more dates for charitable fundraising. With Judith and the Cornish women's help, they would be well on their way to funding a school and orphanage.

Olivia stepped along the grass to see Ian leaning against the buggy with crossed ankles. The man was relentless and confusing, and surely he had more to do at the mine. Her stomach did a strange flip as their eyes met.

"How did it go?" His expression was controlled and cool.

"Well, I believe."

"I did some driving in town." He took her elbow. "There is a confection shop I thought we could stop at and try their refreshments."

Olivia stepped into the buggy and straightened her skirts. "Perhaps another time. I feel as if I've left Katy with the care of the girls too long."

"What if we were to bring them back a treat? Wouldn't they all be forgiving?"

Olivia pictured the smiles on the girls' faces at receiving a yummy surprise. Squeezing her fingers together, she smiled just enough for her small dimple to appear. "All right."

A few minutes later, Olivia stepped from the carriage, noticing the flawless blue sky. Moments like this, when she walked holding his arm, a softness came over her being. It felt so strange, like they'd been together for years. As soon as they walked into the little shop, the sweet aroma of chocolate and sweets made her body tingle in delight. "Oh, this will be too difficult." She spied the cake stands holding the various confections. "You have found my weakness," she murmured.

"I thought I was your weakness." Ian pulled her jacket from her shoulders and set it on a chair behind them. "May we have two cups of coffee?" he asked the woman behind the counter.

"You're right, I have two. Chocolate and Ian Beckner." Olivia's eyes roved back and forth. *Which one for the children and which one for herself?* Her fingers fluttered like butterflies in front of her chest. "These are little cakes." She pointed to a silver tray. "Our cook in Chicago made the most beautiful petits fours. And these are eclairs." She stepped to the side, to a small basket. "Wrapped taffy and caramel? The children will love these." She knew she was rambling, but somehow, the chocolatey richness had already entered her veins.

The woman smiled and set two cups on the little round table behind them.

"Give us four of everything she's pointed to." Ian smiled at the clerk.

Olivia stood back, watching the woman place all the sweet goodness in a paper box. Ian paid and opened the box, and set it on their table with their coffee.

Her eyes widened and she bit down on a large grin.

"If I only knew this was the way to your heart, I would've brought you chocolate earlier." He reached for a small round glazed cake.

"And shopping." She took in a deep breath and reached for an éclair.

They both took bites and watched each other. Olivia felt pure bliss as the custard, mixed with a light buttery pastry and topped with chocolate frosting, melted in her mouth. The sensation assaulting her body should not be permissible, she thought as she kept her eyes from rolling upward.

Ian shook his head, watching her until he took a sip of his coffee. "I'm so sorry you don't enjoy this." A smile curved his lips as he set his cup down. "By the way, speaking of women beaming from head to toe, Mrs. Hocking came to the office to thank me." He took another bite and swallowed. "The only women I see are the thankful ones." He failed to disguise how heartfelt his next words were. "Your letter was kind and sincere."

"Thank you." She caught herself licking some chocolate off her finger, and they squinted playfully at each other. Her heart did a strange flip. Between earlier and now, there was so much more goodwill in his eyes. Her own improved mood must be the sugar affecting her. "The family will have to wait for the adoption paperwork from Sacramento." She sipped her coffee. "But Milton is so excited, and I supposed it wouldn't hurt to let him move in with them now."

Ian nodded. "And did you meet any orphans today? Find any new ones to bring home?" His magnetic blue-gray eyes teased her and held her captive at the same time. Her pulse raced at his gaze, filling her chest with those flutters. It would take only a feather of weakness to make her lean forward and kiss him for such a lovely thought.

"No." Holding her eyes closed, she folded her napkin and dropped it on the table. Her delight was fading. *She was thinking of kissing him?* He must be trying to woo her again—and it was starting to work. But the thought of handing him another painful rejection pulled her backward. The entire morning was a set up from the beginning. Something pinched in her stomach. "We really should get back." She closed the top of the box.

"Wait." He touched her hand. "I think I saw the color in your chocolate-loving cheeks pale. What just changed?"

"I can't do this with you, Ian." Pulling her coat off the back of her chair, she stood and slipped her arms in without his help. "We need to go."

Picking up the box, he had little choice but to follow her from the small shop.

Olivia pulled her skirts up and helped herself into the buggy. How dare he do this? How dare he invade her well-appointed morning? She'd purposely not asked him, because she feared something like this would happen. Just like a hundred times before, he could be kind and fetching, and then while she wasn't paying attention, she'd let her guard down and enjoy herself. He'd then expect… she growled under her breath. How could she make him understand?

A dark and cloudy picture entered her mind. "I want you to know I saw you." Her tone was harried as he stepped in. "When I was sick."

Ian held the reins steady, keeping the buggy in place. "I don't understand."

"I thought it was a dream. Like floating, I would come in and out." She rolled her lips in a line. "But the pain was very real."

Ian set his foot upon the buggy's front board, leaned back, and rubbed his hand over his jaw.

"You'd fallen asleep." She whispered. "Your head rested here." She drew her hand across her middle. "Your hands were heavy over mine." Like she could still feel the thick callouses and warm skin over hers, her skin tingled. "I could feel the burning in my throat, I slipped my hand out from yours. I wanted to touch it, make it stop, but something deep inside me knew you were protecting me from myself, so I would distract myself from the pain by feeling the strands of your hair between my fingers, and then when the floating would thicken, I tucked my hands back under yours."

Ian nodded, looking down. "I was trying to keep you from pulling the pipe out."

"Ian." She touched his sleeve, waiting until he would look at her. "Honestly, believe me, I've never known such love and sacrifice." The words squeezed in her chest, and with eyes filling, she struggled to make sense of it all.

"I did everything I could for you." His brows furrowed. "But I did it for me as well. I knew I loved you. Even before then. All I wanted was for you to live and be mine." His tone dropped lower. "Possibly more selfish than sacrificial."

His words stuck like a sword in her chest. "And that is why I cannot go on with you." She huffed. "It kills me to hurt you." Her voice cracked and she wiped her face with the back of her hand.

"Then don't hurt me." He gripped her raised elbow, pulling them closer. "Be my wife and let me be your husband. Forgive me for the disrespect I showed when I first met you. It will never happen again. Let me be a father to Esther and Bonita." His jaw clenched, and he waited for some response. "I...I...can make no sense of your excuse. To say that I don't really know you?" He released her arm and shook his head. "Here is what I know about you. You are strong." He raised his hands like a preacher proving the content of his sermon. "You are kind and smart, and somehow your loving heart overlaps with your beauty. But not really, because both take me to the edge of hope and desire until I can't sleep." He groaned and ran his fingers through his hair. "I believe with everything in me..." Looking down, he couldn't meet her gaze. "I do know you."

Olivia sank back into the buggy seat. There was no way to bring clarity to his thoughts. Her reasoning would sound like more lame excuses. Looking from left to right, she took a strained swallow. "I haven't been honest, Ian." Her hardened voice almost sounded normal. Leaning forward, she covered her face. A strange thought occurred—*tell him the truth, and then he will understand why they couldn't marry. It's the loving thing to do.*

Her back stiffened and she took a deep breath. "I am not a Bradstreet. I was not sired into the name, given an inheritance, or ever adopted. While knowing this, I've lived a lie before you and everyone."

Ian leaned his chin into his shoulder. "Then who are you?"

Her chest rose and fell in a huff. "I don't know." The fear of how ridiculous she would sound bound her with remorse. "The week after my father died—I mean, Dr. Bradstreet—my brother Wally and I were in the drawing room. I don't even know why he was so upset. He shouted that I'd been coddled and spoiled enough. He said that I'd sucked all the attention to myself and the truth needed to be told. With disdain, he said my father had found me after a woman had given birth down by the docks." Olivia pressed a finger over her lips. "Wally said I was just a dead prostitute's vermin who they'd felt sorry for. I called him a cruel liar." Her voice wavered. "But he gave detail after detail about the day they'd buried a baby girl, his real sister, who had been born dead. Two days later, my father brought an infant home and they all decided to keep it a secret to themselves— to raise me as their own. But he said it was time I knew the truth. There is no Bradstreet blood in me, and certainly no inheritance. It would be an insult to the family name."

A long silence hung in the air. Olivia felt like an empty shell. The words she'd held back for so long now exposed for judgment.

"I don't know what to say." Ian sat back, letting the reins rest on his leg. "I'm sorry you had to find out that way."

Olivia hesitated. "Maxwell is the only one who knows," she murmured. "He took me in when Wally kicked me out." She closed her eyes and shook her head. "I spent so many nights along the wagon trail to California thinking I could have done something. I wished I'd found the building where Dr. Bradstreet found me... maybe ask if anyone remembered her, just to find a name or something." She shrugged. "But it was over twenty years ago." She held her fingers over her mouth and chin looking out to the streets of Grass Valley. "When I was young, so many people said I was pretty, just like my mother." A light breeze tickled a strand of hair over her nose. "It never was true," she murmured. At least with this confession, he would understand why she could not accept his proposal.

She risked a glance at his flexed jaw as he straightened and tapped the horse forward. He'd wanted to talk about their future, and now in his silence, she knew why that could not be. Ian

Beckner would one day be a wealthy mine owner. He would need a wife who could bring forth children from a pure bloodline and represent their station well. Finally, the wretched burden was off her chest.

The truth would be the revelation Ian Beckner needed. He could freely move on.

Forty-Two

The following week, the bleak days of winter passed as Olivia left the door open while sweeping the dust from the guest cottage's front stoop. Mary Ellen skipped down the lane from the main house, and Olivia stepped out to greet her.

"A message for you." She handed Olivia a letter.

"No postage," Olivia smirked. Just the name Miss Olivia Bradstreet, written in script across the front.

"I think it's from Mr. Beckner." Mary Ellen's freckled face pursed. "But maybe I wasn't supposed to tell you that."

Olivia popped the wax and unfolded it. "I would've found out as soon as I saw his signature." She read the few lines and tapped it against her lip. "He has some news about the Oak Street home." Wondering what to do, she glanced back at the girls reading at the table. "He often doesn't leave the mine till late. Would you mind coming by after dinner and sitting with the girls while I talk with him?" She didn't want the impressionable teen to know he'd asked her to meet him in the garden. That was a bit exciting to even Olivia's thinking. But now that he knew her darkest secret, maybe he'd come to say their friendship could have a chance. Mary Ellen agreed to come back, and Olivia walked down the path with her before she turned to face the guest cottage. Funny, with the truth laid bare, her feelings toward Ian had gotten stronger. Would she be able to keep her longing for him in check? *Loneliness, that was all that it was.* Biting on the corner of her thumb, she skimmed over his note and sighed. *The garden, why the garden?*

The day and evening dragged on after the dinner dishes were washed and dried, when Mary Ellen came back. What news about the Oak Street Home could he have? The home was no more, and the mystery had chewed on her all day. She slipped her coat on and asked the girls to prepare for bed. The moon was bright as she walked down the quiet path. A strange quickening in her stomach started, and she pushed her hands against her tingling waist. It was just a talk, and just another kindness. He knew her time at Oak Street as headmistress was important.

Olivia's quiet steps halted. A strange, melodic sound drifted from ahead. Someone was strumming a guitar. "Oh, mercy above." She smiled until she took the first step down the garden path and found Ian Beckner on the bench.

"Have you been drinking, sir?"

He laughed and tried a few more notes on the strings. "No, just practicing." He moved the guitar to the side. "Come, sit by me."

A smile warmed slowly on her face and she sat watching him. "So, why choose the garden to discuss my former workplace at the Oak Street Home?" She blinked. Her heart had deliberated about their estrangement all week, hopeful for this kind of gesture, something that showed some forbearance after everything she'd confessed. "We could've talked at the main house."

He gave her a roguish grin. "I don't think so."

"Now you have my curiosity."

"And you've *always* had mine." He took her hand and held it in his. The stillness lingered as he pressed his fingers against hers. "I've thought a lot about what you said, about feeling as if you've lived a lie." He glanced up as she shook her head slowly.

"I've thought of a solution." All teasing was gone, and she knew this serious, determined expression. "But I want to ask you something first." He took in a deep breath. "If you could go back to Sacramento and take up the work there. Would you?"

Olivia pulled her hand free from his and tapped her chin. Tilting her head, she sighed. "That's too difficult to answer. I've just committed to helping Father Dalton. I...I...don't know." Picturing Bonita and Esther uprooted from their home didn't feel right. What would Katy say to taking Mary Ellen and Lester back to Sacramento? She stilled as another thought occurred, and she lifted her gaze to him. "Do you want me...to go?"

"No." He sat straighter. "I don't."

"There is no Oak Street home." She dipped her chin. "So, I'm not sure why you ask."

Ian pulled a letter from his jacket pocket. "I got this yesterday. I would imagine Sister Patricia might have something to do with it." He handed it to her. "A stewardship committee at the Holy Cross Diocese has committed to rebuilding the house on the Oak Street property. They don't specify that it must be an orphanage, but between you and my mother, I can't imagine it any other way."

"Really?" Olivia turned the letter over in her hand. "That is wonderful."

"It would likely take a year, but you could return to your post if you wished."

Dazed, Olivia stood, blinking, and released a faint laugh. "I don't know." The dry yellow empty plants around the garden held her attention. "I'd put that children's home out of my mind. I can't even picture it." She chewed on her lip and finally turned back over her shoulder. "You command your purpose and goals here at the mine. Everyone knows this is Ian's Empire." She hesitated. "I'm not sure of my place in this world."

After a few moments of listening to the night sounds surrounding them, Ian picked up the guitar and strummed a few chords. "Remember the hymn you sang at the sacrament hall?"

"My solo. 'Just as I am' without any children singing along." She huffed.

"Yes." He smiled. "I've been trying to learn it, but I don't know the words. Sing the first parts."

"My voice is too rough."

"If the crickets or frogs begin to heckle, you can stop." He played the first chord correctly, and Olivia shook her head. Lightly she began,

"Just as I am, without one plea,

But that Thy blood was shed for me,

And that Thou bid'st me come to Thee,

O Lamb of God, I come, I come."

She cleared her throat. "Oh, that was awful. Why are we out here holding this strange musical ensemble?"

"Just be a friend and help my romantic heart." He strummed again, and Olivia fought back a smile.

"Just as I am, and waiting not

To rid my soul of one dark blot;

To Thee whose blood can cleanse each spot,

O Lamb of God, I come, I come."

She surprised herself how clear her tone was.

Just as I am, though tossed about

With many a conflict, many a doubt;

Fightings within, and fears without,

O Lamb of God, I come, I..."

The last line stuck in her throat. Tossed about, with many a fear and doubt…had she really ever listened to these words. She sat quickly. "That's enough of that."

"I thought you sounded beautiful." Ian set his guitar aside. Standing, he looked away and then scratched the back of his head. His serious expression was back.

"So, I said I might have a solution." His eyes locked on hers. "But it was dependent on if you had your heart set on going back to Oak Street."

"What was the solution for again?" Olivia wondered why his cool confidence seemed to be missing as they exchanged awkward glances.

Ian pressed his hands down his jacket and knelt down on one knee before her. Taking a deep breath, he took her hands and held them tight. Before Olivia could catch her breath or open her mouth, he started. "Just hear me out. I've thought about this a lot. When I heard the words of the hymn, I knew I needed…no, not needed. I knew I wanted—really wanted—to ask you something."

Olivia felt a tiny squeak escape her throat.

"My mother is now Mrs. Maxwell Hastings. That is her true name. That is who she is." He nodded, wide-eyed, until she nodded with him. "Good. Umm." Gripping her hand, he wiped his sleeve over his mouth and started again. "So, you struggle with not knowing who you really are. I've thought about the other orphans. They've known from the beginning what happened to their people. And like Milton, a name change and family will give him the security he deserves. But your brother took that from you. Because, Olivia, you were loved and cherished, and he's the one that made you feel it was all a hoax. But it wasn't." He stood and released her hands. "Sorry, my knee was on a rock, and I'm way off from what I wanted to say."

After he brushed off the knees of his pants, he raked his hair behind his ears and then pressed his fingers over his lips. "So here it is." He rocked back on his heels a split second. "You know I love you. Though I don't know how you feel about me." Groaning, he pulled back. "Nope, I'm off again." He glanced to the right and back at her. "I want to give you my name. I want to marry you. See, if you were Mrs. Ian Beckner you would have a new name. I think you should keep Olivia, it suits you perfectly. But I would be your new family. We would share the name and share a new life." He stepped closer and pulled her to standing. "Just as you are," he whispered. "With all your past, and present, and fears, and doubts."

His sincere, caring face searched hers and Olivia felt her eyes misting.

"Of course, you would have to take me just as *I* am." Ian brushed his finger across her cheek. "That might take more grace than most wives would sign up for."

"Your romantic heart is really something to behold." Olivia sniffed. "I think you are asking me to marry you?"

Ian closed his eyes as his face scrunched up. He took her hands again and bent on one knee. Looking up, he smiled. "Miss Olivia Bradstreet, would you do me the honor of becoming my wife?"

She gave him an apologetic look. "I would like to accept, on the terms that we abolish the first engagement that never was."

Ian frowned, expelling a sigh that bordered on a groan. "So, you will marry me and live here with me?"

"Yes," she giggled. Gripping the back of his arms, she pulled him to standing.

Ian moved back and eyed her. "I do love you—more than the mine, more than my life. You are more precious to me than gold."

"Thank you, Ian." She stepped forward and pressed her hands under his coat and around his waist. "Please, believe me, I love you too. I'm sorry for all I've put you through."

"No, it wasn't… just you," Ian murmured as they held each other, feeling their hearts beat in tender awe.

Olivia lifted her face. "There is one thing that hasn't been made right."

"Tell me." He loosened his arms from around her.

"The garden, the guitar." Her eyes narrowed on his. "How long does a young woman wait for a second kiss?"

A slow smile covered his face before the glimmer in his eyes was all she could see as he came closer. Gentle fingers rose into her hairline, and a shiver ran down her back. As soon as his lips met hers, a sweet sensation raced through her limbs. It was every flutter she remembered and more. There was more passion and promise as she returned his desire with her own. The cool of the evening was replaced with trembling heat as their kissing deepened. Never had anything glorious shaken her so completely. She pulled back to find her breath.

"I…I…had no idea." She blinked. "Oh my, Mr. Beckner, this was worth waiting for."

Still holding her tight, his smile caressed her eyes, neck, and lips before he placed a line of breathy kisses up her chin and next to her ear. "As my beloved Olivia Beckner, I won't keep you waiting ever again."

⌒

Three months later…

On a delightful clear spring afternoon on Eureka Creek, north of Hangtown. Morgan Hastings stood so handsome, tall, and proud it made Olivia's heart squeeze. He'd found love and a sweet family to call his own. Baby Gus kicked and squealed, practically rocking off Emery's sister's hip. The simple riverside wedding sparkled like the sun off a bubbling creek.

The beautiful doe-eyed bride was Emery, the young woman Olivia had met before at Morgan's cabin. Her sweet baby, Gus, had grown into a chubby, active little boy. Even though her sister, Gianna, was having a hard time keeping the baby entertained, the beautiful bride in her powder blue and pink dress never looked from Morgan's eyes. A circle of greens crowned her head, bright ribbons floating down her dark locks.

Thankfully, there were no chairs for the few guests, so Ian stood in his black suit behind her with his hands wrapped around her waist, making her feel connected to her amazing love. Another striking woman with light red hair stood with her husband holding her the same. Beaming at the couple, the woman dabbed the corners of her eyes. A soft breeze blew the pine-scented mountain air, the smell mixing with the fertile valley soil. Those standing around watching them were the immigrants, the simple calloused-hand, hard-working gold mining families.

As the wedding couple repeated their vows, Olivia spied a small Chinese woman dressed in a thick, silken traditional gown. Next to her was Francine Boxner, with her hands wrapped around Joshua's shoulders. It was such a delight to see them again. The boy had been such a good friend to Thomas.

Ian chuckled and enfolded her waist as the couple kissed, and she couldn't agree with him more. The love swirling around these two could make anyone swoon, and she was grateful again for Ian's arms around her. Seconds after the reverend pronounced them Mr. and Mrs. Morgan Hastings, everyone broke out in applause. She didn't want to cry, but Maxwell stood proudly with his son and swiped a tear from the corner of his eye. Olivia tried but couldn't stop her eyes from filling. After the loss of Ronald, he was a strong, brave soul to leave everything behind and find a new life out west.

Maxwell had told her at dinner the night before that watching his remaining child marry, gain a daughter-in-law, and have Augustus Hastings as his grandson was a rich reward—something he'd dearly desired but could only imagine. As Judith approached where Maxwell stood next to Morgan, she wrapped her arms around him. Olivia couldn't look away as Emery in turn hugged her parents. They were blessed to be surrounded by family. Olivia dug in her reticule. A hankie was sorely needed.

A tall, thick burly man in the plaid shirt approached and shook Ian's hand.

"Truitt Emerson, and this is my wife, Cassidy."

"Nice to meet you both," Ian replied, and introduced Olivia.

"How is your connection to the new couple?" Olivia asked, wondering about the emotion she'd seen in Cassidy Emerson.

"We all worked and knew each other in Hangtown." Cassidy smiled. "I helped Emery and Gianna learn English." She turned admiring eyes on her husband. "Emery is a precious friend."

"And the small Chinese woman?" Olivia said, curious.

"That is So Chen. She runs Hangtown with an iron little fist." Truitt smiled. "Not really. But besides offering a hot bath and clean laundry, she helps many of the troubled women. For a while, Emery worked for her."

"I see." Olivia wondered, "Perhaps, did either of you know a Janny Long?"

Truitt seemed to stiffen. "I did. And you?"

"No." Olivia's tone dropped. "I was headmistress at the orphanage where her son Thomas lived before he passed." Olivia noticed Cassidy hold her husband's arm tighter as the festive air took a turn for the somber. "I'm working with a new parish in Grass Valley. The school and orphanage for children will be opening soon."

The couple nodded.

"I've asked that the boys' center be named after Thomas Long. The committee has agreed."

Truitt nodded, lines of emotion deepening on his face as he accepted the news.

"Years ago, my father and Dr. Hastings were friends." Olivia smiled. "So I've known the family all my life." She glanced to where Morgan and his father were speaking with Judith. "Dr. Maxwell Hastings' new wife is Ian's mother, Judith."

Truitt scratched his head. "You are the owner of the Empire Mine?"

"I am." Ian nodded. "And you, sir? Do you still find employment in Hangtown?"

"No," both Truitt and Cassidy said in unison before Truitt continued. "We own property by Lake Tahoe, and I'm in the middle of building a house and an inn." Truitt smiled as Morgan and Emery joined the group.

"Congratulations to both of you!" Olivia reached up to hug Morgan. The men shook hands, and the women embraced. "Emery, you looked so beautiful today," Olivia sighed, clutching her chest. "We're just getting acquainted with the Emersons, and then I will have to go give Gus a kiss."

"And congratulations to both of you." Emery smiled at Olivia. "Dr. Hastings, I mean, Maxwell, said you would be marrying soon."

"We will." Olivia smiled up at Ian. "And you're all invited!" Her eyes sparkled. "Morgan is now Judith's stepson, and by marrying Ian, I will be her daughter-in-law. So, though it sounds confusing to me, we are all family somehow." She laughed. The group agreed, and Olivia felt a soft touch deep in her heart.

Ian was right. She'd believed that without knowing her past she could never belong. It was such a lie. From every connection, small or large, a family could be made. Orphans could begin to love and bond again. Friendships, people from other countries and cultures, marriages could make strangers into family. To think she thought love would only happen in the best matches. How ridiculous. Love's pure gold flowed within the gifts of honesty and forgiveness.

As the men stepped away, murmuring something about the arrest and imprisonment of a gold baron named Arnold Snider, Emery and Cassidy talked and hugged again. Olivia glanced at the bubbling creek and breathed deeply of the fresh air. To her left, baby Gus let out a happy squeal, and new excitement and peace settled within her. Esther and Bonita were only months away from calling her mother and Ian father. Out of God's love, He'd created a family just for her. A group of imperfect people all learning how to be truly caring family members to each other. The truth was so evident now: no matter how dark or backward the path people or children come from, trusting God and waiting is the only way forward. Reaching for Ian's hand, she leaned into his side. Truitt followed suit, moving from the men to take his wife's gloved hand and gave it a kiss. Morgan returned to Emery's side, pulling his arm around her shoulder. Emery smiled upward, gazing long at her new husband. Olivia felt something she couldn't put into words. Maybe true gold, true riches, are the things within a person. Oh, how extremely thankful she was for the riches of God's grace.

His faithfulness abounded.

In love, he predestined us for adoption to sonship through Jesus Christ, in accordance with his pleasure and will— to the praise of his glorious grace, which he has freely given us in the One he loves. Eph1:5

Author's Note

If you made it through all three books in Loves Pure Gold, thank you, thank you, thank you!

I always ask God about a takeaway, and I feel something here about identity. God created us for connection. But we live in a world riddled with broken connections. *(Sometimes our own fault!)* Do you suppose that's why the Bible tells us we are new creations in Christ? Putting away all that is behind us to press forward. You are no longer_____, but now you are God's people, God's family of choice! How deep is the Father God identity written on your heart?

He's always wanted you. You belong and are accepted, that is your true identity. With all that swirls around us in our other relationships, aren't you glad for the One who never changes His feelings, His connection with you: daughter, son, beloved, precious, wanted.

Your picture is on His fridge.

Grace and belonging for eternity,
Julia

You are no longer foreigners and strangers, but fellow citizens with God's people and also members of his household, built on the foundation of the apostles and prophets, with Christ Jesus himself as the chief cornerstone. Eph 2:19

Fun facts
(because you know the rest is fiction)

Empire Mine is a State Historic Park in Grass Valley, California, containing 856 acres of land with the original cottage and mine, a magnificent garden, and grounds. The home and mine shafts are open for tours. The Empire Mine produced over 5.8 million ounces in gold, and it ranked at one time one of the largest, oldest, and most prosperous mines in North American history.

From my tour, I learned the real owners (the Bourn family) funded an orphanage in Sacramento. In 1869, Mr. Bourn was only 22 when he took over the management of Empire Mine. Katy Moriarty and her rule of big house and kitchen is fact. She was reported to "have run the Cottage like clockwork and often supplied the local orphanage with home-baked goods."

In the mid-1850s, Cornish workers came to Empire Mine, brought the Cornish pump, and provided the bulk of the mine's labor force. Decades of Cornish families still reside in Grass Valley and celebrate St. Piran's Day. St Piran is also a patron saint of tin miners.

Father Dalton came to Grass Valley on June 10, 1855, as the first resident pastor of St. Patrick's Church. Two years later, he purchased two pieces of land and, with the help of the *entire community*, built a brick church. Father Dalton converted the original wooden church into a school in 1859. Sacramento Diocesan Archives reports that "everywhere throughout the mining region there were serious accidents. Safety measures were only just being developed. Dozens of families found themselves fatherless and others parentless. The big heart of Father Dalton saw a need and wanted to meet it. The generous Sisters of Mercy agreed to work with him. In 1866 with over 30 children, a Mrs. Edward McLaughlin came to their rescue and provided the sisters with blankets and spreads for 30 beds, a kitchen stove, and $150.00."

The Ladies' Protection and Relief Society was among California's earliest charities. As they say, "Their purpose was to support homes where friendless or destitute children may be received and provided for until permanent homes in Christian families can be secured."

Thanks again, and if you ever find yourself in Northern California, Placerville (Hangtown), Auburn and Grass Valley are a load of fun.

I'm standing in the Empire Mine garden with house behind. A better close up of the stone and brick original Empire home.

I have more fun backstory at http://www.juliadwrites.com. Sign up for my newsletter and receive heads up on new book releases and automatic entry into my $50.00 Amazon drawing *(for more books, of course!)*

The Messenger's Mischief

Mine Blast. Watch out! When Calls the Heart just collided with Bonanza.

Virginia City's new schoolmarm is a plucky, pious, cat-loving bible-thumper who can't seem to stop tumbling into the handsome Wells Fargo shotgun messenger's arms. Not a problem for him, but the attraction could ruin her future.

Fresh winning combination of Humor, History, and Happy-Ending Romance.

Now available on Amazon!